THE ACCUSED

OWEN MULLEN

Boldwood

First published in Great Britain in 2021 by Boldwood Books Ltd.

Copyright © Owen Mullen, 2021

Cover Design: Nick Castle Design

Cover Photography: Shutterstock

The moral right of Owen Mullen to be identified as the author of this work has been asserted in accordance with the Copyright, Designs and Patents Act 1988.

All rights reserved. No part of this book may be reproduced in any form or by any electronic or mechanical means, including information storage and retrieval systems, without written permission from the author, except for the use of brief quotations in a book review.

This book is a work of fiction and, except in the case of historical fact, any resemblance to actual persons, living or dead, is purely coincidental.

Every effort has been made to obtain the necessary permissions with reference to copyright material, both illustrative and quoted. We apologise for any omissions in this respect and will be pleased to make the appropriate acknowledgements in any future edition.

A CIP catalogue record for this book is available from the British Library.

Paperback ISBN 978-1-80162-704-7

Large Print ISBN 978-1-80162-703-0

Hardback ISBN 978-1-80162-702-3

Ebook ISBN 978-1-80162-705-4

Kindle ISBN 978-1-80162-706-1

Audio CD ISBN 978-1-80162-697-2

MP3 CD ISBN 978-1-80162-698-9

Digital audio download ISBN 978-1-80162-701-6

Boldwood Books Ltd
23 Bowerdean Street
London SW6 3TN
www.boldwoodbooks.com

To Devon and Harrison Carney

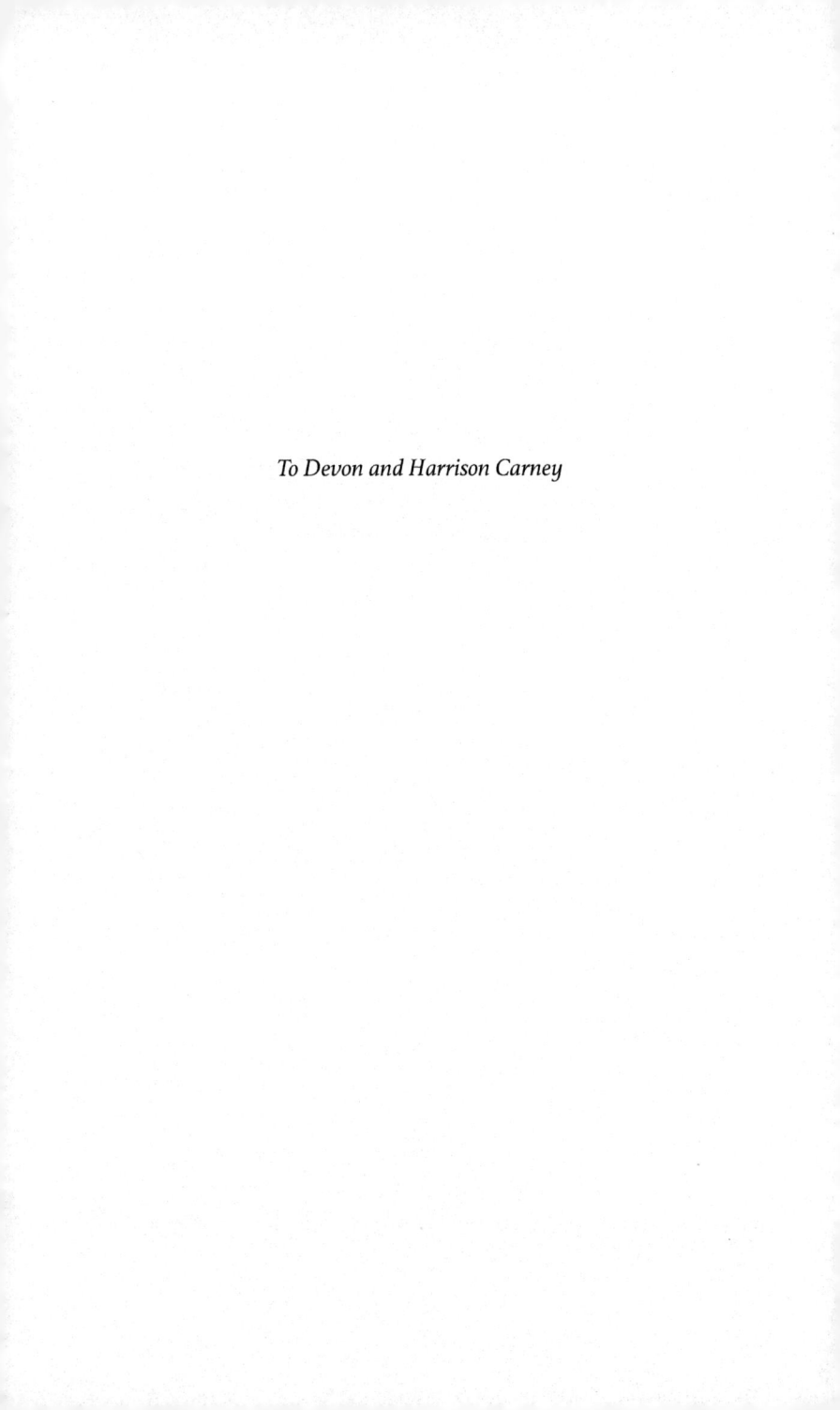

PROLOGUE

Inside the restaurant in Merchant City, people recognised the handsome couple and whispered to each other behind their hands. Tomorrow, they'd have a story to tell.

Sean Rafferty lifted his head in time to catch the half-smile fade from his wife's lips; something had amused her. Across the table, Kim nervously pushed food around the plate, knowing his eyes were on her. Rafferty turned in his seat and saw a guy in his mid-thirties leaning back in his chair, swirling the red wine in his glass; through his designer stubble he was smiling, too. On another day, this was a good enough excuse for Sean to drag him outside and beat him senseless.

Except, that was the old Sean Rafferty.

A PR company was charging him a small fortune to make his family's violent past ancient history. He dabbed the edges of his mouth with a napkin. 'Want to let me in on the joke?'

Kim said, 'What joke? There isn't a joke.'

'Your friend seems to think there is.'

She put down her cutlery, annoyed by the accusation. 'I've no idea what you're talking about. What friend?'

'You fucking slut. Do you think I'm a fool?'

'I was only being polite, Sean.'

He snapped his fingers impatiently in the air for the bill.

The evening was over.

* * *

In the taxi on the way home, he didn't speak. When they got to the house in Bothwell on the banks of the River Clyde, Kim ran upstairs and locked the bedroom door. Rafferty paid the driver and asked him to take the babysitter home. Inside, he peeled money off the wad in his pocket and gave it to the young teenager who looked after Rosie when they went out. Then, he went upstairs. His shoulder connected with the wooden door panel, Kim screamed and he stepped into the room.

PART I

1

Sean Rafferty was in a foul mood – he didn't need this shit.

Behind the wheel of the midnight-blue Mercedes, the driver kept his mouth shut; he knew better. In the passenger seat, Sean slouched, sullen and silent, as they joined the motorway and the procession into the city.

This morning, the face staring back at him from the bathroom mirror was no longer a young man's face, the skin around the eyes dry and puffy above the dark shadow on his jaw, a reminder of his father in his last years after the stroke doused the spark, leaving him crippled and bitter and – if it was possible – even more of a vicious old bastard than he'd been. Sean had splashed cold water on his cheeks, put drops in his bloodshot whites and studied his reflection again.

Better, though not much.

He was getting older. Simple as that. It happened to everybody. Today, he felt it and last night hadn't helped. The idiot at the next table in the restaurant had been on his second bottle of wine and hadn't bothered to hide his lust, staring at Kim, smiling, mouthing words at her when he'd thought Rafferty wasn't looking. Sean understood those words; he'd whispered them to other men's wives and savoured their reaction. It had taken every ounce of self-restraint not to stab the man in the eye with a fork. No point spending a small fortune cleaning up his image to spoil it on some drunken horny clown who fancied his chances; the guy would never know how lucky he'd been.

Kim was another story. There were no excuses for her – she could've shut it down. Instead, she'd preferred to make a fool of him and join in the game.

When would the silly bitch learn?

The answer was obvious: never. And it couldn't have mattered less; she'd served her purpose and given him a daughter. Sex – okay rather than great – hadn't lasted beyond the third year. Kim would've been down the road already, except Rosie adored her mummy. Now, she'd gone past her sell-by date: time to trade her in for a newer model, one with a bit of fire under the bonnet.

Of course, she thawed quick enough when her credit card was maxed out or she needed money for a new obsession – there had been plenty of those. For a while, Ayurvedic massage, then, a series of sessions in a floatation tank in an Edinburgh spa. Christ knew what that was supposed to be about. Colonic hydrotherapy was the latest. The breakdown in communication meant he was spared the details, for which he was grateful.

The back of his skull throbbed in rhythm with his heart; he'd sat in the conservatory and hammered a bottle of Ballantine's till stupid o'clock. In his youth, he'd binge for three days and need a day to recover. Now, it was the other way around. A quack would shake his head and, with a superior smile, deliver a bleak prognosis: cut down on the booze or suffer the consequences. Sean Rafferty's response would be the same as many in the West of Scotland.

No chance.

The previous night, Kim had locked herself in the bedroom. It hadn't saved the bitch. But a decision on his marital situation was overdue.

He'd been tying a Windsor knot in the blue Salvatore Ferragamo round his neck when the call from Vicky had come through.

'Sean?'

'Yeah.'

'Problem at Dowanhill.'

Fuck!

'One of our girls is at the Royal Infirmary.'

He'd bitten back his irritation. Vicky Farrell was worth two of anybody else on the payroll – if she was contacting him this early, there had to be more to it.

'How bad?'

'She'll be out of action for a few weeks.'

'Handle it, Victoria. Isn't that what I pay you for?'

'It's not that simple. The guy who did it says you work for his father.'

Sean had felt the anger that was never far away stir in him. 'I work for... What's this fucker's name?'

'Hunter. Kelvin Hunter. His father is—'

'I know who his father is.'

* * *

They pulled up at a set of traffic lights on Park Road with the spire of Lansdowne Parish Church rising slim and stark into a cold blue sky. Rafferty's fingers drummed impatiently on his thigh, while dull-eyed pedestrians crossed in front of them on their way to another soul-destroying shift in the snake pits. The fool he was going to meet claimed Sean worked for his father, which wasn't even close to being true. Apart from old Jimmy, Sean had never worked for anybody. He tried to imagine what it would be like and failed.

It seemed Bryce Hunter had been building up his part, boasting to his maladjusted offspring what a big shot he was. Apparently, being an influential member of three committees and chairman of another wasn't enough for him.

Wining and dining city planners, slipping brown envelopes under the table while Sean had to fake interest in their long-winded stories was one thing – letting their over-entitled spawn take liberties with his girls was a stretch too far.

Sean's father and brother were dead. Their criminal enterprise, the scourge of the East End for close on half a century, hadn't died with them. Sean had taken over. But his vision of the future was very different. Times had changed; the old ways were gone. He put people in charge of running the streets – Vicky Farrell was one of them – while he faded into the background, engaged a PR company to create his new image, and got involved in well-publicised causes like the one this morning.

Life had never been better. Other than his bitch of a wife, he'd little to complain about. In a few short years, he'd become one of the most respected members of the Glasgow Chamber of Commerce and the driving force behind a much-lauded initiative to provide shelter for the city's many homeless.

Rafferty's role model wasn't his crude, unsophisticated father, who'd punched and gouged his way to the top of the Glasgow underworld. His son had rubbed up against another kind of man and wanted to be like him. He'd visited Emil Rocha's villa, seen how the Spaniard lived, and wanted the same. The drug lord supplied Sean's organisation, but their association went deeper: unbeknown to the city council, one of Europe's biggest criminals was Rafferty's sleeping partner in the Waterside Regeneration

Initiative, the prestigious multi-million pound development on the Clyde. Sean's brainchild slogan 'Good for Glasgow' had helped sway public opinion and overcome objections to the controversial project.

Rocha was happy having a finger in yet another pie and was coming to Glasgow, ostensibly to take a look at what his money had helped build. In reality, and Sean Rafferty knew it, he was checking up on his Scottish connection.

The truth about how Rafferty's fledgling company came to partner Glasgow City Council would never be known. It hadn't made him rich – although he was well on the way – but it sealed the deal on his new persona. And like a butterfly emerging from a chrysalis, Sean Rafferty was reborn and reinvented: to a gullible world, a public-spirited, self-made entrepreneur, who just happened to buy his Ludovic de Saint Sernin suits from 5 Carlos Place in Mayfair rather than Ralph Slater in Howard Street, a stone's throw from the river. The expensive clothes changed nothing. Hidden beneath the façade of do-good sham-respectability was the pitiless gangster he'd always been. Unmistakably, his father's son.

Marrying Kim completed the picture he wanted to promote. Love hadn't come into it. She'd given him Rosie, his daughter, and another piece of the image was in place.

Today was a busy day. Places to go and people to see: a meeting with his accountant scheduled for nine-thirty had been pushed back because of Vicky's call, then a visit to the youth centre in Rutherglen he'd championed, built on a parcel of land until recently a designated green belt. 'Making Glasgow Better' was his new rallying cry as he moved among the disadvantaged, who mistakenly saw him as one of their own.

Not everybody was convinced by the gangster as a renaissance man. Once again, *The Herald* had several pieces questioning the probity of the planning permission process, among other things, stopping short of saying money had changed hands.

Fuck them. If they'd proof, they'd be shouting it from the rooftops. They hadn't and weren't likely to find anyone brave enough to corroborate their suspicions.

He pulled his thoughts back to Rosie; Rafferty liked to give the little girl a kiss before he left and the omission today annoyed him. He blamed Kim and made a promise to himself to call his lawyer to start divorce proceedings. His pounding head promoted another thought: might as well tone the drinking down while he was at it. Always assuming he could.

Beginning tomorrow, of course.

Sean had no regrets about his violence the night before. Kim had got what she deserved. His mind wandered to the solicitor's wife he was meeting later, picturing her naked; they'd met at his place, at a party organised by Kim, a tedious affair – weren't they all? His leggy guest had made her intentions clear early on, running a hand down her thigh to straighten her skirt when she knew he was watching, her eyes on him longer than necessary.

A prelude to sex; she wanted him. Who was he to deny her?

Given the chance, he'd have taken her to one of the spare rooms – God knew there were enough of them – and done her there and then. Kim had sensed something and glued herself to his elbow for the rest of the night. When everybody left, she stormed upstairs and locked the bedroom door.

Her locking the door always amused Sean; his lips cracked in a half-smile, there and gone. Last night he'd shown her nothing would stop him if he wanted to come in.

To hell with her. The woman today would be good; he *knew* she'd be good – the married ones were always the best. Playing golf with Guy, her smug tit of a solicitor husband, added piquancy to the conquest. Rafferty imagined Guy thrashing between her spread legs, convinced he was the only one who'd been there.

Secrets. Everybody had them. The only people who didn't were six feet under.

They crossed Byres Road and Queen Margaret Drive, past the contrasting iconic façades of the Hilton Glasgow Grosvenor hotel on one corner and Òran Mór, the brasserie in the former Kelvinside Parish Church – another fucking church – on the other. Whoever had spotted that opening should be congratulated: a goldmine if ever there was one. Capitalising on opportunities was the name of the game.

Business in the morning, other men's wives in the afternoon.

Before that, he had this crap to deal with.

A left turn, then, further on, a right brought them into an elegant Grade B listed sandstone terrace lined with parked cars. They rolled to a halt and Rafferty got out. He had two more properties like the one he was about to visit – in Mount Florida, a spit from Hampden Park, and in Crown Circus, all bringing in coin. Short of another Ice Age, property was the most solid investment you could make. He didn't own the houses, at least not yet; the banks did. Eventually, he would. For the moment, horny men paid the mortgages and Vicky Farrell managed them.

* * *

Vicky waited inside the door. Her and Sean went way back. Once upon a time he'd been her best customer, using her as much as three times a week: a rough lover with strong hands who'd suck her nipples until they were swollen and tender, then take her from behind. He was never satisfied; when she thought he'd finished he'd mount her again in a different position. Sean Rafferty liked to get his money's worth and it was okay with her.

He was handsome and firm and knew his way around a woman's body. Faking orgasms to placate the fragile egos of inadequate men was Vicky Farrell's trade. With Sean, she'd had no need.

When he married a size-six model with Botox lips Vicky hadn't expected to see him again. And then one day, her mobile rang. It was Sean. Offering her a job. Vicky accepted and they'd sealed it with a fuck for old times' sake, knowing it was a one-off. But he made clear the history between them, however sweet, counted for nothing. Protecting his investment was her responsibility, which meant making sure the girls maximised their potential as revenue streams on legs.

That wasn't always easy. The smarter ones stayed clear of drugs and disease, saved their pennies and got out as soon as they could. Some even found a man and put the skin trade behind them. It happened they were the exceptions. Most hung on too long, lost their youth and their looks and moved down the chain, through the brothels and, eventually, onto the street.

By then, nobody cared if they lived or died or how they abused their bodies, not even them.

2

Vicky saw the anger in Sean's eyes and blanched. He strode into the flat without looking at her and spoke out of the side of his mouth. 'Where is he?'

Quietly, and all the more chilling for it.

'The last door on the left.'

She fell into step with him down the hall. He didn't ask about the girl who'd been injured; she was a stranger to him and always would be – they'd never meet, never speak – somebody he could profit from until her usefulness came to an end.

Vicky volunteered the information anyway. 'She's okay.'

'Who is?'

'Our girl. The attack wasn't as vicious as it might've been. He wasn't trying to kill her, just hurt her for fun. Because he could. Fortunately, one of the others heard her screaming and called me.'

'When was this?'

'Around three. We caught the bastard running down Great Western and brought him back.'

'Why didn't you sort him, there and then?'

'Oh, I wanted to, believe me, Sean. This is the second time he's roughed-up our girls. Left the last one unconscious on the pavement in West George Street. He was getting a hiding until he said you worked for his father. He wasn't scared. Or bothered about the damage he'd done, so I phoned you.'

Rafferty stopped at the end of the hall. 'How long have you known me, Victoria?'

He called her Victoria when he was displeased.

'A long time.'

'And have I ever mentioned working for anybody? I mean, even once.'

'No.'

'So why take this clown's word when you know it isn't true?'

'What if it was? I... I couldn't be certain. You're involved in so many things.'

Rafferty shook his head. Vicky Farrell wasn't the whore she used to be. He'd heard a whisper there was a boyfriend in the wings. A Tony somebody. Tony must be desperate. What kind of man got seriously involved with a tart?

'You know, Vicky, I can remember a time you'd have had his legs broken and left him in the street without even telling me. You're losing it. Maybe I need to give your job to somebody else. Now, show me this idiot. Let's hear what fantasy his father's been feeding him.'

At the door, he turned. 'I'm serious. Do better or get another gig.'

* * *

Kelvin Hunter raised his head when Rafferty came in. Vicky had been right about this guy: he wasn't afraid. Sean pegged him somewhere between twenty and twenty-five, as confident a bastard as he'd met in a while. Kelvin sat on a chair in the middle of the room, examining his fingernails, making a show of being bored. His shirt had blood on it but it wasn't his own. Apart from bruising across his knuckles, he was unmarked. Rafferty caught the amusement in the eyes staring up at him and wanted to waste the young sadist's face. Clearly, Kelvin believed he was fireproof; his father had a lot to answer for. Two men Sean recognised stood behind Hunter – he'd made a run for it once; it wouldn't happen again.

Kelvin clapped his hands and spoke in a privately educated accent. 'At long last, the boss man cometh. Now, can I get out of here?'

He straightened his jacket in a prelude to leaving and tried to stand. Thick fingers digging into his shoulder forced him back on the chair. He shook his head slowly as though he didn't understand why he was being treated this way, mumbling an explanation to himself that revealed his sense of superiority. 'She was a prostitute, for Christ's sake. What's the big deal?'

Rafferty's interest was in what the thug had said to Vicky rather than the harm he'd done to a defenceless girl. His tone was conversational. 'Apparently, I work for your father. Who told you that?'

The question surprised Hunter. 'What? He did.'

'And this "work". What is it?'

'How would I know?'

'Maybe we should ask him. First, you owe me for damage to my property.'

Strong hands dragged Kelvin to his feet and threw him against the wall. For the first time, fear lit his eyes. His misjudged sense of entitlement won; he tried the brazen routine again. 'You wouldn't dare. My father—'

The punch to his gut doubled him over, lining him up to

catch the full force of Rafferty's knee to his chin. Kelvin dropped to the floor and lay still, barely conscious as Sean Rafferty's foot smashed into him, again and again.

'You're due a valuable lesson, then we'll hear what your dad has to say for himself, eh?'

* * *

The bungalow and the neat square of well-tended lawn edged with rose bushes would be considered modest in many parts of the country. In Bearsden, six miles north-west of the city centre, it was beyond most people's reach. One survey put the G61 postcode as the seventh wealthiest in the UK. Posh Glasgow, a world away from the tenements of the East End or the high-rise monstrosities like the now demolished Red Road flats where, on a clear day from the thirteenth-floor, residents could see gangs of junkies shooting up on the banks of Hogganfield Loch.

Councillor Bryce Hunter lived here; he'd done all right for a guy who'd left school at fifteen without a qualification to his name.

The car pulled off the road into the drive. Sean Rafferty got out and walked up the path. Behind him, Kelvin Hunter's feet scraped the gravel. Barely able to stand, he wasn't smiling now. Naked from the waist up, supported on either side by the heavies who'd watched their boss teach him a lesson he richly deserved, he moaned as they dragged him to the door, his pale skin black and blue from the beating.

Rafferty pressed the doorbell and waited. When it opened, Bryce Hunter saw the gangster and the state his son was in. The elected member's tone told Sean everything. Kelvin was his father's boy, no doubt about that.

'You low-life bastard, Rafferty. What the hell have you done to him?'

'Think yourself lucky he isn't floating face down in the Clyde. Kelvin here likes rough sex. Did he get that from you or his mother? The problem is, it costs, and he didn't fancy paying for it.'

A woman appeared from the kitchen still holding the tea towel she'd been using to dry dishes. Hunter raised his arms to stop her getting closer. 'It's okay, Hazel. It's okay.'

Her hand went to her mouth when she saw her boy. 'Oh, my God! Oh, my God! What's happened?'

Hunter shepherded her into the lounge. 'There's been a bit of trouble but I'm dealing with it. Kelvin's all right.'

They dumped the semi-conscious thug inside the door. Rafferty said, 'Because of this piece of shit, one of my girls is in hospital.' He shook his head. 'Messing with Sean Rafferty's property – how did he imagine it would turn out?'

Bryce Hunter bent over Kelvin, whispering to him. From the other room, his wife shouted, 'I'm calling the police!'

Sean Rafferty ignored her. 'You'll be getting a bill for lost income. I'll add on something for the girl.' He pointed to Kelvin. 'If you're wise, you'll keep him on a leash. We've got his shirt and jacket; the hooker's blood is on them and there's a video of him admitting he assaulted her. I own you now, Bryce. Don't forget it. Whenever a request for planning permission comes across your desk with my name on it, persuade your colleagues to approve it without the usual malarkey.'

He moved away, then turned back.

'One more thing. Kelvin tells me I work for you. Who the fuck gave him that idea?'

* * *

Walking into NYB was like walking into a Jack Vettriano painting. All that was missing was a singing butler.

For years this had been a familiar scene when my office was a room above the diner. Moving from New York Blue might have meant seeing a lot less of Jackie, Andrew and Pat Logue. But like so many things, it didn't come out like that. The space Alex Gilby offered me was round the corner, and whenever I went back to NYB it was like visiting the land time forgot; Jackie Mallon still managed the place from her cupboard under the stairs. With me gone from the office she'd lusted after, the need to actually occupy it seemed to have passed. Over next to the Rock-Ola, Andrew Geddes was starting his day with his usual habit of ruining perfectly good bagels by dunking them in his coffee.

Andrew was a detective sergeant in Police Scotland CID: a shrewd, observant old-time copper. We'd been friends a long time. More impressive than it sounded because Geddes wasn't the easiest guy to be friends with. He'd helped me more often than I could remember; he had a good heart. But if you wanted to find it, you had to be prepared to dig.

And Patrick Logue was Patrick Logue: as permanent a fixture at the bar as Sir Walter Scott on top of the column in George Square. He'd worked for me on and off for years and was streetwise and savvy, except when it came to his own business. He was a good guy. I liked him. At a minute to eleven o'clock, he broke from the racing section of the *Daily Record* and his ritual of picking losers to speak to Jackie.

'How long till I can get something stronger than a coffee? Askin' for an alkie.'

She gave him an old-fashioned look and poured his first pint of the day, the first of many.

I saw her the moment she came through the door, her lemon dress and Ray-Ban sunglasses pushed up into her blonde hair –

perfect for the fine weather central Scotland had been enjoying for more than a week – catching the attention of everyone in the bar, including the women: especially the women.

The new arrival scanned the tables, searching for somebody. When she didn't find them, she spoke to Jackie Mallon. Jackie raised an arm and pointed in my direction. High heels clacked on the floor; the vision weaved towards me between the chairs. Then I realised who she was and wished she wasn't coming to me.

Close up, with her slim figure and fresh complexion, she might have been seventeen or eighteen, and if she was wearing make-up on her heart-shaped face, it didn't show. We'd never met though I knew her story: Kim had been a model at the beginning of what was certain to be a successful career, a finalist in the Miss Scotland competition at the Radisson Blu Hotel on Argyle Street the night the man she'd go on to marry introduced himself.

Sean Rafferty was the son of legendary Glasgow gangster, Jimmy. When his father died, he'd taken over and, on the surface at least, moved away from his family's criminal past. But, behind the façade of respectability, Sean was worse than Jimmy had ever been.

For months, pictures of the fairy-tale romance between beauty and the beast had filled the celebrity gossip columns: coming out of a Michelin-starred restaurant in Edinburgh glassy-eyed, smiling champagne smiles; draped round each other laughing at a Kevin Bridges show in the SEC; strolling barefoot on a Caribbean beach, hand in hand as a blood-red sun dipped into the sea. For me, at least, the last photograph I'd seen of this beautiful woman had been on a chest of drawers in a cottage on the outskirts of Peebles.

Her top lip quivered; she was nervous and not because every pair of eyes was on her – a lady like her was used to that kind of attention and took it in her stride. This was something else.

'Mr Cameron. Charlie Cameron?'

I wanted to deny it.

'Yeah, that's me.'

'Can I sit down?'

'Please do.'

'I'm sorry to break into your morning. You have an office here, don't you?'

She was almost correct. I'd *had* an office here. Now, my name was stencilled on the door of a shoebox round the corner in Cochrane Street. I'd gone down in the world, a circumstance I was still coming to terms with.

'Do you know who I am?'

'Yes.'

'Then you know who my husband is?'

I knew only too well. Our paths had crossed more than once and I was fortunate to still be alive to tell the tale.

The problem wasn't that I knew Sean Rafferty. It was that Sean Rafferty knew me.

Like his father before him, Rafferty was a killer. This lady had known his reputation and married him anyway. What did that say about her?

I answered her with a question, suspicion undisguised in my voice. 'Why are you here, Mrs Rafferty?'

She gazed away, as though what she had to say wasn't easy. 'I'm in trouble. You're the only one who can help.'

A tear brimmed in her right eye. She blinked and it cascaded down her cheek. The left eye was closed and swollen, purple and dark where the blow had connected. Painful, though it wasn't why she was crying.

'I take it he did that?'

She nodded.

'My advice would be to go to the police. I can put you in touch—'

Kim cut across me, her voice louder than she intended. 'Do you think I'm stupid? Do you think that hadn't occurred to me?' Her fingers gripped the edge of the table. 'How long do you imagine I'd survive? He'd kill me and take Rosie. He will anyway, it's only a matter of time.'

People turned in our direction, instantly interested. At the bar, Pat Logue was one of them, shaking his head; he'd recognised my visitor and was warning me against having anything to do with her.

I said, 'Here isn't the place to be discussing this. We'll go to my office; it's not far.'

'I'm desperate, Mr Cameron. You don't know how desperate.'

3

We walked to Cochrane Street in silence. As soon as the door of my office closed, she took up where she'd left off, describing the sad reality behind the tabloid fantasy.

'The marriage was over almost from the beginning. He didn't love me. He used me to clean up his image. On our honeymoon, I caught him with one of the hotel's chambermaids. He wasn't sorry; he laughed. Told me to get used to it. Yet, he's jealous, insanely jealous. He sees me as his property. Another man only has to look at me and he goes crazy, while he flaunts his affairs and his whores.'

Kim looked around the modest room, too wrapped up in her own problems to see its shortcomings. 'He'll never let me go because I'd take Rosie. Sean idolises his daughter. She's probably the only person in the world he truly cares about.'

I spoke quietly, trying to keep disbelief out of my voice. 'Am I understanding this? You're asking me to help you leave your husband?'

'Yes. Finding people who've disappeared is what you do, isn't it? Like that child, Baby Lily Hamilton. That was you.'

'It was. But that was very different.'

Kim sailed through my objections. 'Wherever I go, wherever I run to, Sean will come after me.' She paused and smiled a half-smile. 'As for the police... let's just say... your faith in them is... misplaced.' She laid her crazy idea on me. 'I want you to work in reverse. Make me and Rosie disappear.'

The look on my face should've told her all she needed to know. Even if I was foolish enough to get involved, her plan was doomed. Rafferty had eyes and ears on every street corner in Glasgow and connections far beyond. She reached across and squeezed my fingers; hers felt soft and dry. 'You are going to help me, aren't you? At least tell me you'll think about it. Say you'll consider it. For God's sake give me something to cling to. This is my life we're talking about. Mine and my daughter's.'

'Mrs Rafferty—'

'Don't call me that.'

'Okay, but really...'

Her hand slipped into her bag and came out clutching a thick bundle held together by a rubber band. The notes were Bank of Scotland twenties, purple like her eye; thousands of pounds. She put them on the table and pushed them towards me.

I said, 'Look, it's not about money.'

Kim's expression changed, her head tilted, lips parting provocatively. I realised what was coming and tried to stop her before her humiliation was complete.

Too late.

She whispered, 'I'll do anything. Anything. Please, Mr Cameron. Please... Charlie.'

I felt an overwhelming sadness deep inside me. What she was asking was impossible, even if I was the man for it, which I wasn't. The decision was simple – a choice between prudent or rash, smart or dumb. From bitter experience, I understood the reach

Sean Rafferty had and the lengths he'd go to avenge himself on whoever had been stupid enough to help his wife escape.

A stone-cold no-brainer.

Until a voice that sounded like my voice betrayed my desire to go on breathing.

'Let me think about it.'

And I knew I'd made a terrible mistake.

Kim Rafferty seized on my lack of fortitude. 'Thank you, thank you, thank you. I was sure you wouldn't refuse me.'

'Hold on. I'm agreeing to give it some thought. Don't read any more into it.'

She lied. 'I won't. I promise, I won't.'

I didn't believe her. 'Give me your mobile number.'

I added it to my contact list; her face lit up. 'You can't imagine how much this means. You've given me hope there's an end to the nightmare.'

The conversation had got away from me. I made an attempt to rein it back.

'Please understand how difficult life will be for you and your daughter if by some miracle we get you away from him.'

I was talking to myself; she wasn't listening.

'How soon will you let me know?'

My throat was dry. Somehow thinking about it had become agreeing to do it.

'A few days.'

She threw her arms round me and I smelled her scent – beautiful like the lady herself.

What the hell had I got myself into?

Out on Cochrane Street, Sean Rafferty's wife waved and hurried towards George Square, already dreaming dreams of freedom. I envied her optimism and wished I shared it.

*   *   *

As a base, the room in Cochrane Street was okay rather than great. Kim Rafferty had had too much on her mind to notice the spartan decor. Somebody less rattled might conclude whoever worked here wasn't very good at what they did and find another private investigator to take on their case. I wouldn't blame them.

Kim was terrified; it was in her eyes and in her voice, and, though my instinct was to help her, the downside was massive. Getting involved with the wife of the most dangerous gangster in Glasgow was madness, unless I wanted to spend the rest of my life in a wheelchair wishing he'd finished the job. Turning Kim away was the only thing that made sense. Instead, I'd asked for a few days to think about it and given her false hope.

Footsteps on the stairs told me I had another visitor. The door banged open and Pat Logue stood in the frame, his face taut with anger. Before he spoke, I knew what he would say. Patrick had come charging over the hill like the cavalry and saved me on more than a few occasions. He rarely lost his temper. Today, anger flushed his neck and his usual bonhomie was missing.

He sat in the same chair as Kim Rafferty – the only other chair in the room – and stared at me as though he didn't understand what he was seeing. He was wearing his on-holiday clothes: polo shirt, jeans and open-toed sandals, the goatee on his chin neatly trimmed. Patrick had a singular view of life and made me laugh; he hadn't come to joke.

'How long have we known each other, Charlie? I mean, seriously, how long?'

I sighed. 'A long time, Pat.'

'And how often have I given you duff advice?' He didn't wait for a reply. 'What I'm gettin' at is this. A wise man sees trouble and gives it a body swerve; he doesn't seek it out.'

'I haven't taken her case.'

He stabbed a knowing finger at me. 'That the same as sendin' her on her way? 'Cause the smile on her face when she left makes me think it isn't.'

My silence said it all.

'For Christ's sake, when will you learn? Whatever Sean Rafferty's wife wants, the answer is no! It has to be. She's bad news. The fact she even came to you is too close for comfort. Any contact...'

'Patrick—'

The red on his neck rose to his cheeks. 'Rafferty hates you. Have you forgotten? I'd rather slam my tits in a car door than go up against him again.'

'Pat, listen—'

'You should feel the same.'

'I haven't said I'll help her.'

He hammered his fist on the desk and shouted, 'Don't insult me, Charlie! Don't fuckin' do that! I understand you better than anybody in this town! Better than you understand yourself! You haven't said you won't! Find some other maiden in distress to play the knight in shinin' armour with. Not this lady. Not Sean Rafferty's wife.'

'Listen—'

'No, you listen. Another case, a different client, fair enough, I'm here. But there's a line you don't cross. Not recognisin' that will get you killed. Which makes you a man with a death wish or a bloody fool. Either way, I'm out. Commit suicide if you want. I'm havin' no part of it.' He pushed the chair back and turned at the door. 'Never thought I'd say this, but you're on your own, Charlie.'

The outburst was so untypical of Patrick Logue it forced me to reconsider what I'd said to Kim Rafferty. Being married to Sean wouldn't be easy. She'd probably gone into the relationship believing he'd change. Discovering that underneath the promises of everlasting love made in the middle of the night lay a heartless bastard must've been a surprise, expecting him to treat her differently from the rest of the world an error she was paying for. Tossing a child into the mix added a complication other people managed to work round.

Sean Rafferty wasn't other people.

And Pat Logue wasn't wrong about how the gangster felt about me.

Disappointing a woman wasn't a novel experience for me, but Kim Rafferty would need to get by without my help.

* * *

Back in NYB, the first of the lunchtime crowd were arriving from the salt mines. Pat kept his nose buried in his newspaper and ignored me. Jackie poured the takeaway I'd asked for, black with the two sugars, and smiled slyly.

'Aren't you a dark horse?'

'Am I?'

'Have to say I'm surprised.'

'Why's that?'

She paused, considering how hard to twist the knife.

'Without putting too fine a point on it, Charlie, it's fair to say she's not exactly your type.'

'I wasn't aware I had a type.'

She made a noise in her throat. 'You amaze me, you really do. 'Course you have. Everybody does.'

'What's mine?'

She handed me the cup and took my money. 'You usually like them smart and she's... well... blonde.'

I'd noticed.

'Joking aside, it's about time. She's gone home to Malawi and isn't coming back. Get over her.'

She was talking about Alile, my last girlfriend – another great woman I'd let slip away. She'd wanted more than I had to give and gone back home to Malawi. I missed her. Though I was reluctant to admit it, Jackie was right. Not for the first time I'd let something fine slip through my fingers.

'She isn't my girlfriend.'

'Then, who is she and what did she want?'

I kept her waiting – the only victory I was getting this morning.

'If I told you, you wouldn't believe me, Jackie.'

4

He looked different. Prison did that to a man and it had done it to Dennis Boyd. His hair was grey and he'd grown a beard. He raised his face to the sky, for the first time in fifteen years breathing air free from the sweat of a thousand captive bodies. It felt good.

He'd been thirty-seven, still relatively young, when they'd brought him handcuffed and flanked by two officers to Barlinnie, the Victorian building in the East End of Glasgow, almost as famous as Alcatraz. On a cold October morning, Boyd had stepped down from the police van and gazed without emotion at the walls, aware the guards were watching for even the smallest shadow of fear to darken his brow. They'd be disappointed. He was everything they'd heard and more: a hard man from an old school.

In court, Boyd pleaded not guilty to the charge and, before sentencing him for the callous murder of Joe Franks, Lord Justice Connor McGuinness asked if there was anything he wished to say. The question went unanswered and he was taken down.

Now, at fifty-two, his skin was the colour of the Bar-L's accommodation halls.

Two guards walked with him as far as the main door. 'Down the pub, is it, Dennis?'

'No.'

He let the screws draw their own conclusions.

'A minute of her life she's never going to get back, eh?'

'A minute the first time, maybe.'

The guards shook their heads and shared a dirty laugh. 'What about your drawings? Not taking them with you?'

He patted the leather portfolio. ''Course I am. Worth a fortune someday.'

Someday. He'd got through fifteen years dreaming of someday.

Now, that day was here.

As he stood on the pavement the murmur of traffic on the nearby M8 reminded him his old stomping ground was just miles away. It would've changed. Boyd let his eyes adjust to the light and wondered why his sister wasn't here to meet him. That wasn't like Annie, his sole visitor during his time in the Big House. Once a month, regular as clockwork she'd come to see him; in the beginning, fired with outrage over the injustice of his conviction, gushing nonsense about appeals, until reality arrived and resignation to the inevitable took hold. Boyd had already been there. Day after day in the dock, listening to the prosecution argue the case against him, he'd known it would end exactly the way whoever set him up meant it to. And it had, ably abetted by the inexperienced lawyer appointed to defend him.

A car racing down Lee Avenue got his attention; it braked hard alongside him. From behind the wheel a female wearing over-sized sunglasses, a headscarf and a double strand of pearls over a blue silk shirt spoke in a husky voice through the open window. 'Get in.'

Boyd didn't move. He was done with being told what to do and when to do it. She tossed the cigarette she was smoking at his feet and followed its progress to the gutter.

'Your sister isn't coming. Get in.'

They drove towards Cumbernauld Road and the city. When the lights at Alexandra Parade brought them to a halt, she held out slender fingers painted to match her lipstick and smiled. 'Welcome back, Dennis.'

He still had no idea who she was and didn't respond; her shades made it impossible to tell.

Her exasperation was genuine. 'Oh, come on, Boyd, surely I haven't changed that much, have I?'

She swept the glasses away and studied his face for the reaction she was determined to have, knowing the last person he'd expected to be waiting for him was the wife of the man he'd been convicted of killing.

'Diane?'

'The very same.'

The lines at the corners of her mouth were new and her hair was blonde and short where in the past it had been brunette and fallen, long and straight, to perfect breasts. But the eyes remained the same. At night in the early years, alone in the darkness of his cell, he'd conjured them and they'd appeared. Sometimes grey, sometimes green. Eyes that had lied for him and to him.

'For God's sake say something.'

'Can't. What the fuck, Diane?'

They'd been friends. Once. She hadn't come to see him because the doubt in her mind would always be there; it would never go away. The jury hadn't shared it.

'Where's Annie?'

'Told her I needed to speak to you. You'll see her soon enough.'

'Why're you here?'

The question didn't go down well with her; the fingers were withdrawn. He caught the sparkle of a ring on her right hand. Diamonds, what else? Diane feigned disappointment. 'You certainly know how to make a girl feel welcome.'

'That isn't what I meant.'

Her next statement took him by surprise. 'Just for the record, I never believed you did it.'

A decade and a half too late to do him any good. 'Glad to hear it.'

His expression gave nothing. He'd done his stretch, it didn't matter what she believed, what any of them believed. Fifteen years had been taken from him. Nothing could bring them back. She shifted in her seat and her skirt rose up, just as she intended. He ignored it and gazed out of the window at the city.

'Stop somewhere for a quick one, will you?'

'I'll have you know I'm a happily married woman.'

He felt himself stir and turned away. 'I meant a quick drink.'

'Where? Most of your old haunts are gone.'

'Then surprise me.'

The world he'd known no longer existed, that was something he was going to have to get used to. Diane grinned, tapped a Benson's from a packet and passed it over. 'So, how does it feel?'

'How does what feel?'

'To be free.'

'Is that what I am?'

'To get your life back.'

'I'll tell you when it happens. Give me a tour.'

'Anywhere special you want to see?'

Dennis Boyd shook his head. 'Just drive.'

*   *   *

They went west as far as Anniesland Cross and back through the city centre, down Renfield Street, across the river and south. Boyd recognised little of it; it had been too long. After a while, he stopped trying. Occasionally, she pointed to where a building had been and told him the history. He wasn't listening. Almost an hour later, they parked outside a pub on Paisley Road West.

'What do you make of it so far?'

He grunted. 'Not much. Could be anywhere.'

Inside, she ordered Johnnie Walker Black Label for both of them. Large ones. Boyd watched the barman ring up the sale. 'Fucking hell. Drinking isn't cheap, is it?'

'Nothing is, Dennis, as you're about to find out.'

They sat at a table; he nodded at her glass. 'Bit early for you to be starting on the hard stuff.'

Her reply was tart. 'How would you know?'

And she was right. After so much time what did he know about her?

Their affair had been passionate, maybe the most passionate Boyd had ever had. The first afternoon in particular stood out in his memory: Joe was in Amsterdam on business; they had sex upstairs in his house, in his bed. Not the slow melding of a man and a woman in love; the coupling of strangers, brief and intense.

What happened next seemed even more natural. Diane rolled onto her side, her body long and lithe and naked, eyes lowered, desire already building again in them. Words were unnecessary. Boyd understood. The workaholic Franks had a fax machine in the corner – another reason why a man was in bed with his wife; Boyd tore paper from it and rummaged in a bedside cabinet until he found a pencil. The pencil was blunt; it didn't matter. Diane watched his unhesitating strokes capture the moment. When he was done, he joined her on the bed and they went at it again with even more urgency than before.

She'd been somebody else's wife then and she was somebody else's wife now.

After three – or was it four? – years the drawing Blu Tacked to the wall in his cell was damaged by an idiot prison guard during a fruitless search. Boyd taped the pieces together and put it back up. Over time, the edges of the paper curled and he started to go grey. But the woman he'd drawn remained unchanged. Sometimes, in the wee small hours, it was all that was left of him.

One morning he noticed the definition was faded and blurred. His finger traced where the lead lines should be and weren't. Without a second thought he ripped the drawing up and flushed it down the toilet. Today, outside Barlinnie, Dennis Boyd had come full circle and hadn't recognised her. They'd returned to the strangers they'd been.

Boyd let the memory go and topped his whisky up with water. 'Better hope you don't get stopped. Goodbye licence.'

'Fuck them. There's no way I'm joining the mindless morons who order in a curry, download a movie and guzzle Tesco's finest plonk without moving off the couch.'

Dennis struggled to picture her spending her evenings with reheated chicken tikka, Asti Spumanti and *Fifty Shades of Grey*.

'How long have you been married?'

She pretended to have to think about it. 'Thirteen years.'

'Who's the lucky man?'

'Ritchie Kennedy.'

'You didn't hang about.'

'Couldn't afford to.'

She blew smoke into the air and he was reminded what a cold bastard she could be. 'Joe messed up everything. Not just him and me. He was up to his ears in debt and kept me in the dark about it. After he died, I discovered we were overdrawn at the bank and the mortgage hadn't been paid in months. Same story with the guy who owned the office in the Arcade.'

'How could that be?'

'That's the question, Dennis.'

'He was successful when I worked with him.'

'Or so everybody imagined.' The edges of her mouth turned down. 'It was a front. My husband was good at appraising stones but shit at selling them. He was drowning. Owed money all over the place. And the diamonds, the ones that got him killed? Not on the books, so no insurance. I would've gone under if it hadn't been for Ritchie.' She tilted her chin, pride creeping into her voice. 'He'd always had his eye on me. Moved in a couple of times when he came round to talk business with Joe. Cheeky bugger. 'Course, I knocked him back. But with Joe out of the picture there was nothing to stop him trying again. Thank God he did.'

Diane lit cigarettes for both of them and passed one to Boyd. An expensive watch on her wrist caught his attention; he guessed it was the real McCoy. This lady had landed on her feet, albeit via her back. She shifted the conversation away from her. 'Now you're out, what're your plans?'

Boyd sat back, sensing hidden meaning in the words. 'You were at the trial, Diane, what do you think my plans are?'

She tapped ash on the floor. 'Go after them.'

'Got it in one. I took the fall for something I didn't do.' His eyes bored into her. 'You don't look surprised.'

Diane considered her reply. 'Why would I be surprised? Look, Dennis, apart from you, nobody has a bigger investment than me in this thing. They beat my husband to death in his own house, for Christ's sake. I've waited all this time to say what I'm going to say to you. It's why I was at the Bar-L.'

'Thought it was because you still fancied me.'

Boyd's flippancy irritated her. 'In your dreams. Understand this: as a lover you were okay. I'd say you were a seven. Seven and a half on a good night. I've had better. Listen. I want you to hear this. What's done is done. Forget it and get on with your life. I have. So can you.'

'And the bastards who put me away?'

'Keep your voice down. Take the heat out of the situation. Whoever did it knows you're on the street. They'll be expecting you to come after them. Don't. Don't play their game.'

She went into her Gucci bag, brought out two envelopes and laid them on the table between them. 'Joe dying the way he did...' She gripped Boyd's arm. 'Even though I didn't love him I was numb. But I made a decision, and I want to help you make one.'

She lifted her glass in a toast. 'To survivors.'

Boyd didn't join in. 'You can't be serious.'

'Never been more so. Okay, you didn't kill Joe. Except we're the only ones who think that's true. Rake up the past and these people – whoever they are – aren't just going to stand by and let you. Enough of your life's been lost to this.' She pushed the envelopes towards him. 'This will get you started.'

'Your concern is appreciated, Mrs Kennedy. What am I missing?'

She leaned across the table until their faces were inches apart. Boyd thought she was going to kiss him and wouldn't have resisted. It didn't happen. She lowered her voice to a whisper and the moment passed. 'Let's tell the truth, Dennis. You and I – but especially you – should've realised Joe was in over his head. You were his bodyguard, after all. He spent more time with you than anybody, including me. The way I see it, our affair was responsible for you going down. So yes, however crazy you think it is, I feel you're due something. Besides, calling you a seven might not be quite true.'

Boyd put a hand on her shoulder and gently eased her back in the seat. 'You haven't answered my question. Helping me is one thing. Why so keen I disappear?'

She lifted her head and glared. In the old days, the fire in those eyes would have been enough to arouse him. 'You went to prison. I almost ended out on the street. But I got lucky; you didn't. Fifteen years is a long time. Joe screwed both of us over. He kept you in the dark instead of letting you do the job he was paying you to do. Think of me as your guardian angel. Take the cash and get away from Glasgow.'

Boyd drew deeply on his cigarette. 'Nice speech, Diane. Touching. Is Ritchie in on how you're spending his money?'

'Ritchie doesn't have any part of this. The money's mine.'

'Your own little nest egg and you're prepared to give it to me. How did you come by it?'

A smile appeared and disappeared. 'What can I tell you? I'm a saver.'

'Careful with other folk's cash. Admirable.'

Her patience was wearing thin. She snapped. 'Just take it and stop fucking about.'

Boyd shook his head. 'No can do. Sorry.'

She scribbled her mobile number on a beer mat and threw it at him. It struck his chest and fell to the floor. When she spoke, her voice was hoarse with frustration. 'Now I remember why it didn't work out with us. You were a fool then and you're still a bloody fool.'

'That wasn't why. It was never going anywhere. I was your bit of rough. A diversion to keep boredom at bay until a better offer came along. I couldn't afford you and we both knew it.'

Diane lifted the mat and pressed it into his hands. 'Take it. Please. For me.'

'On one condition. Wilson, Davidson and McDermid. Where are they?'

She hesitated.

Boyd said, 'I'll find out. With or without your help.'

'Last I heard Wilson and McDermid were in Glasgow. Davidson moved away after his wife died of cancer. Stays with his daughter on the coast somewhere.'

'What else?'

'Nothing else. Their names haven't been mentioned in years. Now, take this. You promised.'

He slipped the beer mat into his inside pocket, drained his drink and stood. She looked up at him. 'They'll know you're out. What will going after them do beyond putting you back inside? It'll change nothing.'

'They can tell me who was behind it.'

'And then what?'

'I'll settle the score.'

'They'll kill you.'

'Maybe they will and maybe they won't.'

Diane wasn't impressed. 'I'd forgotten talking to you was never easy.'

'I don't recall us doing much talking.'

She stabbed out her cigarette, not amused. 'It was always a long shot but I wanted to give it a go. I may be the only friend you've got left in this town.' Her fist banged on the table. 'I'm trying to do you a favour here!'

'Really? Then drop me at my sister's.'

5

Sean Rafferty tore open a paper finger of brown sugar and stirred it into the coffee cup in front of him. Through the glass frontage of the Radisson Blu Hotel, Glasgow was going about its day. He felt himself relax. It had been a stressful morning, but it had turned out well, all things considered.

At one o'clock, a black taxicab pulled up at the kerb. The woman inside paid the driver and got out. Rafferty smiled. Right on time – keen – he liked that in a female. She saw him and waved. Rafferty didn't wave back. He'd forgotten her name. Awkward, though not a problem – she wouldn't be around long enough to need one. She'd dressed for the occasion: white jacket, flared navy-blue skirt and the highest heels he'd ever seen. She hurried towards him, arms outstretched, wet lips parted. His eyes wandered to the lilac blouse and imagined the breasts underneath.

He kissed her cheek and she said, 'I'm not late, am I? Please tell me I'm not late. I've been so busy I'm exhausted.'

A lie. She'd married her husband because he was good at making money, and so she could sit around on her lovely arse all day; the hardest work she did was on her knees for her tennis coach.

Rafferty smiled. When they got to the room upstairs, he'd show her what exhausted felt like.

'No, you're fine.'

Her eyelashes fluttered. 'Have you been waiting long?'

'Just got here.'

She stepped back to look at him. 'How do you manage to stay in such good shape?'

'Clean living. Avoid it at all costs.'

She laughed on cue and playfully punched his shoulder. 'Fake as fuck', to use one of old Jimmy's expressions. Rafferty took her hand and led her to the lifts. She tossed her red hair over her shoulder in her best I-enjoy-being-a-girl routine.

'What kind of morning have you had?'

'If I told you, I'd have to kill you.'

She remembered this was Sean Rafferty and giggled uncomfortably. 'Then don't.'

* * *

The bedroom door closed behind them. Her arms circled his neck and she kissed him; he smelled her perfume, subtle and expensive. Her fingers ran over the front of his shirt.

'Give me a minute.'

He watched her long legs teeter to the bathroom, then went to the window and looked out. The sun was shining; down below, a line of cars sat at the traffic lights, grey smoke puttering from their exhausts, waiting to make the left turn into Hope Street – the most polluted street in Glasgow. Rafferty had cancelled the meeting with his accountant and made only a brief appearance at the youth centre – just long enough to get his face in the photographs. He didn't identify with the kids; compared to his upbringing with Jimmy as a father, they had it easy.

The bathroom door opened and the redhead came out, naked except for the heels.

Rafferty still couldn't remember her fucking name.

He saw the firm breasts, the tanned thighs, and felt himself grow hard. That body had been used to getting its owner what she wanted from men. For all her ladies-who-lunch and golf-club la-di-da, it was for sale.

She came towards him, rolling her tight arse from side to side, confident she had what no warm-blooded man could resist, circling her arms round his neck like she'd done before.

Rafferty took hold of her wrists and roughly pulled them away. 'What the hell do you think you're doing?'

Not the reaction she'd expected. 'I... I...'

He wanted to punch her pretty face for trying to take control, treating him like a clown who thought with his dick and could be played by a smile and a pair of nice tits.

She stepped away, suddenly afraid, the confidence gone, conscious of the change in him without understanding what she'd done to cause it. 'Sean, I was—'

'Save the act for somebody who appreciates it. You're trying too hard, sweetheart. I don't like it. Put your clothes on and hurry up. I've waited long enough.' He opened the minibar, weighed a brandy miniature in his palm and unscrewed the top. 'Bloody robbery what they charge for this. Somebody should call the police.'

When she returned, he was on the edge of the bed, watching TV with the sound down. He spoke without taking his eyes off the screen. 'Get undressed.'

She peeled the blouse away, unzipped the skirt and stepped out of her underwear. The garments dropped to the floor at her feet and he was on her, lifting her up, throwing her against the wall, his lips parted in a cruel smile. He kissed her neck and took her already hard nipple in his mouth; her legs snaked round his waist, gripping him with the unexpected strength of the aroused.

He buried himself in her and whispered in her ear. 'What the hell's your name?'

* * *

The flat in Shawlands was the nicest place Vicky had ever had. And it was all hers; she owned it. From the beginning, she'd been determined not to end up like so many in her trade: addicted, broken and broke. Her bank account had a tidy sum in it. A 'fuck you' fund for the day she needed it.

The meeting with Sean Rafferty was the first sign that day was coming.

She watched Tony stretch for the half-full bottle of Pinot Grigio and top them up. Drinking wasn't his thing – long-distance drivers didn't risk their licence for a few glasses of wine on a Tuesday afternoon. Tony saw the woman behind the label and loved her. He wasn't handsome but he was kind; the most genuine person she'd ever known. And he was crazy about her. If only they'd met before she went down this path. Vicky couldn't even blame her choices on her upbringing. No, the credit was all hers. An impressionable teenager, she'd jumped at the chance when a friend told her what easy money it was and how much of it she was making. It had sounded exciting and glamorous. It was neither. Too late for regrets; she'd done what she'd done.

Tony cut across her thoughts. 'How many times in the last year – forget year, the last six months – have I asked you to marry me?'

'A few.'

'Not a few, seven. I'm starting to think you don't like me.'

Vicky flushed, uncomfortable with the reminder. 'I've told you why.'

'Tell me again, see if I believe you.'

'It wouldn't work.'

'I think it would.'

'You're wrong, Tony. When a man has a girlfriend, what she did in the past doesn't bother him. Wives are different.'

'How?'

'It becomes... personal... a reflection on him.'

Tony sat up. 'Rubbish. What guy thinks like that?'

'You'd be surprised. Almost every working girl I've known who got married ended up divorced.'

'And you assume it's because their husbands couldn't handle their history. Okay. What's that got to do with you and me?'

She looked into his eyes. 'This. What we have, it's good. Let's not spoil it.'

Tony pressed his case. 'I turn good money. Your job would be to make a home for us. It doesn't need to be Glasgow or even Scotland, it could be anywhere you like. Plenty of nice spots down south. *So*, for the eighth time. Vicky Farrell, will you marry me?'

She kissed the tip of his nose. 'No, Tony, I won't. I like you too much. Consider yourself fortunate and stop asking, otherwise one of these days...'

6

The reunion was more awkward than either Dennis Boyd or his sister had imagined it would be. Annie was Boyd's only relative. She loved him, no doubt about that, but they hadn't lived under the same roof since they were teenagers, and the time he'd spent in prison hadn't helped; they were strangers. With the best will in the world, building a relationship would be slow going and they both realised it.

Most men newly released from the Big House could expect a welcome home party. There was no celebration for Dennis Boyd. He didn't want one. A party took people. Friends. Boyd had no friends.

He laid on the single bed in Annie's spare room killing the hours until he could make an excuse to go. A framed charcoal drawing of a woman, done years ago, stared down at him: his sister. He'd captured her perfectly before life had had a chance to grind her down. Grind both of them down. Dennis wondered if she'd put it there to remind him who he'd been and could be again.

His surroundings were comfortable – beyond that, not so

different from his cell. As soon as he'd done what he had to do, he'd be on his way. Annie would spout the usual stuff about there always being a place for him here, though she'd be pleased to see the back of him. Boyd didn't blame her; he felt the same.

After dinner, they sat across from each other watching television, Boyd's eyes straying to the clock on the wall every few minutes. Around eight-thirty, he put on his jacket and said he was going for a drink. Annie called a minicab to take him into town and settled to her programmes and her routine, already recognising the short-term future of having her brother live with her.

Boyd asked the taxi to let him off in St Vincent Street. Banged up in Barlinnie, he'd dreamed of being able to walk in anywhere he fancied and order a whisky and a pint. Now it was a reality, it didn't feel as good as he'd imagined.

Half an hour and two pubs later, he was heading towards George Square. The Counting House was more to his taste. Big and busy, just as he remembered it. Dozens of people stood at the bar or clustered round tables, talking and drinking. Boyd guessed they were city workers who hadn't made it home yet. He squeezed in between two middle-aged businessmen in suits, asked for a whisky and watched the crowd. After a while, he ordered again. The barman brought the drink and a slip of paper to him and went to serve the other side of the bar. Boyd read the message written in capital letters.

ELMBANK CAR PARK TOP LEVEL 10.30

He called the barman over. 'Who gave you this?'
The man shrugged indifference. 'Some guy.'
'Point him out.'
'He left.'
'Who was he?'

'Just a punter.'

'What did he look like?'

The barman shrugged a second time. 'A guy. Never seen him before. Assumed he was a friend of yours. Sorry, pal.'

Boyd pushed the whisky away. Whatever this was about, he'd need a clear head. It hadn't taken somebody long to make a move. The speed of it was the biggest surprise. Or maybe not. Diane had said they'd know he was out. Of course, she was right. They wouldn't hang around. He wondered which one of them would be waiting for him. Wilson was the favourite – a thug who assumed everybody was as gullible as himself. An obvious trap like this was exactly what Boyd expected from an idiot who lied for money.

He read the message again, picturing Hughie Wilson on the stand, the suit he'd been wearing and the shirt and tie not enough to disguise his true nature. To give the prosecution their due, they'd prepped him well and encouraged him to tell the story in his own words. Carefully chosen words sweated over for hours. The fabrication had come close to being undone when Wilson delivered his lines like an amateur, visibly toiling under cross examination. His testimony had liar plastered all over it. In the dock, Boyd had breathed a sigh of relief, convinced it was too pat to persuade a jury – none of them would believe this guy. Except they had. Wilson swore the defendant approached him and suggested there was a place for him in a robbery Boyd intended to commit. The target wasn't identified – that would've been pushing credibility already stretched by the over-rehearsed numbskull's performance – but, since Joe Franks was robbed and murdered shortly after the alleged conversation took place, it hadn't been hard to join the dots.

With a straight face, Wilson admitted considering the offer before turning it down.

When asked to answer yes or no if he believed the jeweller was the intended victim, he answered yes. The judge sustained the defence counsel's immediate objection, warned the prosecution against leading the witness to speculate, and instructed the jury to disregard what they'd heard.

Pointless and impossible.

Dennis Boyd realised whoever was behind it had to be smiling; they'd laid their plan well and it was working. He was going down for a crime he hadn't committed.

On St Vincent Street, he checked his watch, turned his collar up, and started walking. The message said ten-thirty and it was already quarter past. Elmbank Gardens was a good ten minutes away; he quickened his step. At the top of the hill across from the Alexander 'Greek' Thomson church, a monstrosity if ever there was one, he glanced at the time again: a few minutes to half past. Boyd turned right at the traffic lights at the bottom, then left into Elmbank Gardens. From inside the King's Theatre the sound of the audience applauding filtered through to the street; the show was ending. In a minute, the place would be flooded with people. That thought reassured him. Responding to the message was a gut reaction, though it allowed whoever had sent it to set the rules. Hiding wasn't an option. Tonight, for better or worse, he'd learn who he was dealing with. After that...

After that Boyd had no idea.

Diane's offer would still be on the table – he guessed she was part of the deal. Not entirely unwelcome, except he'd be kidding himself to pretend it had a chance of working any better now. She was a woman who needed more than he was ever likely to be able to provide. In a straight choice between love or money, money would win every time. Fifteen years ago, circumstances were different. Joe had given her financial security; she'd needed something more. She'd needed sex. And it had been fun.

The memories had taken time to die because – whatever she said about him – Diane certainly hadn't been a seven. Her second husband had nothing to fear from him; adultery was a young man's game and Boyd was too old to be sneaking around.

A yellow sign flashed 'No Spaces'. In a few minutes, that wouldn't be true; the theatre crowd would arrive and head home. He took the lift to level five, ignoring the smell of piss and stale cigarette smoke – mild after the Bar-L – until it came to a shuddering stop. The doors opened and he walked into the open air, his eyes taking a moment to become used to the half-light. From the street below, the chatter of excited voices rose to meet him.

If it was a trap, this was when he expected whoever had sent the message to step from the shadows. His fists balled at his sides as adrenaline surged through him and his eyes narrowed, scanning the empty car park. The meeting had been a test to get his attention. Somewhere they'd be watching and had already learned something valuable about him: he could be played.

The door opened. Three women, all speaking at once, appeared and made their way to their car. On instinct, Boyd pressed himself against the nearest vehicle and stood still but they were preoccupied with each other and didn't notice him. Soon there would be more. He took a final look round before retracing his steps.

Then he saw it: at the far end, a pile of rags dumped on the ground. Boyd edged cautiously towards it, hearing the hum of the lift. Two men and two women stepped out and hurried to a black Vauxhall. He fell to the concrete floor and scrambled towards the bundle, knowing it was the reason they'd wanted him here. Closer, it became the body of a man lying in a pool of blood. Boyd rolled it over to see the face and immediately wished he hadn't.

Even without the horrific injuries, time hadn't been kind to Hughie Wilson; he hadn't aged well – having his head beaten to a pulp didn't help. In the semi-darkness there was enough left of the thug who'd lied on the witness stand for Boyd to recognise him; shards of bone poked through the skin from the shattered nose below the temple caved in under the force of a tremendous blow. Wilson's eyes were open, the right socket a milky white where the iris and pupil should've been. Boyd touched the cold concrete and felt scrapes of Christ-knew-what under his fingertips.

Nothing had prepared him for this. Less than twelve hours after his release from Barlinnie, one of the men who'd testified against him was dead. And suddenly, Dennis Boyd understood.

They'd framed him once and they were doing it again.

The hum of the lift returning snapped him into action. He ran across the car park, almost knocking down a middle-aged couple coming through the door. The man cursed and the woman cried out. Boyd didn't stop to apologise. In the distance, a police siren cut through the night. He took the stairs to the bottom and ran out of the rear entrance. In Bath Street, he joined the last of the crowd spilling from the King's Theatre and slowed to a walk so as not to attract attention to himself. Fifteen minutes later, he was standing in Central Station with little idea how he'd got there, or why.

Central was quiet. Boyd bought coffee from a Costa stand and sat on a seat under the huge notice board suspended above the gates to the platforms. Yards away, a teenage boy and girl draped their arms round each other and kissed for Scotland. Near them, a gang of young boys passed round a can of foreign beer he didn't recognise and made obscene comments about the couple, while a homeless man in a grubby overcoat a couple of sizes too big for him scavenged a litter bin. If the tramp dug deep enough, he might come across the plan Boyd had had twelve hours earlier.

A train going to the coast caught his eye. For a second, he considered it.

Then what? Who did he know? Where would he go?

I may be the only friend you've got left in this town

He patted his jacket, unsure if he still had it, and was in luck – the beer mat was still there. Boyd threw the coffee away, walked to a bank of telephone booths at the far side of the station and dialled the number. When she answered, she sounded sleepy. He blurted out his relief at hearing her voice. 'Diane? Diane, it's me.'

'Dennis?'

'You were right.'

'What do you mean? What's happened?'

'It's a mess, Diane. A fucking mess.'

'What is? Where are you?'

'Central Station. Come and get me.'

* * *

Sean Rafferty grunted his dissatisfaction at the darkness beyond the empty conservatory overlooking the river. The fine weather had moved on and rain spattered the windowpanes in a steady drumbeat. He was ugly drunk and spoiling for a fight; there weren't any takers. Kim was upstairs in bed – again – with the new door locked. Rosie was asleep. Rafferty's fevered brain threw up a possibility he hadn't considered: she had a lover. Kim was a great-looking woman, even if she was a pain in the arse. When they'd met, she'd been a model, flashing her tits for the cameras every chance she got. Would any guy be stupid enough to mess with his property? If somebody had the balls, God help them. Bryce Hunter's son had tried and was lucky to still be able to walk.

But with his wife? Veins tightened like cords in his neck under the skin; he cracked his knuckles and grimaced. What a mistake that would be.

Rafferty wasn't jealous. He didn't love Kim. Apart from Rosie, he'd never loved anybody. Kim was a good mother, otherwise he'd have got rid of the bitch long since. There would be a queue round the block to take her place when he did pull the plug.

Rosie would always be okay – Sean Rafferty was her father.

He sloshed more whisky into the glass; some of it fell on the carpet. The redhead would be at home, curled up on the couch, watching television with her husband.

He mimicked the conversation. 'How did it go today, darling? Anything to report?'

'You mean, apart from Sean Rafferty fucking me? Not much. How about you, darling?'

Rafferty gave a harsh laugh and put the whisky to his lips, aroused, breathing heavily. Would he see her again? What was the point? He could get sex anywhere – anywhere but his own bed, apparently.

7

Afternoon sunshine streamed in the window. The blonde sitting in my office casually opened another button on her blouse, her eyes studying my face for a reaction. I didn't oblige; it was an act. Better-looking ladies than her had tried it. Some had had the talent to pull it off. She wasn't one of them.

Two blondes in two days. Maybe my aftershave was attracting them.

I expected her to introduce herself. Instead, she lit a cigarette without checking if I objected and pointed to the sign stencilled on the door.

C Cameron
Private Investigator

'Are you any good?'

Her directness fazed me. 'I'm not sure what you mean.'

She crossed her legs, blew a smoke ring in the air and glanced at me to see if her routine was cutting it. 'Could you handle something a little more... unusual?'

'If I knew who I was talking to, I might.'

The fingers she offered were like the rest of her: slim, well cared for and cool.

'Sorry. Diane Kennedy. Call me Diane.'

'Okay, you've got my attention.'

She paused, considering how to begin, and pushed her credibility over the edge. This lady had decided exactly what to say and how to say it before she'd even met me.

'A friend of mine needs help, he's in trouble.'

'What kind of trouble?'

'The police are looking for him, or they will be soon.'

'What for?'

'Murder.'

The femme-fatale nonsense fell away – it wouldn't be missed; concern furrowed her brow, and something real took its place. 'It's a long story. You may not believe it. Don't know if I believe it myself.'

In the movies, the PI would jut out a square jaw and mouth a manly, 'Try me.' I said nothing. It was her show.

'Does the name Dennis Boyd ring any bells?'

'Should it?'

'Perhaps not. Fifteen years ago, when he was convicted of robbing and killing Joe Franks, it was front-page news. Joe was a jeweller. Dennis was his bodyguard. It looked like a set-up and it was. The police found traces of blood in the boot of his car and a diamond on the floor.'

'Convincing.'

'And convenient. Though on its own, probably not quite enough to persuade a jury.'

'What swung it?'

'The testimony of three people.'

I let what I was hearing sink in. Surely, she wasn't expecting me to solve a crime already a decade and a half old? If she was, like Kim Rafferty, she'd come to the wrong door. Mrs Kennedy indulged her flair for the dramatic, got up, walked round the room and kept me waiting for an answer. 'Last night, one of the witnesses was murdered in a car park at Charing Cross.'

I was ahead of her. 'Boyd is the obvious suspect.'

'Correction. The only suspect.'

'And you want me to do... what?'

'Dennis is innocent. Prove he didn't do it. He got a message...'

I held up my hands to stop her. 'Don't tell me anything else. If you have information, you should be talking to the police, not me.'

'They got it wrong before.'

'So you say.'

'Of course they did. A blind man could see he's being framed again. It's obvious.'

'No, it isn't. Less than a day after your friend gets out of prison somebody who spoke against him is killed.'

'That's what they want you to think.'

'They? Who's they?'

'Whoever murdered Joe.'

I massaged my temple. This was crazy. I wanted her out of my office, and not just because the smoke from her cigarette was annoying me. I'd had plenty of loony tunes with impossible expectations come to me. This one was hard to beat.

'Look, Mrs Kennedy—'

'Diane.'

'Look, Diane. I have no idea what happened at Charing Cross last night. Even less about a fifteen-year-old crime. You say your friend is innocent. Fine. I'll take your word for it. But I won't take your case, it isn't what I do. I find missing people.'

She glared over my shoulder and shook her head. 'I knew this was a waste of time. Dennis insisted. Told him you'd be no use.'

Maybe it was part of her strategy to draw me in. If it was, it had worked – being told you were a waste of time would do that.

My ego raised its ugly head. 'Why isn't Boyd with you? Does he even know you're here?'

'He can't show himself.' She paused, pulled out her big line and laid a giant-sized guilt trip on me. 'You're his only hope.'

For a whole two minutes I'd been a stranger – a useless stranger, according to her. I preferred it. I got out of my chair and opened the window. 'Then he's in more trouble than he realises, because I can't promise to help on the say-so of somebody's girlfriend.'

Her voice took on an edge a long way from the aloof character pissing me off by polluting the air; the elegant fingers gripped the table. 'I'm not his girlfriend. I'm not anybody's girlfriend.'

'That's not my business. Just so long as you understand the ground rules. The police will be looking for Boyd. You believe he's innocent – I hope he justifies your faith in him. I'm not interested in knowing where he is, so don't tell me.'

She stubbed the cigarette out under her high-heeled shoe, took a new packet of Benson & Hedges from her bag and tore off the cellophane.

'And I'd prefer you didn't smoke in here.'

That prohibition affected her more than the rest of my speech. The packet went back in her bag and she didn't look at me; I'd displeased her. Too bad.

My objection had knocked her off her stride. It took a moment to get back on track. I filled the gap. 'What's your connection to Dennis Boyd?'

'I met him when he worked for my husband, Joe.'

Diane stared me down.

'The Joe he was convicted of murdering?'

'Dennis didn't kill anybody. Someone else did and made it look like it was him.'

'Why so sure?'

'Because I know Dennis Boyd.'

'Fair enough. Why did Joe have a bodyguard? That isn't usual, is it?'

'Not unusual. He dealt with trade, not the public, and worked out of an office in the Argyll Arcade. Sometimes he'd be holding stones worth a lot of money. It made sense to have protection.'

'Okay. Tell me about the murder.'

Her husband had been gone a long time. Maybe why talking about it didn't seem to bother her. 'One night our house was burgled. A parcel of diamonds was taken. So far as the police could tell, they'd forced Joe to open the safe then beat him to death. It was horrible. After they searched his car and discovered traces of blood and a diamond on the floor, they suspected Dennis.'

'Did Boyd have an alibi?'

'No, he didn't. But the case against him was circumstantial.'

'Until the three witnesses.'

'From out of nowhere, they came forward and nailed him to the cross.'

'What did they say?'

'A small-time crook called Liam McDermid claimed he'd overheard Dennis and Joe arguing.'

'About?'

'Money Joe owed Dennis.'

'And did he?'

She threw back her head, about to laugh, and thought better of it. 'It would be strange if he didn't. He owed everybody else.'

'Is that a yes?'

'I suppose it is.'

'Then what happened?'

'Hughie Wilson, a well-known thug, swore Dennis asked him to be part of a burglary. Of course, he'd turned him down. But, later, when he got word about Joe, he'd realised that was the job. Dennis was already well on his way to Barlinnie when Willie Davidson testified to seeing a guy matching his description running from the house.'

'Added to the physical evidence, there was no way back.'

'It took the jury less than an hour to reach their verdict. I was there.'

Diane had said a lot though she'd left out why she was in my office, asking me to help the man who'd been found guilty of robbing and killing her husband.

'Mrs Kennedy, excuse me for being blunt. Your husband was the victim. What's your interest in helping the man convicted of murdering him?'

She reached for her bag and the pack of cigarettes, then remembered and changed her mind. This lady had arrived with plenty of attitude. Now the questions were more difficult and she was struggling. I gave her a push in the right direction. 'Before you answer you need to know that no matter what you tell me, I'm probably not taking the case. Anything less than the truth and probably becomes definitely.'

I could almost see the wheels turning behind her eyes as she made her decision. Whatever she was holding back had to be pretty important.

'Dennis got a raw deal. Joe screwed both of us. Nobody would've got hurt if he'd kept the stones in a bank or the office safe like any sane person. What was he doing with them in the house? I wasn't at home or I might be dead, too.' Her cheeks coloured. 'I was lucky. Dennis went to Barlinnie for something he didn't do. I owe him.'

'That doesn't explain why you're here. In fact, it gives you even less reason to put yourself in the middle of it. Last chance, Mrs Kennedy. Tell me the truth or close the door on your way out.'

She stared at me for a long time. 'All right. Dennis and I were more than friends. But it was a fling. Nothing serious.'

'Did your husband know?'

'I think he guessed, and I'm afraid that's why he was so reckless and cut Dennis out of the last job, even though there was so much money at stake. Joe was wrong. Dennis wasn't to blame for the affair. I was the one who made the running. He didn't want to betray Joe.' She bit her bottom lip. 'I met him yesterday outside Barlinnie when he was released and tried to get him to go away.'

'Why?'

'Because fifteen years is a lot to have taken from you. There was no chance he'd let it go. I knew he'd be determined to even the score.'

'By doing what?'

She stopped short of putting a name to it. 'I offered him money. At first, he wouldn't take it. Later, he called me. A witness was dead and Dennis was scared. He realised they intended to frame him a second time. At least now he understands what he's up against. No matter what happens, he swears he isn't going inside again. All he wants is his life back.'

Finally, I was hearing something I could believe.

'Is it all right if I have a cigarette?'

I nodded. She rummaged in her bag again with the enthusiasm of a panhandler, except the silver and gold she was after were dried leaves and paper. Diane inhaled hard enough to suck the oxygen from the room; when she spoke, there was smoke in her voice. 'He's desperate. Please meet him. Please.'

I pushed my card across the desk and saw hope come alive in her eyes.

8

DS Geddes was scribbling notes on a sheet of paper, his lips moving soundlessly as he read through them before the scribbling began again. Patrick, on the other hand, had abandoned the racing section of the *Daily Record* for a book. Whatever it was it certainly had his attention.

It was Pat I was looking for. Diane Kennedy had told me the truth – so far as it went. I didn't fool myself it was all there was. Pat would get the whole story; it was his gift. I tapped him on the shoulder. He greeted me like I was a soldier returning from the Russian front. 'Charlie!'

I nodded at his book. 'Good, is it?'

He turned it over to let me see the title: *World's Best Quotations*.

'Fantastic. You've no idea how much stuff is in here. A gem on every page.'

'A word, when you've got a minute.'

'Absolutely. I'm free now.'

He followed me to a table near the back. NYB wasn't busy; we had the place to ourselves. I didn't dance around it. 'Does the name Dennis Boyd mean anything to you?'

'A blast from the past.' He scratched the stubble on his chin. 'Killed the jeweller he was workin' for, as I remember. Big news at the time.'

'Find out everything you can about him.'

'In the Big House, isn't he?'

'Not any more. He got out yesterday.'

'Why the sudden interest? Must've been a dozen years ago now.'

'Fifteen.'

'Any older and it's an archaeologist you'd need. That it?'

'No. I want to know about Joe Franks and his wife, Diane. Diane Kennedy now. And whatever you can find about her second husband.'

He got up. 'Shouldn't be too difficult. Give me a couple of days. Start first thing in the morning, all right?'

'Faster if you can. One more thing. At the trial, the testimony of three witnesses swung it in the prosecution's favour. Whatever you turn up on them will be useful.'

'Any idea where they are?'

'One of them is in the morgue. Died last night in a car park. According to Diane, these guys were bribed, so the other two have got to be seriously sweating.'

Patrick's reaction was understandable. 'Didn't let the grass grow, did he? Not too clever. Better if he'd held off, although maybe he thought fifteen years was long enough.'

'It might not have been Dennis Boyd.'

'Good luck convincin' the procurator fiscal. Have the police caught him?'

'Not yet.'

'Only a matter of time before they do. Hope it was worth it. Probably cost the rest of his life.'

'Unless he didn't do it.'

Pat Logue's eyes searched my face as he began to see where we were headed. 'That what this is about, Charlie? Because if it is, let me remind you the difference between you and your pal, Andrew, over there. He's police. They pay him to solve crimes. You find missin' people. You used to get that.'

'Appreciate the concern, Patrick. Believe me. I'm not involved in anything.'

'Yet.'

He knew me too well. My mobile vibrated in my pocket. I took it out and opened it. 'Charlie Cameron.'

The deep male voice on the other end didn't waste words. 'Strathclyde Park. Tomorrow at four o'clock.'

Before I could speak, he hung up.

Pat Logue was the most tolerant person I'd ever known. Across the table, he didn't disguise his disapproval. 'One word from me and you do what you like, eh, Charlie? Thought you'd learned your lesson. Takin' cases that would put you opposite Sean Rafferty is bad enough. Questions about fifteen-year-old murders and ten-second phone calls tell me you're off and runnin' again, aren't you? Puttin' your nose in where it doesn't belong.' He shook his head. 'This isn't you, Charlie. Findin' people, that's your game. And if you want to branch out, why the hell can't you do bread and butter jobs? Domestic disharmony's a lot less dangerous. Pay's better, too.'

'Not if you're a man.'

I hadn't noticed DS Andrew Geddes standing behind me, singing his usual song. Andrew had been on the wrong end of a bitter divorce and never missed an opportunity to bad-mouth the holy state of matrimony. Listening to him had worn thin. Somebody ought to tell him to put a sock in it, though it wouldn't be me. My tactic was to ignore it and change the subject. 'Andrew! Any progress on the promotion?'

'Not so far. Have to produce evidence to prove leadership. Whole load of stuff like that. Just making some notes. Not so easy to write about yourself.'

'Will your detective inspector be involved?'

'Of course, Barr will be asked for his input so I'm not holding my breath.'

'Surely he wouldn't stand in your way?'

Andrew looked at me as if I'd come down with yesterday's rain and put a friendly hand on my shoulder. 'Sometimes I wonder how you've managed to get through life, Charlie. Your innocence is touching. DI Adam Barr wouldn't give me a kick in the head to bring me out of a fit. I'm everything he's not, starting with professional. Wouldn't stand in my way? Yeah, right. After what happened with Tony Daly, he'd have me on traffic duty.'

'But you were right about the councillor case.'

'And he was wrong. Not likely to forget it, is he? Can only hope he moves on sooner rather than later because, until he does, I'll be staying a detective sergeant.'

Pat Logue said, 'It's a hard world,' and cleared his throat. I knew what was coming. Hoped I was wrong. I wasn't wrong. He said, '"If you can meet with triumph and disaster and treat those two imposters just the same." Rudyard Kipling.'

Geddes glared at him.

Alex Gilby coming through the door broke the tension. Alex was around sixty and had been on the Glasgow hospitality scene longer than almost anyone, in his time, operating some of the best-known restaurants and café bars in the city. The clothes he wore were expensive, yet he always looked as if he'd dressed in the dark. Today, it was jeans, a jacket and a white open-necked shirt. He grinned at us and put an avuncular hand on the shoulder of the blonde with him.

'This is my niece, Michelle. She's coming to work here.'

Michelle smiled at everyone and no one. I guessed she was in her mid-twenties: bright-eyed and eager. Alex explained her to us. 'Michelle isn't sure what she wants to do with her life. My sister suggested I give her a start in hospitality. See how she takes to it.'

He was the boss. He could do what he liked. At least, that was the theory. His next statement set off alarm bells in my head. 'Jackie's going to show her the ropes.'

I wondered if he'd talked to Jackie. For his sake, I hoped so, otherwise – boss or no boss – a shitload of trouble was about to fall on his head.

'Is she in her office? I'll go and speak to her.'

With Alex gone, Pat Logue straightened his shoulders and stepped forward, ready to go into his Mr Charm routine. Patrick had a thing for barmaids. Considering how much of his life he spent in their company, it was hardly a surprise. What he was building up to – to borrow one of his many sporting phrases – was called 'playing away from home'.

Andrew Geddes stared righteously at the floor. Pat moved beside Michelle and whispered something we couldn't hear; she laughed. Geddes shot a disapproving glance at me and shook his head. 'How in God's name do you put up with him, Charlie? Man's no better than a rutting animal.'

'No, he's just a middle-aged guy trying to prove he's still got it.'

'Wish I had your tolerance.'

'So do I, Andrew.'

Out of the corner of my eye, I caught Jackie marching towards the bar with a red-faced Alex trailing behind her. She put out her hand to the new-start. 'Jackie. I hear you're joining us. Welcome to NYB.'

To anyone who didn't know better, it sounded genuine. I knew better. Jackie Mallon made the decisions in New York Blue, especially the hiring and firing. Having the owner give somebody a job – a relative, of all people – without squaring it with her first wasn't on. Jackie guarded her territory like a lioness protecting her young, the reason my office was in Cochrane Street now and not upstairs. Any threat would be met and matched, even if it came from the owner. Through no fault of her own, Gilby's niece was in for a difficult time. Michelle was too unworldly to realise that, thanks to her uncle, she'd unwittingly become part of a power struggle. I didn't envy her.

Gilby hovered in the background, smiling like an idiot, willing things to go well. Pity he hadn't thought about it earlier. An old hand had made an amateur's mistake and was already regretting it.

Jackie's smile was frozen in place. 'So, when can you start?'

'When would you like me to start?'

She led Michelle behind the bar. 'What's wrong with right now? Let's see you pour a pint.'

'A pint of what?'

'Something easy. Make it a pint of Guinness.'

9

Kim Rafferty wouldn't be expecting to hear from me so soon after our meeting. When she saw who was calling, she'd assume I'd had a brainwave and was on with great news for her and her daughter. Letting her down didn't sit well. Neither did drinking my food through a straw. Sean and I had crossed swords twice before and I'd come out still breathing. I didn't fancy my chances a third time.

Expectation was alive in her voice from the first words. 'Mr Cameron?'

'Yeah, Kim, it's me. Look, there's no easy way to say this so I'll come right out with it. If I thought I could help you, believe me, I wouldn't hesitate. I can't. It just isn't possible.'

Her tone was flat; she sounded numb. 'You promised you'd think about it.'

'I have.'

'You said to give you a few days.'

'A few days won't change things. You told me yourself there's nowhere your husband won't find you. My opinion hasn't changed.'

'You mean go to the police.'

'I mean go to the police. They'll protect you.'

Her next words would stay with me for the rest of my life.

'You're afraid of him, aren't you? You're afraid of Sean.'

I wanted to deny it. Wanted it not to be true; the heat in my face said it was.

'Most fathers would hurt anybody who took their child away. Rosie's father, your husband, is Sean Rafferty. I'd be insane not to be.'

The call was over, yet we both stayed on the line. I heard her sobbing at the other end and wanted the ground to open up and swallow me. Finally, Kim Rafferty pulled herself together. She whispered, 'Goodbye, Mr Cameron,' and hung up.

The rest of the day was a bust after that. I watched the shadows lengthen in the room around me and listened to the constant hum of traffic on Cochrane Street heading into George Square. Outside, people were finishing work and going home.

I'd do the same.

Eventually.

* * *

Kim threw herself on the bed, feeling more alone than at any point in her life. The private investigator had been, at best, a long shot. No one in their right mind would mess with Sean, not if they wanted to keep breathing. Except, Charlie Cameron had. More than once. Knowing that had given her hope he'd do it again.

There was a moment in his office when she'd felt he was close to ignoring the risk of going up against her husband. His 'Let me think about it' told Kim her story had touched him. But it wasn't enough – the phone call shouldn't have been a surprise. There was a line only a fool would cross. Cameron wasn't a fool and helping a gangster's wife run away was over it. Well over it.

Her husband hated Charlie Cameron. With good reason; he'd been a thorn in his side from the beginning. Killing him wouldn't cost a man like Sean a second thought, yet so far, he hadn't. The PI's connections in the police meant his death or disappearance would attract more attention than the thug she'd married could handle.

The framed publicity photograph on the bedside cabinet mocked her. On the surface, they were the couple with everything – him a prominent and successful figure in business circles, her a former beauty queen turned model – smiling for the cameras at the end of an evening as they got into the car taking them to the luxurious home on the outskirts of the city, where the gorgeous child they'd created together was waiting for her mummy and daddy.

Only, it was a lie. The marriage was a sham. For Kim, just being in the same room as him was unbearable. He'd never hid his many affairs, slipping into bed beside her with the smell of his latest whore still on him.

Kim was losing weight, her nerves were shot; yesterday, she'd noticed her hair was falling out. Even without the insane jealousy and the violence, she couldn't take any more. Physically she was coming apart. Mentally and emotionally, she was already there. Sean had no use for her. Any day now, he'd have her declared an unfit mother. She'd lose Rosie. If that happened…

* * *

Buying the house in Bothwell overlooking the river had been a landmark for Sean Rafferty – three and a half million, complete with Jacuzzi, sauna and billiard room. He didn't play billiards and was yet to climb into the Jacuzzi. Not the point. Not the point, at all. It was only fifteen miles from the East End streets he'd played in as a boy, while his father built his illegal empire on broken bones and worse, but it was a tangible sign Sean had travelled worlds away from his upbringing. Like him, his neighbours – if you could call them neighbours, they were so far away – had done all right for themselves and didn't care who knew it. For most, this was as high as they were destined to fly. And that was the difference. There was more and Sean wanted it. When the time was right, he'd have it. Tomorrow, the man who'd help him get it was arriving at Glasgow Airport. Emil Rocha was central to Rafferty's plans. Sean would be there to meet him when he landed because the Spaniard held the keys to the kingdom. Impressing him was important.

In the kitchen, Rosie moved around in her baby-walker oblivious to the tense atmosphere between her parents. Kim was unloading the dishwasher – still giving him the silent treatment. Rafferty studied the outline of her underwear through the beige slacks. She sensed his eyes on her, stopped what she was doing and faced him, her expression hostile.

He saw her eyes red-rimmed from crying and mistook their cause. 'Isn't it about time you put the other night behind you and started acting like Sean Rafferty's wife? If you don't want the job there's plenty who do.'

'They're welcome to it.'

Rafferty drew a hand over the Aga, inspecting it for dust that wasn't there.

'All in good time, my darling. All in good time. Tomorrow night, I need you to be at your brilliant best.'

'I don't feel like going anywhere, Sean.' Her hand touched her cheek. 'Not like this.'

Rafferty breathed an exaggerated sigh. 'Maybe I'm not making myself clear. It isn't a suggestion. What you "feel like" doesn't come into it.'

'Where're we going?'

'You'll find out.' He smiled. 'We'll be taking our award-winning impersonation of a happy couple on the road – the successful husband and his gorgeous wife. The one the newspapers are so fond of.' He took her chin in his fingers; she shuddered at his touch. 'Smiling isn't optional. Emil has an eye for the ladies. Quite a stud in his younger days, I understand. I expect you to have him eating out of your hand. Can you do that small thing for me? You used to be able to. Showing your tits was your party piece, as I remember.'

Rafferty dropped the games. 'Be on your best behaviour. Don't fuck this up. I'm serious, Kim. Cause a scene, you'll get the same again. And it'll take more than a bit of make-up to cover it up. As soon as Rocha's on the plane heading back to his villa, you can hate me as much as you like.'

He lifted Rosie into his arms and kissed her forehead. 'Now, what's for dinner?'

10

Sunlight flashed on the wing of the Gulfstream G650 making its descent out of a blue sky into Glasgow Airport with its three passengers on board – Emil Rocha and two bodyguards. Sean Rafferty shielded his eyes. He'd visited Rocha's villa in the hills above the Mediterranean and recalled the heavy security around it. He'd drunk iced tea in the shade of an orange tree the Spaniard had planted himself, listening to him talk about his family: orange farmers, who'd worked hard and died poor. The tree was a symbol, he'd said – a reminder of where he'd come from and how different it might have been.

Clearing Passport Control was a formality. For all his notoriety, the drug lord had no criminal record and was able to travel freely, although who he was and what he did was well known. Sean Rafferty envied him.

They'd met just once but spoken on the phone dozens of times. It was Rocha's millions behind the waterside development. The Scottish gangster didn't have that kind of money. Not yet.

The visitor threw his arms around him, as though he was welcoming a long-lost son back into the fold, grinning his pleasure. His English was flawless, spoken with barely a trace of accent. 'It's been so long. Too long. I can't believe it.'

Rafferty examined the lean bronzed face, the white hair and dark eyes. Emil Rocha didn't seem to have aged. At close to sixty, he was still a handsome man, who'd never married and bedded more females than he could remember.

'Good to see you, Emil, you're looking well.'

The Spaniard put a hand on his shoulder and whispered, 'Unfortunately, Sean, I've been given some bad news.'

'Surely not?'

'Yes, the doctors tell me I've only fifty years left to live.' He roared at his own joke. 'How can I accomplish anything in such a short time? Seriously, I am well. How are you? How is your lovely wife?'

Rafferty was expecting the enquiry and had his answer ready. 'She's fine. Nervous about finally meeting the great Emil.'

'She has no need to be nervous. Women are God's gift to us and we must cherish them. When will I see her?'

'Tonight, at the restaurant. I'll drop you at your hotel and hook up later. Let me take your bag.'

Mistrust clouded the Spaniard's eyes. 'No, thank you, my friend. This bag is my mistress. It sleeps with me and never leaves my side. But, unlike a mistress, it never tells me lies.' He laughed again. 'We have a lot to discuss, you and me, eh?'

Rafferty led the way through the concourse and made for the car park.

'We have, indeed, Emil.'

* * *

Dennis Boyd's instructions had been intentionally vague, and as I left the city in the early afternoon and headed east on the M74 I wondered what it must be like to be the prime suspect in a violent murder on your first day of freedom after a decade and a half. To find yourself back where you started with whatever plans you'd had in the gutter and the police after you would be more than enough to make anybody careful about who they spoke to and where. Probably why Boyd had wanted a daytime meeting out in the open. If I was bringing the police, he'd see them and melt into the crowd.

I had no opinion on whether Dennis Boyd was guilty or innocent. In truth, I'd no idea. In the circumstances, why he might choose to meet at Strathclyde Park, twelve miles from the scene of the latest crime, was easy to understand. It was harder to see where I fitted.

At the Bothwell roundabout, a left turn took me past a Holiday Inn Express and the M&D's theme park, where three children had been seriously injured in a classic example of wrong time wrong place, when a roller coaster derailed and plunged twenty feet to the ground. Not so with Boyd. Luck, bad or otherwise, had had nothing to do with it. Putting him next to the body lying in a pool of blood on the floor of a West End car park – if his friend Mrs Kennedy was to be believed – was exactly what somebody intended.

Four men and two women in their seventies jogged Indian file, determination fixed on their sweat-stained faces. I gave them a friendly toot of the horn, parked on a square of grey asphalt facing the man-made loch, and waited.

Out on the water, a dozen pairs of rowers bent to their task, tracing white lines that glistened in their wake. On a different day, just watching would've been a pleasure. Doubt nagged me and already I regretted getting involved.

Dennis Boyd was the most wanted man in Glasgow. What the hell was I doing?

The Accused

This week had started badly and fallen away. The similarity between Kim Rafferty's situation and where Dennis Boyd found himself was hard to miss – they were both on the losing end.

I wasn't aware of him until the door opened and Boyd got in, filling the car with an intimidating presence. Introductions would have been laughable. We didn't go there. He half turned to face me and I saw a man wearing thick-rimmed glasses who'd been handsome in his youth. His hair was short and grey and his clothes weren't what I was expecting from someone who, only two days earlier, had been detained at Her Majesty's pleasure. The suit, shirt and tie under an oatmeal herringbone coat – inappropriate for the weather – gave him the look of a successful businessman rather than an ex-convict. Even his shoes were expensive.

But it was an illusion, not destined to last – Boyd brought out a pouch of tobacco and a packet of Rizla papers from his pocket. Thick fingers deftly rolled and shaped the materials into a thin white cylinder. I'd been quick enough to nip his former lover's smoking habits in the bud. Dennis Boyd deserved no better, except he was a man with the weight of the world on his shoulders; good manners were well down his list. When he was satisfied, he gently smoothed the ends and struck a match. Through a sulphur cloud hard eyes assessed me with a detachment I found unnerving. But for Mrs Kennedy coming to my office we would never have met and life would've been a little bit less complicated.

Boyd spoke and I remembered the gruff voice from the telephone. 'Diane said you'd help me.'

I laid down a marker, setting the tone for the conversation we were about to have.

'Diane's exaggerating. I agreed to meet you. Speak to you. Nothing more.'

'What do I do to convince you?'

For me, there was more to it than that. 'Tell me the truth. Anything else and I'm gone.'

'Simple. I didn't do it.'

'Didn't do what, exactly?'

'Any of it. Not then. Not now. The guy in the car park last night wasn't me. I wouldn't be so stupid. Twelve hours after I'm released one of the people who put me away is murdered. A bit obvious, don't you think?'

'It's what the police think that counts. Describe what happened in Elmbank Street.'

Boyd removed his glasses. 'Can't get used to these bloody things.' He put the spectacles in his pocket and ran a hand through his cropped hair. 'They set me up before and they're doing it again.'

'Who did? And why you?'

'Honestly, I haven't a clue. I was having a pint in a pub at George Square when the barman handed me a note telling me to be in the car park at ten-thirty.'

'Where did the note come from?'

'I asked the barman. He'd no idea. Don't know what the hell I was thinking – must've left my brains in the Bar-L – because I went.'

'And?'

'Wilson was on the ground in a pool of blood. It was dark but I could see he was dead.'

'Did you touch anything?'

'Can't remember. I fucking hope not.'

'What did you do?'

'Ran. Ended up at Central Station. That's when I called Diane.'

'And you don't know who might've set you up?' Boyd had to

have thought of little else in fifteen years. 'Is it possible somebody has a grudge against you?'

'It's possible, I suppose.'

'You see, I'm asking myself why anybody would bother, unless they had a reason. A good reason. They had to realise you'd come after them. Why not just kill you and be done with it?'

Boyd stared at me as if he'd suddenly come awake and wasn't sure where he was.

'When you got out of Barlinnie, what were your plans? Did you intend to let it be? Move on?'

His gravel voice boomed in the car. 'I was going to find the lying bastards and make them tell me who was behind it.'

'Kill them?'

He didn't shirk from answering. 'If that's what it took, yes. Year after year in Barlinnie that's exactly what I planned to do.'

'What changed?'

'I was free. Whatever happened, I swore I wasn't going back inside. The fuckers who set me up didn't know that. I wasn't about to tell them.'

And now I believed him.

'Did you know the men who testified against you?'

'No.'

'Not at all?'

Boyd pulled on his roll-up and studied the rowers, the mind behind the eyes considering how serious I was about the truth. 'Wilson asked me for a job once. I hunted him.'

'Why?'

'Because he was a thug.'

'Mrs Kennedy said he told the court you asked him to do a job with you.'

He blew smoke against the windscreen. 'Never happened.'

'Never? Could Wilson have taken you turning him down badly enough to hold it against you?'

Boyd flicked ash onto the floor and casually dismissed the suggestion. 'Who knows? The other two were idiots; he was an animal. Hurting people was fun for him. Plenty of punters in the city will be glad he's dead.'

'What about McDermid and Davidson? Any history there?'

'Until the trial, I hadn't even heard their names. Small fish. Turned out McDermid did two years for resetting. Released early for good behaviour. The notion anybody would trust a word that came out of his mouth is laughable. Davidson was even less impressive, if that's possible. Got caught with a dodgy credit card in Marks and Spencer, trying to buy a present for Mother's Day. Nobody in their right mind would credit anything they said. It was ridiculous. Davidson just happened to be passing Joe's place and saw a man who looked like me running away.' He shook his head. 'Unbelievable.'

The jury hadn't agreed.

'Mrs Kennedy says her husband knew about you two. What do you think?'

He blinked and avoided looking at me. Odd behaviour for a cold-blooded killer.

'I think Joe Franks was a victim in more ways than one. Doing him down never felt right.' He ran a restless finger over the tobacco pouch. 'The marriage was a mismatch from the off. People called them the Odd Couple behind their backs. Diane was a looker and Joe...' Boyd let the assessment go unfinished.

'All I'm saying is, she could've had her pick, and she picked Joe Franks. Joe wasn't interested in anything except gems; diamonds mostly. The novelty of a sexy wife wore off pretty fast. If it hadn't been me it would've been somebody else.'

'What was your relationship with Franks?'

'We got on well but we weren't friends, if that's what you mean. Keeping me around was business. Joe didn't deal in wedding rings, engagement rings, or any of that crap. He bought and sold. Been in the game most of his life; knew it inside out. Had suppliers in Rajasthan, Cape Town, all over. Occasionally, he'd be asked to hunt down a stone with a defined cut, colour, clarity and documentation. When that happened, he was obsessed, wouldn't bother to go home. Slept in the office. Faxes would arrive from all over offering him stuff. Joe wouldn't commit to buying until he'd assessed the gem himself. That meant travelling to wherever it was. He'd go to Amsterdam or India or somewhere to touch base with people he worked with and pick up stones.'

'Did you go with him?'

'Hardly ever. Joe would only be gone a few days. Taking me would tell the world he was carrying.'

'How did he find out about you and his wife?'

Boyd shrugged. 'Joe wasn't stupid.'

'What was his reaction?'

'Started acting strange. Secretive. At the time, I assumed it was because he'd sussed what was going on. I believed that was the reason he kept me in the dark about the diamonds in his home safe. I've had a lot of time to think, and it doesn't add up. Joe wouldn't do that. It was reckless. Didn't make sense. I mean, if the guy working for you is fucking your wife, firing him is the least you'd do. Franks kept me on. Six weeks before he died, I heard him on the phone in the Arcade, talking to his contact in Greece. Three hundred grand was mentioned. A lot of money back then.'

'It still is.'

'Joe wasn't happy; he was shouting. I asked if he needed me. He told me he'd handle it himself.'

'So, probably the biggest deal he'd ever done yet he cut you out. If that wasn't to do with his wife, what was it?'

'All I can tell you is that Joe was strange those last weeks. Like I said, secretive.'

'What was the contact's name?'

'Yannis.'

'Ever meet him?'

'Once.'

'Whereabouts?'

'Crete. It was 1953 down there. No customs to speak of. Easy to walk in and walk out.'

'Then it's possible Franks and this Yannis character might have fallen out, the Greek had Joe murdered and took the stones. You were just somebody to blame.'

Boyd rejected the notion. 'As far as I knew, they had a good relationship so I find that explanation hard to swallow. Besides, he'd have no reason to pin Joe's murder on me.'

'To get that level of attention you'd have to have seriously pissed somebody off. Who might fit the bill?'

'If I knew that, I wouldn't need you, would I?'

A clever reply, though not the answer to my question. 'The thing is, we're dealing with murder.'

I didn't mention my cases often included a dead body and Boyd took my little speech in his stride. 'No problem. Whoever murdered Joe Franks has been missing for fifteen years. Find him.'

He opened the car door. Apparently, the meeting was over. I said, 'One last question. Why me? How did you get my name?'

Boyd took a final draw and threw away what little remained of his skinny cigarette. 'Yellow Pages. And no offence, you looked like the only one I could afford.'

* * *

Rocha glanced at Rafferty behind the wheel, confidently weaving through the motorway traffic. Sean deserved credit; when the opportunity had arrived to take over his father's operation, he'd seized it with both hands. And he'd done well for both of them; their partnership had flourished. His mistake was in imagining he was different from the man who'd sired him. He wasn't. Jimmy had been an ignorant thug who'd got lucky. In the Spaniard's judgement, his son was no better. Ambition and animal cunning could never be substitutes for intelligence. The expensive clothes were a façade hiding his true nature and character – there was no guile, no substance to him. He was, in the alleged words of Vladimir Ilyich Lenin, 'a useful idiot'. But while there was money to be made in this city, Rocha would keep his unflattering opinion to himself.

He said, 'How is married life treating you?'

Sean hesitated. 'Some days are better than others, you know what females are like.'

'Most men would envy you. Your wife is very beautiful. I've seen her photograph.'

Rafferty grunted. 'She's still a woman.'

Rocha laughed. 'Yes, indeed. Being married comes easily to them, it's their natural state. Us men find it more difficult.'

'You never married, Emil. Didn't you find the right woman?'

'On the contrary, I found her many times, which convinced me it was unnecessary to settle for just one.'

11

I sat for a while, turning Boyd's story over in my head while the sun dipped over the treeline, throwing shadows on the loch, and the noise of the motorway grew louder. Rush hour. Getting back to the city would take patience. In the space of forty-eight hours I'd been offered two cases a wiser man would walk away from – one so old that solving it was almost certainly an impossibility, the other liable to get me killed. What an exciting life I led.

Strathclyde Park wasn't as busy as it had been when I arrived. Even the rowers had had enough. Dennis Boyd seemed to have disappeared into thin air – a talent I guessed would be useful in the weeks ahead. Fine by me. Not knowing where he was gave me deniability. I hoped I wouldn't need it. Every police officer in Central Scotland would be looking for him: a good excuse to stay well clear. More than once, DS Andrew Geddes had warned me about the line between my business and his. I'd crossed it before. He'd made it clear the next time would be once too often.

And that was my dilemma.

There was nothing I could or even should do for Mrs Kennedy's friend. As far as the murder in the car park went, Boyd was on his own. No amount of money could persuade me otherwise. Proving he didn't kill Hughie Wilson would have to be somebody else's responsibility. I wanted no part in it. Not least because Andrew was a good guy and I valued our relationship. But incredibly I was considering taking on a fifteen-year-old crime Dennis Boyd had already served time for. After all, that was old news nobody else was interested in.

Patrick Logue wanted me to do divorce work. Of course, he had his reasons. There was plenty of it around and it was easy money. I hated to disappoint him; it wasn't for me. What I did was challenging and took me to unexpected places; at times, places I didn't want to go. Andrew Geddes often accused me of being a frustrated copper; could be he was right.

Dennis Boyd was a case in point. A jury had delivered a guilty verdict when the evidence trail was still relatively fresh. The chances of discovering anything to alter that finding were beyond remote. Yet, I was struggling not to be drawn in.

Boyd had made no effort to curry favour with me and I'd believed him when he'd said he didn't do it, then or now, though my interest would need to stay firmly anchored in the then. And if the murder in the car park had put him at the centre of a manhunt, meeting again was out of the question. Mrs Kennedy would have to be my contact, adding to the improbability of solving a case from the long-gone past.

On the road back to Glasgow, traffic moved at a reasonable speed until the infamous Junction 16, close to Blochairn, where it ground to a halt. In ten minutes, I drove as many yards. Ahead, I could see the black granite of the Royal Infirmary and the Necropolis, where once-prominent citizens of the city would spend eternity.

Stuck in the line of stationary vehicles, I understood how they felt.

My last visit to the Victorian cemetery had been to confront Colin McMillan, another man in prison for a crime he didn't commit. Now, it was Dennis Boyd in my head. With nothing better to do I thought about his undisguised intention to seek out his accusers and force them to tell the truth.

kill them?

if that's what it took, yes

Convincing. But it was worth remembering both he and Diane Kennedy were people with a capacity for deception.

The late Joe Franks would agree.

* * *

The city was quiet. For most of the people who worked in town, business was over for the day. Unless you were in the same business as me. I parked the car and walked, enjoying the evening sun on my face. In NYB, the only customers were men not in a hurry to go home, maybe because there was nobody waiting for them. Or maybe because there was.

Michelle smiled when she saw me. I ordered an espresso and watched her make it; she seemed to have mastered the process.

'How's it going so far?'

Her reply was less than convincing. 'Okay, I suppose.'

I trotted out the standard lines. 'Every job's scary at first. You'll get used to it and wonder what you were worrying about.'

'It isn't that.'

'No? Then what?'

She brought the coffee and put it down. 'Jackie doesn't like me.'

I wanted to say, 'Listen, kid, some days she doesn't like me, either.' That wasn't what I told her. 'I've known her for years. She comes across as hard, but if you were in trouble, Jackie Mallon would be there.'

Michelle shook her head. 'I doubt it. And I understand. My uncle was wrong to assume because he owns New York Blue he can just bring anybody in without speaking to the manager. It was a mistake and I'm going to pay for it.'

'What's happened?'

'Nothing. Couldn't be nicer, except I know she isn't pleased. Apart from showing me what she wanted me to do, she hasn't spoken.'

'Give her time. She'll mellow.'

A guy at the far end of the bar signalled for service; Michelle went to him. I took my coffee and found a table. As soon as I sat down my mobile rang: Mrs Kennedy, following up on my meeting with Dennis Boyd. She sounded out of breath, as if she'd been running. 'You met him? What did you think?'

'I think he's in a lot of trouble.'

'But did you believe him?'

'It doesn't matter what I believe. My advice is to contact a good defence lawyer and get Boyd to turn himself in. He'll get his chance to prove he didn't kill Wilson.'

This wasn't what Diane Kennedy wanted to hear. Silence screamed on the other end of the line. Eventually, when she spoke, her tone was cool. 'Like the chance he had before? That kind of chance? You're not listening. Dennis was framed for killing my husband. The people who did it are doing it again. He needs somebody on his side.'

'He's got you.'

She shook her head. 'I can't help him. I don't know how. But you can.'

I wasn't persuaded. 'What happened in Elmbank car park

isn't something I want any part of. You say Boyd didn't do it. What makes you so certain?'

'Dennis isn't a murderer.'

She'd said that already. 'Look, Mrs Kennedy. Cards on the table. You asked me to meet Dennis Boyd, and I have. I've no way of knowing if he's innocent. No offence, I'm not prepared to take your word for it. Sooner or later, he's going to have to surrender himself to the police and, when he does, I don't want to be involved.'

She fought back. 'Don't talk to him, then, talk to me. I can be the go-between. If the police catch him, your name won't come up.'

Diane Kennedy was back where she'd started and what she was suggesting was so ridiculous, I almost laughed out loud. 'Let's get something straight. As for Boyd's current dilemma, he's on his own. I could look into your husband's murder, though even if I prove Dennis Boyd didn't do it – and after fifteen years the chances of finding anything are close to zero – the police will need to be brought in. One way or the other, at some point, he'll have to give himself up.'

'Are you saying you'll take the case?'

'I'm saying what's happening now isn't my business. Joe's murder is different. Before you get carried away, understand this: any new evidence will be handed over to the authorities.'

'I still have some of his stuff if you want it.'

'What kind of stuff?'

'Invoices, bank statements, his address book.'

'Why keep them?'

The hesitation in her voice was a clue: she was still in love with Dennis Boyd. 'Never got round to throwing them out. Didn't seem right, somehow.'

I drummed my fingers on the table. Across the almost empty

NYB, Michelle was chatting to two guys in their twenties. I heard her laugh at something one of them said. Maybe the job would work out after all.

'Okay, I'll collect it all tomorrow.'

Her gratitude was spontaneous and for a moment I caught the woman behind the brassy veneer. 'Thank you, Mr Cameron. Thank you so much. I'll pay whatever it costs.'

'Very generous, Mrs Kennedy.'

'That's what friends are for, isn't it?'

12

The drive from the house in Bothwell to Crossbasket Castle in Blantyre, where Rocha and his bodyguards were staying, took less than fifteen silent minutes. Sean and Kim didn't speak until they pulled up outside the hotel. She'd come downstairs looking as stunning as he'd ever seen her, wearing a black off-the-shoulder dress and a single-strand pearl necklace with matching earrings. Her hair was pinned back, the bruising at her eye disguised, barely noticeable, and for a moment Rafferty remembered why, in a room full of gorgeous female flesh, it was her who'd caught his attention.

None of that admiration was in his voice. 'Don't forget what I told you. The next couple of hours are crucial. Rocha pretends he's here to assess land for future projects. That's only one of the reasons. He's checking up on me before he commits himself and his money more than he already has. He needs to see a loving spouse, supporting her man, hanging on every word he says. Anything less...' He tipped her chin. 'And in case you don't remember, if I fall, I don't go down alone.'

Kim didn't protest. Her last best hope had died with Charlie

Cameron's rejection. To his credit, he'd sounded sorry. Sorry or not, his answer had still been no.

Sean went around the car and opened her door. As she got out he leaned closer and whispered, 'No silences. No sulks. The performance of your life for an audience of one, or I'll break your lovely legs. What a waste that would be.'

Emil Rocha was at the bar. Kim had expected an old man with wrinkled leather skin. The Spaniard was far from that. His white suit and sky-blue shirt open at the neck highlighted a perfect tan. He ignored Sean, gathered her in his arms and kissed her on both cheeks, then added another.

'In my country we kiss twice. But my mother was Dutch and I inherited her tradition.' His keen eyes darted over her face. 'I approve. There should be more traditions like it.'

He shook Sean's hand and waved at the room. 'You have taste, my friend. This is a splendid place.'

'I'm sure the meal will be just as good.'

'What can I get you to drink?' Rocha snapped his fingers like a man not used to being kept waiting. 'And don't tell me you're driving. I don't want to hear it. That's why taxi drivers were invented. So, what? Brandy? Wine? Champagne, perhaps?'

Kim said, 'Sparkling water with a twist of lime.'

'Really, is that all?'

'I don't drink.'

'Never? Not even for me?'

She smiled. 'Not even for you.'

From his jacket pocket he brought out two small boxes and pushed them across the table, the first squat and square, the second thin and rectangular. Rocha said, 'Sadly, as you'll remember, it wasn't possible for me to attend your wedding. The loss was mine.' He sighed. 'Work steals so many of life's happy moments from us. Please accept these gifts by way of apology and as a token of my friendship.'

Rafferty unwrapped his and flipped it open. The watch inside was a black Longines, stylish and fashionable. Not outrageously expensive, though more than most people would pay. Rocha tapped the box with his finger. 'I have this one myself.'

Sean's reaction was genuine. 'Emil, I don't know what to say.'

'Then, my advice would be to say nothing. Wear it in good health.'

He moved closer to Kim. 'Go on. I might bite you but this won't.'

Sean felt a stab of annoyance at the blatant flirtation but let it go. Rocha was a womaniser – he couldn't help himself; it was who he was. Kim did as she was told and gasped. Inside was a necklace studded with emeralds and diamonds, the gems sparkling in the light. 'I... I...'

The Spaniard supplied the history. 'It was my mother's. Now, it's yours. My family weren't always poor. Once, many decades ago, we were wealthy. This was given to my great-great-grandmother on her wedding day by her husband. She passed it down to my mother. Through hard times she could easily have sold it but never did.'

'I can't accept it.'

His hand closed over hers. 'This treasure sits at the bottom of a drawer in my villa, bringing happiness to no one. If I had a wife, it would belong to her and I would insist she wear it for me always. Sadly, I don't and doubt I ever will. At least try it on.'

Kim removed her strand of pearls and laid them in her lap. Rocha fastened the necklace's delicate clasp, his finger tracing the soft skin at the nape of her neck beyond her husband's sight. She bowed her head and smiled; the Spaniard wanted her.

'Your wife, Sean, isn't she beautiful?'

'Very.'

The Spaniard's hand rested on Kim's shoulder, gentle yet firm. 'Do me the honour of taking it. My mother would approve.'

Kim blushed and bent her head. 'If you insist, Mr Rocha.'

'Emil. Call me Emil.'

'If you insist, Emil.'

A waiter appeared at his elbow. Annoyance at the interruption flashed in Rocha's eyes.

'Your table is ready, please follow me.'

Kim moved to put the pearls back on. Emil stopped her. 'No, no, leave it where it is. It's perfect.'

'I have to look.'

'Then, look. We'll wait for you.'

When she'd gone, Rocha sat down; he was smiling. Sean said, 'You're a fox, Emil.'

'Am I?'

Rafferty smiled. 'Absolutely. You forget, I've seen the orange tree and heard the story of how you planted it as a symbol of where you'd come from. The jewellery's wonderful – she loves it – but it never belonged to your mother, to a farmer's wife from Murcia.'

Rocha pursed his lips and nodded. 'You're right, of course. And you've reminded me why I agreed to go into business with you. One of my better decisions.'

'I don't miss much.'

The Spaniard agreed. 'Not much, Sean, not much. As for the gift.' He shrugged. 'If he desires an easy life, a wise man tells a woman what she wants to hear. I assumed you already understood that. Perhaps, I was wrong.'

* * *

During the meal, Rocha spun stories of an idyllic childhood in the countryside near Valencia, where money was scarce and family everything. Sean glanced across at Kim taking it all in, believing every word. The Spaniard could certainly talk, skilfully larding his fantasy tales with history lessons. 'The orange was probably grown in southern China or India and brought to the Mediterranean by Italian traders or Portuguese navigators around 1500. No one can be sure.'

Kim was clearly impressed. 'You know so much, Emil.'

Rocha accepted the compliment. 'I know what I know. Because we were poor, I started working when I was nine but vowed to make up for it. Later, I did, reading most evenings, sometimes late into the night.' His dark eyes fixed on Sean Rafferty. 'Do you read?'

'I'm too busy.'

'A pity, there's so much to learn about the world.'

Under the table his foot touched Kim's ankle and lingered. She didn't draw away. There were very few people Sean was afraid of: this man was one of them.

When the dessert plates were cleared and the coffee served, with nobody to interrupt or contradict him, Rocha summed up his philosophy. Rafferty observed his silent partner, ruthless and still ambitious in spite of his wealth, lying for the fun of it. He'd called him a fox; he was more. Emil was a con artist. Apart from the odd fragment of truth, most of what he revealed about himself was false. Sean almost laughed out loud.

'My parents were good people, noble in their own way. They taught me the values that have guided me to this day. I'll always be grateful to them.' He spoke to Kim. 'You have a daughter now. Believe me when I tell you, power, money – even the exquisite necklace you wear with such grace – mean nothing compared to the light in the eyes of a child. What's her name?'

'Rosie.'

'Rosie is why God put you on this earth. Cherish her. Protect her with your life.'

He sipped from the cup in his right hand while, out of sight, the left squeezed her thigh.

Kim said, 'I'd love her to meet you.'

'I'd love that, too. You should bring her to my villa. I'll arrange for the young ones in the village to play with her.'

Rocha's villa had impressed Rafferty; he'd never forgotten the luxurious furnishings, the turquoise water of the swimming pool and, the most vivid image of all, the armed security guards at the gate and on top of the whitewashed walls, bronzed faces hidden behind black sunglasses, Israeli-made Uzis ready to defend the bleached citadel against Rocha's many enemies.

Sean had had enough. He couldn't listen to any more of Emil Rocha's crap; he excused himself and went to the bathroom. As soon as he was gone the Spaniard moved in on his wife, taking her hands in his, staring at her as though she was the only other person in the room.

'Don't speak; there's no need. I can see for myself.' He pointed to the injured eye and the heavy make-up. 'Did Sean do this?'

'Yes? He accused me—'

Rocha broke angrily into the explanation. 'It doesn't matter what you did or didn't do. A man who strikes a woman, especially the mother of his child, is lower than a snake.' He edged closer, his index finger scratching her palm. 'I want the truth. This has happened before, hasn't it?'

Kim lowered her head. 'Yes. Yes, it has. I'm scared of him, Emil. If I leave, he'll find us and take Rosie. Don't tell him I spoke to you, you've no idea—'

Rocha patted the back of her hand. 'You're wrong, my dear, I do. And it can't go on. I won't let it go on.'

'Please don't say anything, Emil. He'll kill me.'

Rocha whispered, 'No, he won't. I promise you, he won't. Meet me tomorrow afternoon in the city and we'll make a plan for you and Rosie.' Their faces were inches apart. 'Will you be there?'

'Yes. Yes.'

'Give me your mobile number. Expect my call and, please, wear the necklace for me.'

13

When I stopped at NYB for breakfast on the way to my office, Jackie Mallon threw a tight smile at me and went on with what she was doing.

It was too early for Pat. I'd given him a tall order. But if anybody could pull it off, it was Patrick Logue. Part of me hoped he hadn't been able to discover anything significant so I could legitimately turn the case down.

Andrew nodded and kept on reading his newspaper: a sign he wanted to be left alone. Given what I'd agreed to, I was happy to oblige. I ordered scrambled eggs on toast and a cappuccino. Jackie brought it over. A smarter man would've said nothing. Today, I wasn't him. 'Saw Michelle in action last night. Looks the part.'

It was meant to be positive. It failed. The plate of scrambled eggs hit the table like a brick dropped from a great height. Bits of congealed yellow flew into space. The coffee got the same treatment, spilling in a dark brown puddle in the saucer. Jackie glared down at me.

'That your professional opinion, Charlie? Because you can

shove it. It's about respect. Gilby comes waltzing in with somebody I haven't seen and announces she's working here. Still, it tells me how much value the owner puts on what I do for the business. Now I know. Worth it for that alone.'

Jackie had a right to be upset. 'Alex was out of order, no doubt about it. But you'd be wrong to think he doesn't appreciate you. He does.'

'Really? Got a queer way of showing it.'

Unbelievably, she started crying and stomped away leaving me to scrape my breakfast off the table and wonder what I'd done to upset her. Andrew didn't bat an eye. His mood must be dark, and it would be a whole lot darker if he knew I'd met Dennis Boyd the night before. New York Blue wasn't the place to be. I was happy to leave.

* * *

It would've been less trouble to ask Diane Kennedy to bring Joe Franks' stuff to my office, but then I'd miss the opportunity to see the Kennedys in their natural habitat.

Diane lived with her second husband in Newton Mearns, seven miles from the centre. After Giffnock, signs directed me to golf courses – Williamwood, Cathcart Castle and Whitecraigs – and the houses got bigger.

I rang the bell and checked out the neighbours while I waited for somebody to answer. Across the street, in the driveway of an impressive, detached villa with a mock-Tudor façade, a metallic matador-red Audi A5 coupe with new reg plates was parked in front of a double garage. Further along, a top of the range Lancia shared space with a grey Mercedes, together costing more money than I made in a year. Some people had taken that 'have a nice life' stuff seriously. Like everybody else, the people who lived here would have their share of problems. Paying the rent wouldn't be one of them.

Diane Kennedy opened the door. 'You're early. I wasn't expecting you so soon. Come in.'

I stepped into the hall just as a tall, heavy-set man with short black hair was coming downstairs. Ritchie Kennedy reminded me of somebody I couldn't put my finger on. He ignored me and spoke to his wife. 'I'm late.'

'When will you be back?'

His reply had an offhand edge. 'No idea.'

'Remember we're having dinner with Roland and Janice.'

Kennedy shrugged on his coat and swore under his breath. 'You go. Tell them something came up at the hotel.'

'But we cancelled last time. We can't let them down again. Try to make it, will you?'

He brushed past without committing himself or acknowledging me, and it was impossible not to notice the chemistry between them: there wasn't any. When he'd left, we went into the lounge. Diane lit a cigarette, inhaled defiantly and dared me to disapprove. A waste of time; her house, her rules. What I'd witnessed had angered her.

I said, 'Joe's things. You said you still have some of them.'

'Yes. They were in the loft. I dug them out.'

She lifted a cardboard box filled with a jumble of paper from behind the sofa and handed it to me. 'Do you think there's likely to be anything that can help you?'

'Who knows? It's a place to start. We always come back to the same problem: none of it happened yesterday.'

Mrs Kennedy moved towards the door. Giving me her late husband's paperwork was enough; she'd done her bit. Not how it was going to play. 'I want to discuss Joe Franks with you. Who he was and how he conducted his business. You're better placed than anybody to understand.'

The mention of her late husband seemed to affect her the way it hadn't previously. Her smoking took on an exaggerated flourish; the cigarette became a prop. Suddenly, she seemed vulnerable. 'Of course. Though I doubt I'll remember much. What do you want to know?'

We sat facing each other on two wine leather couches. Diane said, 'I haven't offered you something to drink.'

'I'm fine.'

'No, really. Have something. Please. Whisky and water?'

'No, thanks, it's too early in the day. But don't let me stop you.'

She opened a dark-wood cabinet hiding a not-so-minibar and poured a stiff one from a bottle of Dewar's that had already been given a good kicking, then topped it off with mineral water. When she rejoined me the nerves, or whatever it had been, had passed. Maybe the glass in her hand reassured her, but the Diane Kennedy I'd met in my office – laid-back and aloof – was back. She stubbed the first cigarette out and immediately lit another. Finally, she was ready to explain. 'This is the house I shared with Joe. You're sitting where his body was when they found him. Blood soaked through the carpet and stained the floorboards.' She pointed at the wall. 'There used to be a built-in safe. I had it taken out.'

'I can imagine it must be upsetting.'

'Most of the time it's as if it never happened and I'm okay. Dennis's release brought memories I hoped I'd forgotten.'

She caressed her right eye with a suntanned finger. Brushing a tear away? I couldn't be sure. 'Ask your questions, Mr Cameron. I'll do my best to answer them.'

'Let's go back to the beginning. Tell me about you and Joe Franks.'

She sighed. 'There's not much to tell. That was the problem. Joe was a simple man. There was no depth to him. Precious stones were his business and his life. Back then, whatever I lacked, it wasn't sparkle. Joe saw it and wanted it.'

'Were you in love with him?'

She smiled a smile that had been years in the making, a mixture of sadness and amusement. 'Did I love Joe Franks? It depends on the mood I'm in.' Diane allowed herself a brittle laugh.

'Is that a yes?'

'It's a sometimes. Best I can do. For a while we both got what we wanted out of the relationship. Joe had the good-looking young wife, and I had security. Or, so I thought. Then he was killed and the truth came out.'

'Which was?'

'Like I told you. He was in trouble. I thought it was just me he wasn't paying attention to. I was wrong. It was the business as well.'

'How do you end up on the wrong side of selling stones to the trade?'

She laughed again, and this time there was genuine humour. 'Excuse my French but fucked if I know. All I can tell you for certain is my husband managed it.'

'This last deal, the one he kept Boyd away from. Tell me about it. If it was so hush-hush, how did the police realise there had been a robbery? What led them to that conclusion?'

'The safe had been cleaned out and everything in it taken except a small uncut gem in the corner; the police assumed there was a struggle, and in their hurry to get away it got missed.'

I tried not to let my disbelief show. A diamond conveniently spilled in the back of Dennis Boyd's car and a second stone left beside the jeweller's dead body; somebody had tried hard. Too hard. Five minutes on the case and already for me the circumstantial evidence was unravelling.

'And you weren't aware Joe had a big deal on?'

'I had no idea. That wasn't unusual. Joe didn't discuss his work with me.'

'Where were you when the robbery took place?'

Mrs Kennedy hesitated. I waited her out. 'I was with a friend.'

It was only half an answer. I let it go. 'The three witnesses. Did you know them?'

'Not until the trial.'

'And since?'

'Of course not. Why would I?'

She went to the minibar and poured herself a refill.

'Sure you don't want one?'

'Thanks, but no, thanks.'

Diane lit another cigarette and studied me the way Dennis Boyd had at Strathclyde Park. 'I think I may have underestimated you, Mr Cameron.'

It might have been meant as a compliment. I couldn't be sure. 'Boyd tells me he went to Crete with Joe on business. Did he ever take you?'

'Yes. Said it was a holiday. Some holiday. We were only there a few days and I spent most of it by myself while he met his contact in a bar in the harbour.'

'Yannis?'

She seemed surprised. 'Yes.'

'What was his second name?'

'I never knew it. I was in his company for about ninety seconds.'

Mrs Kennedy swirled the amber liquor around in her glass. 'I'd say he was about thirty, maybe. With a beard. His English was perfect, that's what struck me most about him.'

'And that was the only time you met him?'

'He called the house a couple of times looking for Joe.'

'Would you say your husband and this Yannis were on good terms?'

She considered her answer. 'I think they were, yes. Why do you ask?'

'Because Boyd heard Joe on the phone arguing with him.'

'Joe argued with everybody and their granny, including me, including Dennis. He could be an awkward bastard when it suited him.'

I glanced at a framed photograph of her and Ritchie. She caught me. 'You're too smart not to have noticed things between me and Ritchie could be better. Don't deny it.'

Denial hadn't crossed my mind.

'He's unhappy this has started again. Dennis Boyd is a no-go subject in this house. Ritchie's the jealous kind, against me having anything to do with him. I don't blame him. Dennis was my lover, after all.'

I carried all that was left of Joe Franks to the door. Diane put a hand on my arm.

'Don't let my husband bother you. He can be an arse sometimes.' She had that right. 'Got a lot on his plate right now. We own a hotel on the Ayr Road. Daltallin House. Do you know it?'

'Can't say I do.'

'We won our first Michelin star last year and we're anxious to hold onto it. Every day brings another problem for Ritchie to sort out. Good managers are as rare as hen's teeth.'

Jackie Mallon would be pleased to hear it.

'When will you talk to Dennis again?'

'I'm not planning on speaking to him again. And if you tell me where he is – even by accident – I'll drop the case. Trust me on that.'

'You can relax, Mr Cameron. I can't tell you. I don't know where Dennis is.'

* * *

There was a change in the Spaniard. Sean Rafferty sensed it. The night before he'd been urbane and utterly charming and had Kim eating out of his hand. This morning, he was edgy and distracted, not interested in what he was being shown. Sean caught him gazing off into the distance as though he had something on his mind.

His two bodyguards didn't speak. It wasn't what they were paid for. Behind the sunshades their eyes constantly scanned the line of trees. At one point, Rocha excused himself and moved away to make a call. Rafferty heard him, intimate and persuasive, talking to a woman no doubt. He returned, smiling to himself, and Sean knew he was right. The land they were assessing was on the outskirts of Glasgow. For the moment, beyond the reach of developers. As Sean animatedly outlined his vision about how they would acquire it and how much it would cost, Rocha listened in silence. When Rafferty finished, Emil was less than enthusiastic.

'I admire your energy.'

Sean detected a but coming.

'It's a question of timing and... visibility. I'm told the controversy over the Waterside Regeneration Initiative hasn't gone away. With that in mind, further involvement with the council is better avoided. Our profile – your profile, actually – is too high. I'd feel more comfortable if it was lower.'

His handmade Italian shoe toyed with a tuft of grass.

'You have to understand, Sean, a man in my position is offered opportunities every day of the week. For example, the island of

Menorca is vastly under-exploited compared with its big sister, Majorca. Just before I flew here a company looking for funds approached me. For reasons too tedious to go into, the banks have decided not to grant the loans they seek and they came to me.'

He swept a hand across the horizon.

'Whether I go with them or not is neither here nor there. Unlike you, I'm not in a hurry. Playing the long game. Of course, if you'd presented a gilt-edged investment perhaps my answer would be different. As it stands...'

The rebuff was unexpected. Rafferty reacted like a rejected lover. 'Are you saying you don't want to do business with me?'

Rocha took his arm and guided them back to the car. 'If and when you have something less public, by all means bring it to me. Meanwhile, our other interests are closely aligned and very successful. Demand outstrips supply and always will. There's a reason people love drugs. They dull the pain of their grey little lives and make them feel fucking great.'

Sean swallowed his disappointment. 'I'll find another project.'

'Do that. I won't be hard to get hold of.'

Rafferty checked the new Longines on his wrist and tried to salvage what he could from a wasted day. 'I've booked a table for lunch. I thought we—'

Rocha put a hand on his shoulder. 'A splendid idea. Unfortunately, I already have an appointment.'

Rafferty didn't hide his surprise. 'Anyone I know?'

Emil Rocha patted his arm. 'I think I can confidently say it isn't. But I'll see you tomorrow. We can chat on our way to the airport. Drop me in town, would you? Anywhere in the centre will do.'

14

Back in the office I trawled through what I had. At first glance it didn't look good. The paper sheets were yellowed and dusty, some of them torn from rough handling; fifteen years in the attic hadn't done them any favours. Underneath, in the bottom of the box, were a small black address book and a leather-bound Filofax with the gossamer threads of a spider's web clinging to the crack along the spine. Inside, the pages were stiff and dry to the touch and had the musty smell you'd expect off an old book. Nobody had opened it in a very long time – probably the police had been the last.

I turned to the beginning and read the last two years of Joe Franks' life. The first had been very busy: appointments, flights, meetings with his accountant. Nothing jumped out at me other than the name Yannis.

In January of his final year, the entries were in blue pen, capitalised and neat, the name, time and place of every meeting carefully recorded, along with flights to Amsterdam and Chania every other week just like before. February was business as usual.

Around March, the handwriting deteriorated into hastily made scrawls and initials replaced names. For reasons of his own, Franks had decided to make whoever he met with less obvious and there were fewer appointments. Was Joe Franks losing interest?

A typical entry read:

BS/10. TM/6. CL/6.

In May, everything changed again. No flights, no appointments, and the letter Y appeared more frequently. Towards the end of June, an edge was smudged and worn where information had been crudely erased. I tried and failed to read the imprint of what had been written. The story wasn't hard to follow – page after empty page told how it had been. The author stuck with his rudimentary attempts at disguise even when the scribbles in the margin were fewer because trade had all but ceased. Franks' business was in trouble. Probably why he'd got in over his head on the diamond deal.

Two contacts were regularly mentioned: BS and somebody called CL. Joe Franks was with one or other of them a total of ten times in the last seven weeks of his life.

Maybe they'd murdered him and set Dennis Boyd up for it? Without knowing their identities, it was impossible to say.

A month later, the jeweller would be dead, though on the twenty-eighth of June he was very much alive when he wrote his final reminder to himself. A single letter. Capitalised and underlined.

<u>Y</u>

Y for Yannis?

Almost certainly.

Pat Logue came in without knocking and broke into my train of thought. He sat down, put his hands behind his head and stretched like a cat, the row we'd had forgotten.

He was pleased with himself. He'd been given a difficult task and cracked it in record time. I'd come to expect no less from a man at home on the streets of a city where he knew everybody and everybody knew him. In another life, he might have been a high-flying politician or a self-made millionaire. In this one, he too often depended on the third favourite in the four-thirty at Wincanton to get him out of a hole. Often it did. And when it didn't, there was me: his very own lender of last resort. He had talents, lots of them. Unfortunately, nothing inspired him as much as drinking. That said, Patrick wasn't destined to die with his music still inside him. He loved life more than anybody I'd ever come across and was happy with who he was.

I let him enjoy his moment before I spoke. 'Surprised to see you so soon.'

'Time is money, Charlie. So they say. And speakin' of money, I could use some.'

'I paid you a couple of days ago. Surely you haven't gone through it already?'

I sounded like his mother.

He stared for a minute and shook his head. 'You and me have a fundamentally different understandin' about the nature of finance. Not your fault; you can't help it. Folk from money are desperate to hold onto it. They're used to havin' it. It's important to them. Whereas people like me – who've never had much and aren't likely to – instinctively grasp the truth. The world's full of the stuff. Knowin' somebody who's well fixed is nearly as good as being well fixed yourself. In some ways better.'

'And you know me, that right?'

'Got it in one, Charlie. Even if I was born rich...'

'I wasn't born rich, Patrick.'

He wouldn't be deflected. 'I'd spend every day obsessing that some street urchin in Singapore was cleanin' out my bank account and end up givin' it to somebody like me. Then I'd worry about not havin' it. This way, I minimise self-doubt.' He raised his hands to make his point. '"Money is only a tool." Ayn Rand said that.'

'Did she?'

'She did. And she was right.'

'Yeah, yeah. What've you got for me?'

He rested his elbows on the desk and pulled a bunch of pink betting slips from his inside jacket pocket. 'Let me refer to my report.'

'Stop fucking about. What did you find?'

'Okay. Long story short: on the surface, there's not much to tell. Franks and Boyd had a good relationship. I haven't found anybody who heard them argue, about money or anythin' else. Franks trusted Boyd and Boyd didn't let him down. Until he did.'

'The affair with his wife?'

'A foregone conclusion. She was a man-eater from way back. Big surprise when Joe left his wife and married her.'

A small detail Diane Kennedy had neglected to mention.

'Doomed from the start but, hey, it happens.'

A generous spirit was one of Pat Logue's gifts.

'His widow says Franks left her in bad financial shape. Anything on that?'

Patrick scratched his chin. 'Give me another day. Same with the guy who stepped into his shoes.' He meant Ritchie Kennedy. 'Likes them to have a few coins, doesn't she? Joe must've been doing all right when she met him. Never heard of a poor jeweller.

Contradiction in terms. If he was on the ropes at the end, nobody I spoke to was aware of it.'

'What about the witnesses?'

'Nonentities to a man. Couldn't lace Boyd's boots, accordin' to my sources.'

'Any link to Franks?'

'No. Not in the picture until their fifteen minutes of fame at the trial.'

'And since?'

'Didn't hang out together before or after they testified against Boyd. Doesn't look like they're connected.'

'Tell me about them.'

Patrick read with a straight face from his betting slips. 'Hughie Wilson was a misfit and a loner. No job. No wife. No kids. No interests at all, unless you count drinkin' his gyro. He had a reputation as a hard man and put some time in as a bouncer. He enjoyed his work until he smacked a punter harder than he needed to and the club had to let him go. A big mouth when he'd had a few. Claimed he'd sorted Dennis Boyd. Proud of it, too. Told a pub full of people if Boyd came after him, he was ready. Not many cryin' because he's gone. Wilson was scum, and not in a good way.'

'Where did he live?'

'In Baillieston. He lived there with his mother before she died. She was a widow. Father died when Hughie was a boy.' Patrick put the notes down. 'What kind of hard man lives with his mammy?' He read on. 'And here's the thing. Wilson didn't have a pot to piss in, but the house belonged to him.'

'It must've been left to him.'

'It was. Of course it was. Mrs Wilson bought her council house fifteen years ago. Not long after Dennis Boyd was convicted. Where did Mrs W get the money?'

'Her son gave it to her out of what he was paid to testify?'

'Makes sense.'

'Any idea what the going rate was for telling lies at the high court back then?'

Pat Logue returned to his balancing act with the chair and gave the question his attention. 'Five grand? Ten? Depends on who was payin', doesn't it? Enough to see your old mum right and still afford to get drunk for the next six months.'

'I'm guessing that's how it was. The dates work. Did McDermid and Davidson suddenly come into funds around the same time?'

The betting slips made a comeback. 'Haven't much on them yet. I'll keep diggin'. McDermid's a barman, currently workin' at a pub called the Schooner Inn, near Gallowgate. Lives in Possil. Been in and out of the Bar-L. Nothin' serious. The guy isn't very good at breakin' the law. Keeps gettin' caught. If he was a stick of rock, he'd have 'Loser' runnin' through him. Nobody's seen him since the night Wilson was murdered. He has to be terrified.'

'And Davidson?

'Willie Davidson's the quiet man. A joiner to trade. Self-employed. Shop-fitting mostly. Packed it in. Word on the street is his health wasn't good. Hasn't been on the Glasgow scene in years. Might even be dead.'

'Is that it? Nothing on Kennedy?'

He looked away and back. 'I'm sensin' ingratitude, Charlie. It's only been a day.'

'You're right. It's a good start. Thanks, Pat.'

I waited, expecting him to leave. I should've known better. The optimism in his voice was forced. Not difficult to spot if you were looking for it. He said, 'Anyway, as I mentioned, I'm off the pace. It's happened before though it's never lasted as long as this.'

'What're you saying, Patrick?'

'Mojo isn't workin'. I'm skint.'

He was singing a song I'd heard often from him. 'How skint?'

'Skint skint. Haven't a razzoo. Worse than that. Don't even have the entrance money to NYB.'

'Since when do you need entrance money there? Jackie lets you drink on the slate, doesn't she?'

'That option's tapped out until I square up what I owe. Fifty would get me back in the game. If I'm on this case with nothin' comin' back at the end of it, that's just how it is.'

'What about Gail?'

'Gail's all right. I make sure she's always the first name on the team sheet.'

'Glad to hear it.'

He toyed with his goatee. 'God hates me. Did I ever tell you that?'

'More times than I can remember.'

I took five twenties from my wallet and handed them to him. Now, he had more money than me.

'Thanks, Charlie. Appreciate it.'

He got up to go, his faith renewed, and anxiously checked the time on his watch. William Hill was about to have another customer. 'I'll get you what you need on these guys. Stand on me.'

'I know you will, Pat. And I do. One more thing. Looks like Franks' business really was struggling. Keep digging on that and find out if he was the faithful type.'

When he'd gone, I settled down with the contents of the cardboard box. The sheets of paper hadn't fared as well as the Filofax or the address book. At some point, coffee had been spilled, making them look like the Dead Sea Scrolls. Most of what had survived was trade information: a brochure for a conference in London and the odd invoice that hadn't made it to Franks' earnings.

That thought drew me to the black address book. The jeweller's accountant would be able to tell what Franks had been thinking those last months.

At the back of the book, the firm of Turner and McCabe sat near the bottom with about forty others in a list that ran over the page. Y, BS and CL weren't there, which made sense. What would be the point of writing in code then leaving the key? I rang the number and heard a hum: unobtainable. Maybe they'd packed their tent and disappeared into the night. Not so. Directory Enquiries put me through. A bright female voice – the kind of voice it would be nice to come home to – said, 'Turner, O'Neil and McCabe.'

I cleared my throat. 'This may sound like a strange request. I'd like to speak to whoever acted for a Joseph Franks. Mr Franks died fifteen years ago. Your firm handled his accounts.'

'I expect that would be Mr McCabe. He retired. I could give you an appointment with his son, Barry, if it's any good to you.'

'Can he see me today?'

The gentle laughter cascading down the line wasn't meant to offend. Nevertheless, it did and altered my opinion about hearing her call my name after a tough day.

'Who did you say you were?'

'Cameron. Charlie Cameron.'

'You're in luck. He has a window at two.'

'Fine.'

'Do you know where we are?'

I read from the address book. 'Battlefield Road, Mount Florida.'

The laugh returned; I could almost see her smile. 'No, that's where our offices used to be. We're in Bath Street now. Number 1427.'

Joe Franks' old accountant firm had added a partner and

changed address. In itself, unremarkable. Except, it highlighted the problem at the heart of uncovering who had murdered the jeweller: fifteen years. It might as well have been fifty. People had lived and loved and died during that time, some taking their secrets with them. Joe Franks was one of them, his life boiled down to a collection of junk revealing little about who he'd been.

Parts of it I could guess. His wife's affair must have been a blow to a man already drowning financially and probably guaranteed the end of the marriage. Add in the betrayal by Dennis Boyd – a man he trusted – and it was possible to imagine his state of mind.

Beyond that, all I had were questions. Had Franks, in a desperate bid to get back on his feet, got involved in a diamond deal way out of his league? Was Yannis in it with him? Had the Greek killed him or had him killed? Boyd didn't think so but if the deal was big enough to let the thieves leave two stones behind, anything was possible.

The two remaining witnesses were the only real hope of discovering the truth. Andrew Geddes might know something if I could get him talking about it.

* * *

Bath Street was busy. Cars at the traffic lights revved their engines impatiently as if they were under starter's orders and ready for the race to begin. Above them, the sun was losing its battle to break through, and it was humid; rain wasn't far away. God hadn't come to a decision on the weather; when he made up his mind, we'd be the first to know.

On the pavement across the road outside an Italian restaurant, a sallow guy in T-shirt and jeans hunkered to chalk today's specials on a blackboard. I'd taken a woman to dinner there a lifetime ago and could still see her toying provocatively with the stem of her wine glass as she lied to me. Even if I'd known I wouldn't have minded. Later maybe, but not then.

A block further up the street, a gold rectangle mounted on the wall next to a heavy door told me I'd found where Joe Franks' former accountants lived these days.

Inside, a female receptionist glanced from behind a mahogany desk and smiled. Behind her, a large grey Perspex sign with the Turner, O'Neil and McCabe logo etched in burgundy reassured anybody who needed reassuring they'd come to the right place. During our brief phone conversation, something in her voice had drawn me in and I'd imagined coming home to that sweet sound after a day in the snake pit. Then, without trying, she'd turned me off. Seeing her auburn hair and angel face made me change my mind about changing my mind.

'Charlie Cameron. I'm meeting Mr McCabe at two.'

She checked my name off against a list in front of her and put a tick beside it.

'Of course. I remember. I'll see if he's available. Have a seat, Mr Cameron.'

I didn't have to wait long. Barry McCabe collected me himself, tired-looking, balding and somewhere in his fifties with a pallor that matched his clammy handshake.

I followed him up several flights of wide stairs to the third floor. At the top, he stopped to get his breath back. 'Make more sense to be closer to the door, wouldn't it?'

'Or take the lift.'

'Building doesn't have one.'

'Alternatively, quit smoking.'

'Believe me, I'm considering it. Can't see me surviving another ten years of this.'

McCabe senior had retired. I guessed the son wouldn't mind

following his example. His office was big. About as much as you could say for it. Apart from a desk – the twin of the one at reception – a couple of chairs and some lifeless landscapes on the walls, there was nothing in it. If I'd expected banks of filing cabinets I was off the mark. Somewhere in the bowels of the building an army of drones dealt with the real work, while their leader lunched with clients.

When he was seated, he leaned his elbows on the desk. 'So, what can I do for you, Mr Cameron?'

'I'm a private investigator and I'd like to speak to your father about a client of his.'

He made a hissing sound through his teeth to warn me how impossible my request was. 'My father hasn't worked in the business for eight years.'

'He's retired, I know. But I'd still like to talk to him. Does he live in the city?'

'No. My parents moved to Millport. "Far from the madding crowd" and all that. Hard to believe how different the weather is. Supposed to be because of the Gulf Stream. Dad loves it. If you tell me what it's about, I may be able to help, although you must understand confidentiality forbids me from going into details.'

'Of course. Does the name Franks mean anything to you?'

He scratched the side of his balding head. 'Franks. Franks. Can't say that it does. How long ago was this?'

'Fifteen years.'

McCabe flattened his hands on the top of the desk, as if I'd solved a particularly baffling mystery. 'Well, there you are. No wonder I didn't recognise it. We started storing files electronically before we moved from Battlefield Road. Couldn't afford the space, quite frankly. Anything prior to then is long gone.'

'I'm hoping your father might remember the name.'

Barry considered what I was saying and agreed. 'He might, though don't depend on it. His memory isn't what it was.'

'Can you arrange for me to meet him?'

His eyes narrowed and I sensed him withdraw. 'You haven't said what this is about. Nothing that involves the firm, I hope.'

'Not at all. Joe Franks was murdered. I'm trying to establish how solvent he was at the time of his death. As his accountant, your father would've been better placed than anyone to know.'

McCabe was still suspicious. Understandably, his instincts were to protect his family and his business. Ancient history or not, he was closing down on me and didn't bother to hide his reluctance; his arms spread in a gesture of powerlessness. 'I'm not sure Dad will meet you. That would be for him to decide. Anyway, it's all a bit academic.'

'Academic, how?'

'They're away on a cruise of the Mediterranean. Flew to Palma yesterday. Won't be back for ten days. Sorry.'

He didn't sound sorry.

'When he returns will you tell him I'd like to talk to him about an old client of his? He doesn't have to come to Glasgow. I'll go to Millport.'

Barry had no talent for lying. 'I'll mention it to him, of course. Be prepared for him to say no. Can be a stubborn bugger when he feels like it.'

'Can't we all.'

McCabe showed me out though it meant climbing the stairs yet again. At the front door he pointed to the sky. 'Rain by the looks of it.'

I left the weather forecasting to him and shook his moist palm a second time.

'Tell your father a man's freedom may depend on what he can remember.'

He smiled, only half believing me. 'You make it sound dramatic.'

'It is.'

15

Dennis Boyd stood with his hands deep in his coat pockets and gazed at the rain falling on the water. No rowers or joggers today. Strathclyde Park was deserted. The roll-ups were gone; the cigarette stuck in a corner of his mouth was an Embassy. Boyd glanced at the grey sky and asked himself what the fuck he was doing here; a question needing no answer.

Three days earlier – three days and three sleepless nights, to be exact – the warmth of the sun on his face for the first time in so many years had made him more determined than ever to fight for his freedom and not have it taken from him again. That fight had already begun. Diane's fears had been way off; Cameron was a straight-shooter. Better than that, he was smart.

Boyd thought back to Central Station. While he'd waited for Diane, he'd stayed in the phone booth thumbing through directories, pretending to be speaking to someone so he could stay out of sight. The private investigator's simple advert in Yellow Pages had found him.

Diane was against it. There was a train leaving for London in five hours; she urged him to quit Scotland and get on it. Her argument was sound; Glasgow was too small to hide him for long. Scotland was too small. Eventually, they'd catch him and charge him with murdering Wilson. Although what she was saying made sense, Boyd overruled her. But when she'd offered the cash again, he hadn't refused. He had both envelopes with him now. For the moment money wasn't a problem.

Getting out of the station had been his first priority, though going back to his sister's house was out of the question. If the police hadn't already been there, they soon would be. He thought of Annie and how hard this would be on her. She'd believed in him. Her faith would be shattered. Another bridge gone in a long line of burning bridges.

They drove for over an hour – going nowhere – until Diane parked the car in Lynedoch Street. Around the corner in Woodlands Road they found an all-night café and sat with their heads close together, holding hands, playing the part of the lovers they'd once been. Boyd asked what the time was. Diane told him it was after one o'clock.

'Won't Ritchie wonder where you are?'

'He's staying at the hotel tonight.'

'He runs a hotel?'

'No. We own a hotel, and I wish to God we didn't. More trouble than it's worth.'

She steepled her fingers over a half-finished coffee, too harsh to drink, too sweet to leave alone. 'But even if he was at home, I doubt he'd notice I'd gone.'

The reply might have been an invitation to take up where they'd left off and Boyd hesitated. He wanted sex; this wasn't the moment.

'I really do think you'd be better off catching that train.'

'Running's the same as admitting I killed Wilson and I didn't. I went to Barlinnie for something I didn't do once already. I'm not going back. Whatever happens. Besides, the cops will be all over Central by now.'

'You could turn yourself in. Tell your side of the story.'

Boyd's eyes bored into her, his voice a monotone, the anger behind it controlled but real. 'Is that a serious suggestion? Because if it is you can fuck off right now, Diane. I mean it.'

She covered his hand with hers. 'I'm only trying to do what's best. For you. Surely you understand that much? I've never stopped caring about you, Dennis, and I'm not about to start. Let's not kid ourselves. It looks bad and it is. Less than a day after you're released, one of the witnesses who testified against you is murdered. Here, London or anywhere, it doesn't matter. Face facts. You're on the run. The question is where to run to. Any ideas?'

'I was hoping you might have some.'

'I have. London. Get on the train. I'll drive you to Motherwell to catch it.'

'No. Even the cops could work that out. The private investigator I was telling you about in the station, Charlie Cameron, ever hear of him?'

Diane's exasperation boiled over. She drew her hands away. 'Oh, for Christ's sake, Dennis. You're losing it. You don't know the first thing about him. He could be a sleaze with bad breath and dandruff who specialises in pictures of people with their clothes off. Talk sense.'

'I am talking sense. Somebody needs to ask the questions I was going to ask. Find out who framed me. Cameron could do that. It's worth a try.'

She glanced at her watch. 'The London train? Last chance.'

Boyd shook his head. 'Non-starter. Forget it.'

They toyed with their coffee cups. A passing waitress offered them a refill. Finally, Diane said, 'All right, Dennis, have it your way. What do you want me to do?'

'Contact Cameron. Get him to agree to meet me.'

'And in the meantime?'

Boyd ran a hand through his beard. 'Get rid of this, stay out of sight and pray Cameron is more than a low-life muckraker.'

'What if he isn't interested?'

'Then I'm fucked, aren't I? They'll catch me and I'll go down.'

'If this Cameron agrees to meet you, where will you be?'

'I wish I knew.'

She pushed her chair away from the table and stood. 'You can stay at my place, at least until morning. Then I'll drive you wherever you want.'

Boyd looked up. Diane had always been a strong woman; a lady who knew what she wanted and wasn't afraid to go after it. She'd made the move that started the affair. Boyd hadn't objected then and he didn't object now.

'It's coming up on 2 a.m. Ritchie won't be back until lunchtime at the earliest. That gives us time.'

The 'us' didn't escape Dennis Boyd and he remembered why he'd been so attracted to her. In truth, he'd never forgotten.

He paid the bill and followed her into the street. On the journey to her house, Diane kept her eyes on the road, while a late-night music station murmured in the background. She didn't believe some private investigator, advertising in Yellow Pages, had any hope of discovering who murdered Joe Franks. Neither did Dennis Boyd, but Charlie Cameron – whoever he was – was all that stood between him and the rest of his life in the Bar-L.

Boyd allowed the motion of the car to gently rock him. Sleep would've been welcome; his mind wouldn't let him. The image of Hughie Wilson lying on the car park floor appeared, and with it the knowledge he'd fallen into a trap conceived long before he walked through the gates of Barlinnie prison. They'd known exactly what to expect from him and been ready.

* * *

For Boyd, seeing the house was a journey back in time. He'd been there so often with Joe Franks. And with his wife when Joe wasn't around. His affair with Diane had gone on in hotel rooms in the city and upstairs in the master bedroom. In those days, Diane had had the place decorated in Laura Ashley floral prints with matching curtains. Not to Dennis Boyd's taste; *she* certainly had been. For almost a year they'd met, often in the jeweller's home, and fucked each other's brains out, while giant lilies bowed their heads and watched from the walls.

Inside, memories flooded over him, mostly of Joe, discussing what he wanted him to do or where he needed him to be and splashing whisky into a glass that already had plenty in it. Franks had been a generous employer, often, for no reason, paying Dennis an unexpected bonus. When that happened, his conscience complained and he made excuses to avoid having sex with Diane. Only, the sensual power of Franks' wife was too strong to resist. Soon they were at it again, harder than ever. And Boyd couldn't have cared less about Franks.

Diane took her coat off in the lounge and bent forward to remove her shoes. The V-neck sweater she was wearing showed the top of her bra and her breasts. Beautiful breasts.

'Bathroom's at the top of...' She smiled. 'But you know that, don't you? You know where everything is.'

It was as much as Boyd could do to stop himself from throwing her on the floor and having her. She was aware of the effect she was creating; the smile followed him to the door. In the bathroom, Boyd took off his coat, jacket and shirt and stared at his reflection. The last time he'd looked in this mirror a different face had looked back: a younger fresher guy with his best years still in front of him. Boyd didn't lie to himself. The decade and a half in the Big House were those better years. And they were gone.

He ran the tap and squeezed Ritchie Kennedy's shaving gel into his palm. Once again, he was in another man's home with another man's woman. Wanting her. Joe Franks hadn't deserved to be treated the way he'd treated him. Boyd wondered if Kennedy – so quick to squire Joe's widow – was as deserving.

The arms circled his chest before he realised she was there. Hot breath on his neck made him cut himself; in the mirror a red line appeared on his chin. She kissed his back and drew her nails across his belly. Boyd tensed. He turned to face her, fingers already underneath the sweater. Beneath the bra, the nipple was stone-hard, waiting. Ritchie might have saved her when she'd needed saving but for a woman like Diane there had to be more than security on offer. Kennedy had only done half the job. The rest should be played out slowly between her smooth slender thighs. She was up for it. After fifteen years, so was he. Until an image of Wilson's body on the cold concrete came into his mind and Boyd stepped away.

'Bad timing, Mrs Kennedy.'

'It didn't stop us before.'

'The police weren't after me before.'

He was right and she knew it. 'Some of Ritchie's clothes are on the bed. You're about the same size. They should do well enough. Shoes too. The man's got more pairs than me.'

Boyd mumbled thanks, finished shaving and tried on the clothes: expensive and a decent fit. Seeing himself in the shirt and tie was startling. When he came downstairs, she handed him a whisky – her first husband had done the same thing once, less than an hour after Boyd had been with his wife.

Diane pointed at the ceiling. 'Sorry about that. Couldn't help myself. Imagine sex is the last thing on your mind.'

She had to be joking.

'A pressure you don't need right now. They say men who've been in prison struggle to—'

Boyd grabbed her and pinned her against the wall. In seconds, he had her naked and was pounding into her. Diane cried out and bit his shoulder, eyes closed, lips parted in a sly grin.

It didn't last long; it didn't need to. They were back where they'd been before Joe Franks was murdered, before Barlinnie, before Ritchie Kennedy.

When it was over, they didn't speak. It wasn't necessary; they both knew what it meant. Diane picked her clothes off the floor and walked to the kitchen. 'I'll make something to eat then we'd better leave in case my husband decides to come home early.' She laughed. 'That would complicate things, wouldn't it? Where am I taking you?'

'Anywhere, as long as it's away from Glasgow and anybody who might recognise me.'

While he waited, Boyd remembered his conversation with the guards in the Bar-L.

a minute of her life she's never going to get back, eh?

a minute the first time, maybe

He had exaggerated.

Over poached eggs on toast, she asked again where he wanted to go. His answer remained the same: out of the city. Diane fished in a drawer and found a pair of thick-rimmed spectacles. 'See how these are. Ritchie's too vain to wear them. They're not very strong and nobody's seen you with glasses.'

Boyd put them on. 'How do I look?'

'Like Clark Kent's geeky older brother.'

'That'll do.'

Before they left, she gathered his old clothes, put them in a bag and emptied the ashtrays on top. Ritchie didn't smoke, and, even if he had, he was too much of a snob to go near roll-ups.

They got into her car and left at seven-thirty. At the Ayr Road junction, she threw an option into the mix. 'We could be at the coast in half an hour. No?'

He let the suggestion pass without a word and they joined traffic heading towards Glasgow. Lack of sleep made them subdued. Boyd's thoughts were dark. Diane sensed his mood and stayed quiet. Three miles from the city centre she broke the silence. 'Please tell me where the hell we're going.'

In the passenger seat, Dennis stared straight ahead. At Mount Florida he said, 'Take a right. Drop me in Hamilton. Get a hold of Cameron. If he agrees to help, tell him to expect my call.'

He'd lost her. 'The investigator I understand, but why Hamilton?'

'Why not? You said I look different. Different enough to walk down the street? We'll soon see. Wherever I go it has to be somewhere Cameron can reach me. Otherwise, I may as well turn myself in and be done with it.'

Diane Kennedy sighed. There was logic to what he was saying; she didn't have to approve. 'Okay. Hamilton, it is.'

* * *

The last three days had been the longest days of Dennis Boyd's life. Now, standing on the shore with rain plastering his hair against his head, he came to a decision. This would be the final night he'd spend here. It was time to move on.

A lone rower strained against the elements, cutting through the water in a show of strength and determination. It would take more than that to bring the result Boyd needed. He'd been impressed with Charlie Cameron. The PI had made it clear he'd come to talk. Only that. If Boyd lied, the talking would stop. Every question had had a point. He'd probed, searching for inconsistency in the answers, which would make it easy for him to pass. Boyd kept it simple, sticking to what little he knew. There were no inconsistencies in the story. He didn't do it. Not then and not now.

Later, he'd called Diane and heard the news: Cameron was on board. Since then, nothing. Nothing except a fear that grew with every hour spent trapped like an animal.

At the far end of the loch, the rower slumped across his oars, recovering from the effort. To the south, a shaft of sunlight broke through the clouds and a rainbow arced in the sky over the racecourse: a sign of good luck. Boyd grinned humourlessly and started walking back the way he'd come. If it wasn't for bad luck, he'd have no luck at all.

One more night.

* * *

Emil Rocha looked out of the hotel window at the rain falling steadily on the city. To his right, the Kingston Bridge spanned the river; a very different landscape from the barren hills surrounding his villa. A bottle of champagne sat in an ice bucket beside two fluted glasses on a table by the TV. He glanced over his shoulder to the bathroom door and smiled. Kim was making him wait. Good for her. The Spaniard was confident that when she finally appeared, it would be worth it. Getting her to meet him at the Hilton hadn't been difficult; she believed he'd save her and her daughter from Sean. Even if he hadn't suggested it, she would have come anyway – he'd met her type before: it was who she was. His objective was less complicated. And Emil Rocha usually got what he wanted.

The room at the Hilton was booked for one night; he'd no intention of sleeping here. Rocha lost his virginity at sixteen and had a long history of bedding females – unattached, married, divorced, he didn't mind; the world was awash with wives unhappy with their husbands – so long as they inspired something in him. Kim Rafferty certainly had. When Sean introduced them, Rocha's sharp eyes immediately noticed the marks on her face and he'd known she was his for the taking. Sympathetic words and a generous gift were all it needed. Emil had both.

The door opened. Kim Rafferty stood in the frame, naked apart from the present he'd given her sparkling at her throat. They kissed, then kissed again. Rocha lifted her in his arms and laid her gently on the bed. Kim said, 'I wore the necklace just like you asked.'

He caressed her soft flesh with the tip of his finger, tracing a line between her breasts to her belly and beyond. Kim gasped and Rocha whispered, 'I like a woman who does what she's told. Now, turn over.'

* * *

He was a good-looking man, but Kim wasn't attracted to Emil Rocha. Despite the show she'd put on for him, she'd hoped he'd get the sex over with quickly so they could talk about how he intended to help her and Rosie. For all his old-world charm, Kim had expected the Spaniard to be easily satisfied. She'd underestimated him.

Kim lost count of how many times he had her: on the bed and on the floor, his lean body crushing her; bending her over the upholstered arm of a chair, moaning with pleasure, as he ploughed her from behind with the sound of his flesh slapping against her buttocks; up against the wall, her legs wrapped round his waist, and back to the bed.

Rocha was insatiable. Yet, he still wasn't done. Kim had had her share of lovers; none had been like this. He poured champagne and handed her a glass, eying her nudity like a horny schoolboy.

She said, 'I told you, I don't drink.'

Rocha sat beside her. 'We all do a lot of things we say we don't. Drinking is one example. Spreading your legs for a man who isn't your husband, another. This afternoon, it appears you do both.'

Kim didn't appreciate his joke, pushed the glass away, and changed the subject. 'Have you thought about me and Rosie?'

'Of course. Since last night I've thought about little else. The situation disturbs me. It cannot be allowed to go on.'

Kim moved closer. 'I've been thinking, too, Emil. Perhaps, we could stay in your villa. The three of us. Rosie's sweet, you'll soon be very fond of her.'

Rocha sipped from his glass. 'If she's like her mother, I'm certain I will. Alas, my darling, when you get to my age you like things just as they are. Relationships are a complication better avoided. And, in spite of his obvious failings as a husband, Sean's a valued associate. The ties between us are deep. We make a lot of money together.' Rocha kissed the slope of her neck. 'He doesn't appreciate what he's got.'

'And never has.'

'Did you ever love him?'

Kim replied candidly. 'In the beginning, yes, maybe I did. It didn't last. Like most folk in Glasgow, I'd heard of the Rafferty family. The stories he told me about his upbringing were terrifying – his father, Jimmy, was a monster, who beat his sons and set them against each other. Stupidly, I believed Sean wasn't like him.' She sighed. 'I can't say I wasn't warned. Everybody pleaded with me to have nothing to do with him. Of course, I knew better. By the time I realised I was wrong, Rosie was on the way and it was too late, I was part of his plan. The Rafferty name was despised in the city, something Sean was determined to change. Having a wife and a daughter was, and is, important to his image of appearing ordinary.'

Rocha corrected her. 'Not ordinary. Sean Rafferty's a lot of things, ordinary isn't one of them. To appear *respectable*.'

'Respectable, you're right.'

'Didn't you have family of your own? Couldn't they have helped?'

'My parents were dead. As for the rest – I hadn't seen them in years.'

Rocha caressed the inside of her wrist. 'And what do you think would happen if your respectable husband discovered his lovely wife, the mother of his child, had spent the afternoon in a hotel room being fucked?'

'I don't need to think, I know. He'd kill me. Kill me with his bare hands.'

* * *

Through the shadows at the end of the garden, the River Clyde flowed to the city and on to the sea. Sean Rafferty was in the conservatory – not drunk, but getting there. He was considering his decision to divorce Kim. It needed more thought. She'd fight for custody and get it – the woman always did. The newspapers, bastards that they were, would jump all over the story. His carefully contrived image would be damaged; once Kim started talking, he'd never get it back. Rosie was a child, too young to understand her mother was a bitch.

As usual, Kim and Rosie were upstairs and he was alone, still seething over the morning meeting. Rocha had used his public profile as an excuse to turn his proposal down, then kicked his lunch invitation into touch. The relationship had cooled; he didn't understand why. Tomorrow, the Spaniard was flying home. All Sean had to show for his efforts was a nice watch.

He started to pour another drink, thought better of it and lifted his mobile. Fifteen miles away, Vicky Farrell answered. A call from Sean was never good news; she faked it as she'd been doing with men all her life.

'Sean. To what do I owe the pleasure?'

Rafferty said, 'Set me up with one of the West End girls. I'll be there in twenty-five minutes.'

'Anybody in particular?'

'No. On second thoughts, make it two.'

'You really are in the mood.'

'Actually, Vicky, I'm not. But I will be.'

16

Sean kept his eyes on the road and his hands firmly on the wheel to conceal the trembling, his mood as sour as the taste in his mouth; hangovers were becoming a habit. Vicky had organised a blonde and a black chick from Liverpool for him. They'd done their best to please the boss. He'd performed poorly – too much on his mind – and ended the night back in the conservatory, finishing what he'd started, getting drunk.

Rocha had only a few hours left in Scotland; this afternoon, he'd be in Spain. Nobody needed to tell Sean the visit hadn't been a success. Rocha's interests went beyond the drug empire that had made him wealthy, which meant constantly fielding calls. Apart from chauffeuring him to and from the airport, Sean had been with him exactly twice and couldn't shake the suspicion Emil was avoiding him.

Outside, temperatures were in the low twenties; inside the car the atmosphere was heavy. The bodyguards sat in the back, impassive. Rafferty had yet to hear them speak, even to each other. Their boss liked the sound of his own voice, pontificating on every subject under the sun: politics, history, music, women;

the world according to Emil Rocha. Expecting whoever was there to listen.

Today, he was subdued.

This quiet Rocha unnerved Sean; he tried to make conversation. 'I'm sorry your trip wasn't more fruitful, Emil.'

The Spaniard faced him. 'I wouldn't say that. I got to meet Kim. An interesting woman by any standards. Worth making the journey for that alone.'

Rafferty didn't respond and settled for driving. Something was definitely wrong.

When they reached Departures, the bodyguards unloaded the suitcases from the boot. Rocha stayed where he was, shifting in his seat so he was looking directly at Sean, his tone uncharacteristically formal. 'In a week, the latest delivery will arrive. I'm assured it's already been dispatched.'

'Good. Very good. Like you said, demand is always greater than supply. This shipment is the biggest yet.'

Rocha's mouth was a thin line. He said, 'The biggest and the last, I'm afraid. After this, make your arrangements with somebody else. Doesn't matter who, I don't care. Our work... our association... is over.'

Rafferty hadn't seen this coming. His legitimate revenue streams paled compared to the money he made from the marijuana, cocaine and heroin he bought from Rocha.

'Have I offended you in some way, Emil?'

Rocha leaned forward, the Rocha of old, his piercing eyes black coals against his dark skin.

'Offended, no. Caused me concern, most certainly. You have a problem, Sean, one it seems you're unaware of.'

Sean Rafferty tensed. What the fuck was coming?

'Kim asked me to get both her and your daughter out of the country. Somewhere you couldn't get to them.'

Surprise mixed with anger on Rafferty's face. Rocha said, 'If she's willing to betray you to me, she'll betray both of us to the police. It's merely a question of when. And that's a risk I'm not comfortable with.' He opened the door. 'Of course, your first instinct is to kill her. I would be the same.' The Spaniard shook his head. 'I'd counsel against doing anything before you're sure who else she's spoken to. Your fine wife is in a position to destroy you. Act carefully.'

Over his shoulder his bodyguards patiently waited for him. Through the windscreen, he looked up at the sky, resigned acceptance in his voice, almost as though he was speaking to himself. 'We've had a good run. A shame it has to end. When you've done what's necessary, call me and we'll talk. With the threat gone, perhaps there's a way to reinstate our arrangement and our friendship. I hope so.' He offered a regretful half-smile. 'Otherwise...'

Emil Rocha held out his hand.

Sean didn't take it.

* * *

In the wing mirror, Rafferty watched Rocha head into Departures, his burly henchmen in his wake. When the automatic doors closed behind them, Sean hammered the steering wheel with his fists, screaming with rage. He'd welcomed the visit, seeing it as an opportunity to forge an even closer relationship with the drug lord. Now, he regretted Emil Rocha ever setting foot in Scotland. Outwardly, he treated Sean like a son, complimenting his success, admiring his wife – 'your fine wife', he'd called her – in a caricature of old-fashioned respect. In reality, he'd enjoyed sharing the danger he'd uncovered, the danger Kim had put both of them in. The quietly spoken words weren't the commiserations of a friend to a deceived husband – they were a thinly disguised ultimatum. In his urbane way, he was telling him to fix it or there would be more than the future of his business at stake.

otherwise...

A memory of the Spaniard excusing himself, breaking away to make a call, his voice soft, gently wooing the woman on the other end of the line, came to him. And he understood. Nobody knew how many men had died on Rocha's orders. Scores, maybe hundreds.

Behind the gifts and fawning charm in the restaurant lay an ice-cold killer the equal of any. That man had fucked his wife. Offering sinister advice even as he boasted about it.

Rafferty closed his eyes, picturing how it would've been: Rocha pinning a naked Kim to the bed, relishing his power as she shuddered and climaxed under him, smiling a tight smile at her faith in him as her saviour. Sean struggled to keep control of the fury burning like acid inside him. Kim had been history long before Rocha's private jet landed in Glasgow. But her betrayal with the Spaniard had condemned her to a fate more awful than anything she could contemplate. Cuckolding him would've been enough. What she'd done was worse. Much worse. Plotting to take Rosie was a sin beyond mercy. Death would come – that much was certain – but before she breathed her final breath, she had to suffer as few had suffered. And she would; he'd see to it.

He punched the buttons on his mobile. Vicky assumed her boss was on with a complaint about the girls the previous night and answered reluctantly; two conversations in twenty-four hours with Sean Rafferty were more than she could handle. More than anyone could handle.

'Sean.'

'Send a girl to the airport hotel.'

'Any particular one?'

'Yeah, actually, you. I want you.'

* * *

Most of Vicky Farrell's adult life had been spent in the skin trade; nothing about men surprised her. Some were considerate, others rough, almost animals. Sean was neither.

It had gone on for ninety minutes. But it wasn't sex. There was no joy. No lust. He'd been relentless, emotionless, almost like a machine, repeating the act but taking no pleasure in it. When he'd finished, he'd thrown money on the bed and told her what he needed her to do – the only words spoken since she'd arrived. Vicky heard them and felt sick.

PART II

17

I'd committed myself to Dennis Boyd. Now, it was time to get serious. In the office, I emptied the cardboard box onto the desk and set about arranging the contents into some kind of order. I didn't kid myself. Apart from the Filofax with its code, there wasn't much. The relevant entries covered a period of three months.

BS/10. TM/6. CL/6.
CL/7. BS/12. Y/2.
CL/3. CL/4. BS/5.
BS/8.
TM/6 BS/10. CL/5.
Y/2. BS/4.

I turned my attention to the papers. Reading the dog-eared sheets confirmed my original opinion that there was nothing of importance amongst them. Franks had thought them so unimportant, he hadn't bothered to file the last couple of invoices he'd received. One of them – from his accountant, McCabe Senior –

had a personal note tacked to it thanking the jeweller for his business, signed with a sprawling A.

Unfortunately for Dennis Boyd, 'A' was sunning himself on the deck of a cruise liner or trailing around Pompeii along with three dozen sweaty tourists determined to get their money's worth, even if it killed them. Hopefully, we'd talk when he returned. Until then, all I had – apart from a few scraps from Pat Logue and Diane Kennedy – was right in front of me. My gut told me I was looking at the answer; it wasn't often wrong.

With luck, Patrick would find something useful; meanwhile, the late Joe Franks remained a mystery.

I called Diane Kennedy and got her husband. Ritchie was a man of few words, at least where I was concerned. 'She isn't here, she's in town.'

The phone went dead.

Diane, on the other hand, was pleased to hear from me when I dialled her mobile.

'Have you found anything to help Dennis?'

'No. Sorry to disappoint you.'

Her expectations – so far beyond reality – surprised me, and I had to stop myself from reminding her it had only been days. Now I knew where Pat Logue had been coming from with his 'ingratitude' comment. On cue, the door opened and the bold Patrick came in. I waved him to take a seat while I finished my conversation.

Diane said, 'Then why're you calling me?'

'I need to speak to you. Today if possible.'

'Why?'

'I'll tell you when you get here. There's something I want you to do. I'll be in my office till three this afternoon, does that suit?'

She seemed unsure. 'Yes, I suppose so.'

'Good. See you then.'

For all his shortcomings as a husband, Pat Logue understood people. 'Didn't sound too keen, did she? Considerin' she's the client and her old boyfriend's on the run.'

'You're not wrong.'

'How does the husband feel about it?'

'Kennedy doesn't have much to say. He's clearly uncomfortable with it. Boyd's an old boyfriend after all.'

'Think he's jealous?'

'She's still a good-looking woman.'

Patrick said, '"The jealous are troublesome to others but a torment to themselves." William Penn.'

He was starting to bore me. 'What've you got?'

He took the hint and consulted a fresh set of betting slips. 'Ritchie Kennedy's a man on a mission.'

'How so?'

'Went from runnin' a pub in Govan to owning three in record time. Plus, he has some property he rents out. All before he hooked up with the merry widow.'

'Maybe he's a hard worker.'

'Or just hard. Plays his cards close to his chest. No partners; a genuine self-made man.'

'Any suggestion he had something to do with the Joe Franks murder?'

'No. But he moved in on the wife double-quick.'

'Yeah. He'd been after her for a while, she told me. Tried it on with her more than once. She only took him up on his offer when she discovered she was headed for the poor house, thanks to Joe.'

'Her very own knight in shinin' armour. Kennedy squared the mortgage so she didn't lose the roof over her head. Two years later, it was marzipan all round. Later on, he got shot of the pubs and went into the hotel business.'

'How's it doing?'

'Same as everybody else in hospitality. Every year's a bumper year accordin' to VisitScotland. Never seems to reach the people on the front line. I talked to a guy whose sister was employed there for a while as a silver-service waitress when there was a big wedding on. Apparently, Kennedy has a temper. Jumps up and down and shouts a lot. Can't keep staff.'

'But so far he hasn't killed anybody?'

'Not yet.'

'Is the hotel in financial trouble?'

'Nothing a couple of decent trading quarters wouldn't put right. To give Kennedy some credit, he's on the premises every day.'

'And his wife?'

Patrick tucked his notes in his inside pocket; he didn't need them. 'Now and again. She's wheeled out occasionally to have dinner with some visiting bigwigs. No danger of gettin' her hands dirty, if that's what you mean.'

'You haven't said anything about Franks.'

'Not much more to say. Haven't come across anybody who didn't like him.'

'Even though he owed them money? Strange.'

'That only happened in the last three months. Thinkin' is the diamond deal was an attempt to get out of the hole he was in. And the debts weren't huge. The mortgage was behind and he hadn't paid the office in the Argyll Arcade in a while. Beyond that, the cars and household bills had been allowed to slide, but nobody I spoke to had been shafted. Seems Franks wasn't that kind of guy. The big surprise was that when he died, he was penniless. No insurance. No savings. Nada.'

'His wife was the big loser.'

'Not for long, thanks to Ritchie Boy.'

'Yeah, but there's something not right here, Pat. I feel it. Why didn't he sack Boyd? Wouldn't that be the obvious thing to do? And why do you need a bodyguard if you're not doing any business? And why cut him out of your biggest deal ever?'

'Good questions, Charlie.'

'Why do we believe Franks knew about the affair?'

Patrick gave it some thought and came back with the correct answer. 'Because Dennis and Diane said so.'

'Right. But maybe he didn't, or maybe Boyd's right and he did know. He just didn't care.'

Patrick sat forward in his chair. 'She saw the writin' was on the wall and... and what? Cooked it up with her lover?'

'No. She was in the dark about the diamond deal and had no idea she was broke. Boyd didn't do it, according to her, and she's paying us to prove it. Diane doesn't fit.'

We stared at each other across the table. In Cochrane Street, a car horn tooted.

Patrick summed it up. 'Bollocks, isn't it?'

I agreed. 'Absolute bollocks.'

'So, what do you want me to do, Charlie?'

'We need these witnesses and while you're at it, Pat,' I scribbled down the initials and handed them to him, 'see if you can kick up anything on these.'

'What are they?'

'They show up a lot in the last few weeks of Franks' life. Boyd says he was secretive around him. What you're holding in your hand bears it out. Joe was meeting people and hiding their identities. Has to be people connected with the deal.'

Before Patrick had a chance to comment, Diane Kennedy stepped through the door wearing a beige cardigan, a brown and cream dress and sunglasses; very *Breakfast at Tiffany's*. Diane didn't speak. She just stood, clearly waiting for Pat Logue to make himself scarce. He took the hint. 'I'll see what I can do, Charlie,' he said and left. On his way out he eyed Diane from head to foot. Later he'd give me his verdict.

18

The shades stayed on and I realised that, behind them, Diane's mood was dark. The you're-his-only-hope woman was missing; she seemed tense, her tone clipped. 'You wanted me here so here I am.'

Her old boyfriend was on the run yet she was displeased with having to see me at short notice. Mrs Kennedy was a complex woman, impossible to read. Before I could begin, she blurted out what was on her mind. 'The police have been. They think I might be in danger.'

'From Boyd?'

'Yes, so I gave them the reaction they expected.'

'Do they have any idea where he is?'

'No. They don't.' She moved back into confrontational mode. 'So why am I here if you haven't found anything to help Dennis?'

I threw the Filofax on the desk between us; it landed with a dull thud. 'Ever look at this?'

She eyed me suspiciously, sensing a trap. 'Why would I?'

'Oh, I don't know. Maybe to figure out what the hell Joe was up to before he died.' Her expression was stone; my sarcasm wasn't welcome. I ignored the signs and encouraged her. 'Go on. See if anything jumps out at you.'

She lifted the Filofax with her manicured fingers and flicked through the pages with the speed of somebody with no interest in reading.

'Start at the second year.'

The shades came off, replaced by a frown, her mouth set tight with barely concealed temper. Perhaps the visit from the police had rattled her. Whatever the reason, Diane Kennedy wasn't keen to help all of a sudden. Her lips moved silently over the words as the pages turned. She said, 'Give me a clue. What am I supposed to be looking for?'

Telling her would've been too easy.

'What do you see?'

She stroked her nose, deep in thought – or pretending to be. 'Nothing very much. Dates. Times. Initials.'

'Recognise any of them?'

She closed the Filofax and withdrew behind her shades again. 'No. Should I?'

Diane was giving up too easily. Her attitude confused me. She was the one who'd asked for help; I'd assumed we were on the same side. Today, Joe Franks' widow seemed bored and impatient.

'I'd say your husband was hiding what he was doing, wouldn't you?'

'Joe was a very private man.'

'You say private. Boyd said secretive. Which is it?'

She stared at me like I was speaking a foreign language and changed the subject with a question of her own. 'Have you found the other witnesses?'

I told the truth. 'We're working on it. Let's get back to Joe. You didn't mention he'd been married before.'

'I didn't think it was important.'

'What was his first wife's name?'

'Marion. He never talked about her. I heard she'd died a few years ago.'

I took a shot in the dark and hit what I was aiming at. 'Did he leave her for you?'

Diane had been close to snapping since she arrived. Now she did. Her cheeks reddened; anger or whatever it was she'd brought with her rose to the surface. 'What has this got to do with proving Dennis didn't kill Joe? You drag me in here, give me some empty pages to look at, and now you're on about a woman I've never met. Where the hell is this going? Cut the crap, Cameron. Do what I'm paying you to do. Help Dennis.'

Her outrage was impressive though difficult to believe. Diane Kennedy was as hard as nails. The idea that a visit from the police would be enough to upset her was fanciful at best. She was nervy and reacting all right, though not from anything I'd done.

'You said Ritchie tried it on with you at your house. What was he doing there?'

'He had business with Joe.'

My next question pushed her over the edge. 'What kind of business?'

She stood up, unhappy at the line I was taking. 'What is this? Joe's first wife? Ritchie? If there's something you want to say, spit it out. On the phone you said when I got here, you'd tell me why you had to see me. Well, I'm here.'

Behind her, afternoon sunshine from the window cast a golden aura round her head. For a moment, she was almost beautiful and I understood how Joe Franks had fallen for her. But it was an illusion. Diane wasn't anybody's idea of an angel. She'd proved she was a lady more than capable of looking out for Number One; her overplayed annoyance wasn't down to me.

I picked the Filofax off the table and held it out. 'Why don't we both cut the crap? The answers we're searching for are probably in these tired old pages.'

Diane slumped into the chair, suddenly exhausted. 'Sorry. I'm sorry. Ritchie and I haven't been getting on. Before I left the house, we had a huge row. Screaming at each other.'

I guessed what she was about to tell me. Pat Logue had taken the opportunity to lay another quote on me, but he'd been on the money: the Kennedys were a couple at odds with each other and Dennis Boyd was at the centre of it.

'What's his problem?'

'He doesn't like Dennis. Doesn't like me being involved with him. Wants me to drop the whole thing.'

'It isn't hard to see where he's coming from. After all…'

'Dennis was my lover. You don't have to remind me. It's all I hear. Ritchie's threatening to leave. He's given me an ultimatum. Him or Boyd.'

'What did you expect?'

She rubbed her eyes and asked a question only she could answer. 'What Boyd would do when he came out was easy to guess. I was only trying to stop him from going back in again. Why the hell didn't I just mind my own business?'

Now she was being silly. Whatever happened once the gates of Barlinnie prison closed leaving Dennis Boyd on the outside would always be Diane Kennedy's business. Boyd had been found guilty of murdering her husband. Not caring wasn't an option.

She pulled herself together and explained. 'I expected him to take the money and go. Just go. Anywhere, it didn't matter. It wasn't supposed to cost me my marriage.'

'Look, for what it's worth, I get how Ritchie must be feeling. Are you in love with Dennis Boyd?'

My directness caught her off guard; for a moment she faltered and bought herself time by repeating what I'd asked. 'Am I in love with him? I'm not sure. But I am sure he didn't murder Joe.'

I wondered what it must be like to be a husband whose wife prefers another man. Especially this man. For a second, I forgot the boor who'd ignored me twice and felt for Ritchie Kennedy. Their relationship, born out of tragedy, and quickly – too quickly perhaps – progressing to the altar, was in trouble.

Diane spoke in a voice more like a lost little girl than the brassy piece who'd blown smoke rings in the air and flashed her knickers. 'What can I do?'

'Tell Boyd the truth. Tell him where he stands. A friend would.'

She shook her blonde head. 'You've spoken to him, think he'll listen? Would you?'

* * *

Before she left, I wrote the puzzling initials down on a sheet of paper and asked Diane Kennedy again if they made sense to her. Her blank expression said it all. She shrugged and handed them back. 'Sorry. Not much help, am I?'

When she'd gone, alone in the office with the constant purr of traffic in Cochrane Street heading for George Square, I fell back on an old standby. I made a list. Not exactly high-tech but useful for clarifying how things stood. Joe Franks had been a jeweller, not a spy. He hadn't landed me with the Enigma Code. No consolation. I started with questions and the scraps of what I knew about him and the case.

The diamond deal:
Who knew about it?
Who was in it with Franks?

How did it go wrong?
Why keep Boyd out of it?

Franks:
Did Joe Franks know about the affair?
If so, why keep Dennis Boyd as a bodyguard?
Why was he secretive around Boyd?
BS. TM. CL. What do they mean?
What do they tell us about Franks?
How did the business get in trouble?

Dennis Boyd:
Is it possible it was all about settling a score with Boyd?
Whose feathers did he ruffle while he worked for Franks?
And before Franks?
Where is Boyd now?

Speak to:
Andrew. See what he knows about the case.
Alex Gilby. Kennedy is in the hospitality business. What's the word on the street?

Interview everybody with any connection to Franks, Dennis Boyd or the trial:
Diane Kennedy.
Ritchie Kennedy.
Dennis Boyd? Not advisable but necessary.
McCabe, Joe's accountant.
The two remaining witnesses, McDermid and Davidson.
Yannis the Greek – friend or killer?
Joe Franks' old lawyer.
Arcade office owner?

BS, TM and CL once their identities are known.

Plenty of threads. I started with the obvious – Y.

The number rang out. Nobody answered. Next up, the Arcade owner. A bright voice at the other end of the line informed me Mr Shanklin was before her time and no longer worked for the company. I scored him off the list and moved on to the others. Threads, yeah, but none I could tug on for the moment. Finding out who murdered Wilson might have been possible, except – as Pat Logue had underlined – that was what the police were paid to do. A memory of Diane Kennedy stayed with me. She'd been unhappy when she was married to Joe Franks. Fast-forward and not much had changed. The same went for Dennis Boyd: falsely accused – if you believed his story – of killing Franks, and now the prime suspect in the murder of a man whose testimony had sent him down.

The old lovers had more in common than they knew.

19

My mobile vibrated on the desk. Before I could speak, Pat Logue said, 'Charlie? Think I know where Liam McDermid is. I'm outside the Schooner Inn. Pick me up.'

'I'm on my way, Patrick.'

I closed the door of the office and walked to the car park with a spring in my step. My original intention had been to talk to all three witnesses. With Wilson dead, that wasn't possible. It also wasn't necessary; one would do.

A left turn at Glasgow Cross and the Tron Steeple took me along Gallowgate past the Barras, the city's largest and most popular weekend market. On a corner across the road from the Barrowland Ballroom's gaudy neon façade, the Schooner Inn looked like yet another pub that time forgot – the city was full of them. Inside, I guessed nothing had changed in decades, including some of the customers. In a picture above the door, a ship in full sail battled rough seas. Once upon a time it had proudly flown the Union Jack until, early one Sunday morning, an unknown artist took it on himself to add the Irish flag in protest at a bad result for his football team in the Old Firm derby the day before. Somebody had redressed the affront by daubing red, white and blue on top.

Welcome to Glasgow.

Pat Logue was hunkered on the pavement talking to a wild-looking guy with a beard and dirty hair, sitting against the wall with a paper cup beside him. His face was gaunt, with skin the colour of old wallpaper paste. Stick-thin arms told an all too familiar story of heroin addiction and the hopelessness that came with it. His shoes were worn at the heels and had no laces; they'd be in his pocket, reserved for a more important use: tying-off his blood supply when he injected to increase the size of the vein. He couldn't have been more than twenty but in a year or two – maybe sooner – he'd be dead. One day, his traumatised brain wouldn't send the message to his body, his heart would stop beating, and it would be over.

Patrick said something that made him smile and patted his bony shoulder under the faded denim jacket. When he saw me, he got up, stuffed a ten-pound note in the cup and shook the beggar's hand. From the light in the guy's eyes he'd been given more than money.

DS Geddes disliked Pat Logue for living on the margins and didn't care who knew it. Jackie Mallon thought he was a good customer and a terrible husband. Personal experience had taught me he could be a manipulative rogue. But there was more to him than any of us were seeing. To Patrick, people were just trying to make sense of their lives in a world where the odds – from the cradle to the grave – were stacked against too many of them. He didn't judge what they did to get by and would help if he could.

Tomorrow, maybe later today, he'd be after me for a sub to keep him going, yet here he was giving cash to a stranger. I'd caught him at his best and was reminded why I liked him.

He got in, fastened his seat belt and gave me directions, the encounter already forgotten. 'Head for Bellshill.'

We drove deeper into the East End of the city. Off to our right, Celtic Park was a giant alien spacecraft. Patrick gave me the potted version of his visit to the Schooner Inn.

'McDermid's givin' the pub a miss, at least for a while.'

'So, where is he?'

'Barmaid's in the dark. Literally in that dive. Electricity hasn't caught on like it has everywhere else. Or somebody didn't bother putting fifty pence in the meter. But she liked me. Didn't come right out and say it, mind. No need. Her body language did the talkin' for her. Thank God for Buckfast shot. McDermid lives in Possil. Zero chance he's still there. She let slip his son Rory works on the rigs. Isn't married. Same as his father. Has a house in Bellshill. I'm bettin' that's where his old man's hidin'.'

Patrick pulled the visor down and admired his goatee in the mirror. 'Good to know the old magic's still there.'

'You've got an address?'

He grinned. 'Not too many Rory McDermids in the phone book. 'Course I've got an address.'

We edged out of the city. Gallowgate became Tollcross Road then London Road. At Carmyle, I joined the M74 and carried on. Patrick stayed quiet, maybe thinking about his imagined success with the barmaid in the Schooner Inn or the boy and his addiction.

At the turn-off for Bellshill he said, 'Still surprised the witnesses hung around for Boyd to come out of the poky. Would've disappeared like snow off a dyke if it had been me. Surely they didn't think he was goin' to let it go?'

It was a point we'd already discussed; heading for the hills was the logical thing to do. Wilson, McDermid and Davidson must've realised they were in danger. Why stick around? Unless they'd done nothing wrong or thought they were protected.

We left the motorway at Bothwell and stopped at the traffic lights at the bottom of the off-ramp. Strathclyde Park, where I'd met Dennis Boyd, was across the roundabout.

The lights turned green and I drove up the steep rise to Bellshill. In the town, Patrick asked a woman pushing a go-chair for directions to the address he'd found for Rory McDermid. The child was bawling and she was harassed and embarrassed. She shook her head and walked on. A grey-haired man with a dog on a leash was more helpful; he knew the street and told us how to get there. As we pulled into the housing estate, Pat said, 'If McDermid's here, what's the script?'

'Get him to talk about his part in the trial.'

He laughed. 'Break down and tell us who paid him to commit perjury? Don't see it.'

'Agreed. I think we should push the if-we-can-find-you-so-can-he angle.'

Even as I spoke, it sounded far-fetched. Patrick damned me with faint praise.

'Say this for you, Charlie, you're an optimist.'

No, I wasn't. I was faking it.

The house was an ex-council pebble-dashed three-bedroom semi-detached, with a dark-wood garage at the end of the drive; a rusty padlock hung from the hasp. There was no sign of a car, the Venetian blinds were drawn and the slim hope I'd had of finding Liam McDermid hiding in his son's place evaporated. I knocked on the front door. Nobody answered because nobody was home. I tried again with the same result then peered through the letter box, seeing the empty hall and on into the kitchen. Neither the father nor the son was here; the house was deserted.

Patrick said, 'I'll try the back.'

Seconds later he called to me and I joined him standing with the padlock in his hand and the wooden door dragged aside.

'Think we've found him, Charlie. And it won't do Dennis Boyd's case much good.'

He was right about that.

I stepped inside the garage into an invisible cloud of fumes. A black rubber hose ran from the exhaust of a green Astra to the window on the driver's side. I put my hand over my mouth and opened the door, careful not to leave fingerprints.

In the front seat, a man sat upright. Liam McDermid's eyes were closed, both arms strapped to his side, his cheeks cherry-pink, as if he'd recently had a blood transfusion; duct tape covered his body like a mummy from his ankles to his neck and over his mouth, fastening him to the headrest. Moving even a little would've been impossible, assuming he'd been conscious enough to try. The end would've come quickly – in the confined space somewhere between five and fifteen minutes – though he'd been dead much longer; the Astra's bonnet was cold to the touch and the petrol gauge showed empty. Suicide it wasn't.

From behind me, Pat Logue summed up what both of us were feeling with a question I couldn't begin to answer. 'What've you got us into, Charlie?'

We closed the garage and walked back to the car. We didn't speak until we were back at the Bothwell roundabout when Patrick broke the silence. I heard anxiety in his voice. 'I'm guessin' it's a call to the police. Tell me I'm right?'

'You're right.'

'An anonymous call?'

'Yep.'

'We were never there?'

'Right again.'

My responses were glib though the implications of our gruesome discovery hung heavy with me; the last time I'd seen Dennis Boyd he was only a few miles away from the scene of the crime. Diane Kennedy's passionate pleading in my office on her old lover's behalf seemed sadly off the mark. She'd put her money on the wrong horse. Again. One dead witness had looked bad for Boyd, yet I'd been prepared to believe him. And her. Two put the issue beyond doubt. At his trial, three witnesses had testified. Only Willie Davidson remained alive. Wherever he was, he needed to pack a bag and get out of Dodge before Boyd found him and made a clean sweep of the men who'd spoken against him.

In the city, I went into a pub on Shettleston Road and made the call. Patrick waited in the car. When we got to High Street he got out and leaned on the half-opened door, needing to speak, reluctant to go. I thought he was going to give me one of his quotes but I was wrong; he was serious and he was trying to help. Except it would take more than a kind word and a tenner.

'Promise me you'll be sensible and let the CID do their job?'

Not having an answer for him was becoming a habit. He tried reason. 'Charlie, listen. This isn't what we do. Findin' who killed the jeweller in the dim and distant... that was one thing... This... is somethin' else. Murder. Double murder. Dangerous waters to be swimmin' in. Know what I'm talkin'?'

His eyes bored into me, willing me to see it as he did. And he was right. No doubt about it, he was right. I cut him a break. 'You can take a step back, Patrick. I'll understand. No harm done.'

His fists clenched and unclenched in frustration. 'Low blow, mate. That's not what I mean. You know I can't leave you with it. How could I?'

In spite of myself I smiled. 'Then keep looking for Davidson. Speak to you tomorrow.'

His reaction was close to comic. Except there was nothing funny about it. 'Fuck, Charlie. Fuck! Fuck! Fuck!'

20

In the office I pulled the blinds on the window and sat in the dark, glad to be alone. Alone, that was, apart from the pictures in my head and the tightness in my chest.

Pat Logue was neither a brave man nor a coward. For as long as I'd known him, he'd been driven by many things; fear wasn't one of them. With the Joe Franks case, his thinking was difficult to argue against. What we'd found in Bellshill would've been more than enough to convince most people. It had certainly convinced him.

This wasn't what he'd signed on for.

There were times when even I realised my dog-with-a-bone mentality was out of step. This was one of those times. 'Won't give up can't let go' had limits, and a barman who looked healthier dead than alive had taken me to them and beyond. I lifted the phone and dialled Diane Kennedy's number.

'Diane Kennedy.'

'Diane, Charlie Cameron.'

Her hesitancy on hearing my name came down the line. She

had no idea what I was going to tell her, though instinctively she sussed it wasn't going to be anything good.

'Is there news?'

what've you got us into, Charlie?

'Not in the sense you mean. I'm quitting the case.'

She gasped. 'No! You can't!'

'I can and I am.'

'What about Dennis?'

'Boyd can look after himself. He's doing an okay job so far.'

'But without you they'll put him back inside.'

'They'll do that anyway. With or without me.'

She mumbled to somebody in the room and returned to me. 'Why now? What's happened?'

'You don't want the details, trust me on that.'

'Tell me why.'

'Let's just say it's better for all concerned that I'm off the case.'

'It isn't. It isn't better for Dennis. He's out there somewhere, on his own, with the police after him. He believes in you. I believe in you. You can't just quit.'

Powerful stuff; not powerful enough to make me change my mind. 'Afraid you're wrong. I can and I have. I'm done.'

Her breathing on the other end of the line was like the rustle of the wind, a portent of the coming storm. She was owed more of an explanation than I was able to give her and was unhappy with the suddenness of my decision.

Her tone was dry, dismissive. I'd gone from hero to zero. 'So. Just like that you drop him.'

'Not just like that.'

She laughed that brittle laugh of hers. 'Poor Dennis. Should've taken the money and got well away from Glasgow when he had the chance. Instead, he pinned his hopes on you. What a loser.'

Did she mean Boyd or me?

'I'll post Joe's papers to you.'

Diane snapped, 'Please don't go to any trouble on my account.'

'They belong to you.'

Her voice rose, angry and accusing. 'Well, I don't fucking want them. What good are they? I'm the one who's going to have to tell Dennis he's been abandoned. Not you.'

I'd given her the best advice I had: sooner or later Boyd would be caught; better if he gave himself up. At the time, a reasonable shout so far as it went. But that was then. In Bellshill, Liam McDermid's body was on its way to the morgue. The search for his killer would be a manhunt with Boyd at its centre. Capture had always been the most probable outcome for Diane Kennedy's old lover. Now, it was inevitable.

The police would let her know the latest development in due course and maybe she'd understand, though I doubted it. As the bringer of bad tidings, I was all she had to unload on. In the circumstances, she held it together pretty well, until her husband said something in the background that made her scream at him.

When she returned to me, she was curt; there was a tremble in her voice. 'Forget the papers. Send me your bill.'

Then she was gone, leaving me staring at the phone in my hand, wondering why the hell I'd got involved in the first place. Diane's loyalty was admirable but her blind faith in Boyd could be setting her up for a big let-down. His innocence or guilt in Joe Franks' death fifteen years ago was less important than it had been; events since his release from Barlinnie had overtaken it.

I needed air. George Square had plenty. A grey-haired woman wearing a scarf and a tan raincoat sat on a bench near the cenotaph feeding broken biscuits to the pigeons from a brown paper bag, her shoes buried beneath the birds flocking around her feet, dipping and diving for the crumbs, always looking for more. When the bag was empty, she crushed it in her hands and held it in the air, smiling. 'All finished.'

She brushed crumbs off her coat and walked towards Queen Street and the trains, her job done.

The absolute ordinariness of it and the lady's quiet pleasure were timely reminders that normal still existed. Most of what I did was undramatic. Sad sometimes, though no more than you'd expect from life: a daughter or a son falling out with their parents and running to a world they were unprepared for; a wife or a husband quitting the marital home, leaving a bewildered spouse behind; a business partner emptying the company bank account and taking off. In short, the usual. The Joe Franks case had never been that, but with two murders its novelty value paled; any association with it was unwise.

I stayed in the square for over an hour, people watching, until the sun disappeared and the clouds darkened, returning the sky to its grey default position in these parts. Lightning flashed followed by a distant growl of thunder. The pigeons rose as one, circled and flew to their rooftop nests and safety. I headed for NYB with rain spattering the pavement. By the time I got there it was coming down hard.

This late in the afternoon, New York Blue was deserted apart from Patrick leaning on the bar deep in conversation with Alex Gilby's niece, animated and smiling; on the surface at least, recovered from our grim discovery. Saying hello didn't feel right. I ignored him, ordered a coffee to go and took a seat beside the Rock-Ola. He got the message and refocused his attention on the girl.

Back in the office I hung my jacket over the cast iron radiator. Thunder crashed over the city chambers, loud enough to make the window rattle in its wooden frame. The latte was cool and unpleasantly strong. Michelle had a lot to learn. Pat Logue was offering to teach her.

I heard footsteps on the stairs, then the door opened. The glasses Diane had given him had been ditched, his coat was soaked, his hair plastered to his head. Rivulets of water ran down his face; he blinked them away. The last time we'd met, Dennis Boyd looked like a typical businessman. Words were unnecessary. Flinty eyes narrowed as rain dripped off him onto the floor. My decision to quit the case had obviously reached him and, wherever he'd been, he hadn't wasted time in getting here.

His opening sentence left me in no doubt how he felt about it.

'Charlie. I'm disappointed in you. I thought we had a deal.'

21

Thunder crashed across the black sky above the car gliding through the steel gates and up the drive to the house. Three men got out, oblivious to the rain, scanning the exclusive neighbourhood for prying eyes. There were none. Like everywhere, the people in this part of South Lanarkshire had their own secrets and kept themselves to themselves.

Sean Rafferty stood aside to let them pass, pointing to the stairs. 'Left at the top. Do what you have to but don't mark her face.' He raised a threatening finger. 'And don't wake my daughter.'

In the kitchen, he switched on the Oracle espresso machine Kim insisted they had to have and tipped Blue Mountain beans into the bowl of the grinder. The noise wasn't enough to blot out the screams above him. Sean Rafferty cursed – the idiots were going to disturb Rosie. Rocha would be at his villa, probably sipping a glass of chilled white wine, wondering how Sean would handle the situation back in Scotland; he needn't be concerned. It was taken care of.

Sean's laugh was forced; Rocha really was a pompous arsehole and Kim was about to discover there were worse things than dying.

* * *

She was sitting at the dressing table in her underwear, removing make-up with cotton pads, massaging lotion into her skin, carefully applying it to the swollen area around her eye. Rocha hadn't called – the sooner he did, the better she'd feel. The sex with him had been the most intense she'd ever known. He'd dominated her from beginning to end, though made it clear he'd no interest in a permanent arrangement. Fine with her. Once they were safe, she'd decide what to do with the rest of her life. Hers and Rosie's. First things first. Getting Rosie away from her father was the priority. They'd start again somewhere else with new names; the world didn't need another Rafferty. The prospect excited her and she smiled at her reflection in the mirror.

Usually, Rosie went down without a fuss. Tonight, she'd been restless, eventually drifting into a fitful sleep, almost as though she'd sensed something wasn't right. Sean loved his daughter – no doubt about that – and she'd miss him. But her young mind would forget. Years down the line questions would start about who her father was and why they weren't with him. When she was old enough to understand, her mother would tell her. All of it.

Kim heard footsteps on the stairs and prayed Sean wasn't coming to make a scene. He'd been a heavy drinker when they met – now, it was out of control. As long as he left her alone, she couldn't care less how much he drank.

The footsteps stopped. The door handle turned. Kim

watched, terrified, aware how vulnerable she was. She called to him, trying to sound unafraid. 'Please, Sean, go away! Please!'

The frame cracked and buckled, the lock sprang loose and three men came through the door; hard-faced thugs with pitiless eyes, dressed like burglars in jeans and black polo necks – Sean had an army of them. One she'd seen before, the others strangers.

Kim lifted a hairbrush, brandishing it like a knife, screaming at them. 'Get out! Whoever you are, stay away from me! I'm warning you, stay away!'

They edged towards her, blocking her escape. The leader said, 'Shut the bitch up. Sean wants this done quietly.'

'If he's finished with her, I'll take her on.'

'Yeah, I'll tell him you said that, shall I?'

'For Christ's sake, don't.'

Kim ran to the window, banging on the glass, shouting for help. One of her attackers went after her and made the mistake of getting too near; her nails ripped bloody lines on his cheek. His reaction was instinctive; he punched her with his clenched fist, rocking her head back on her shoulders. His mate pulled him away. 'Are you fucking crazy? Didn't you hear what Sean said? He doesn't want her marked.' He took plastic ties from his pocket. 'For fuck's sake get these on her. And where's the tape? Get it over her mouth before she wakes the whole fucking neighbourhood, never mind the kid.'

Kim twisted her head, yelling, 'Sean! Sean! This is wrong!'

They bound her hands and feet, finally managing to hold her long enough to get the gag in place, then carried her like a sack of laundry, still kicking. On the landing, they passed the bedroom where Rosie was asleep. The door was ajar – her baby was in there. Hot tears blinded Kim. She'd been a fool: Rocha had used her, had his fun and tossed her aside like the silly woman she was.

At the bottom of the stairs Sean was waiting. Rosie started to cry. Kim bucked and fought but her strength was gone.

Sean barked at his men. 'I told you not to wake my daughter!'

'She had the door locked. We didn't have a choice.'

He cradled his wife's head, gently wiping her tears. Kim smelled whisky on his breath as he leaned closer and whispered, 'Did you really believe you could double-cross Sean Rafferty and get away with it? You're a fool, my darling. And a whore. A tart too stupid to have around. Rosie will miss her mummy.' He sighed. 'But in a month, she won't remember you. As for us, we won't meet again, at least, not in this life.'

He ran a finger tenderly over her face. 'Get her out of here.'

* * *

Rough hands hauled her to the car, dragging her bare legs on the wet concrete drive, cutting her feet, scraping her thighs. She strained to look back at the house, knowing she'd never be here again. What she saw broke her heart: Sean was at the bedroom window holding Rosie in his arms, her small fingers in his, both of them waving goodbye.

Kim's anguished moan was lost in the storm. She retched, acid bile burning her throat, choking her. Lightning lit the night, the blow struck the side of her head, and the world went dark.

* * *

The blue neon sign hanging from the crumbling building in Renfrew Street flickered in and out as it had for as long as anyone could remember. Nobody fixed it. Nobody cared enough, certainly not the Johns who made their way up the hill from the town centre, arm in arm with the women they'd picked up in the pubs on Sauchiehall. The arrangements struck depended on how much money the guy had in his wallet or was able to get out of the cash machine.

Sean Rafferty had inherited this place from his father, tucked between a row of unloved low-rent bed and breakfasts at the top of stone stairs, green with mould. Nothing had been spent on the exterior in decades and it showed; the building was black, decaying like a rotted tree, the guttering broken and overgrown with weeds, paint peeling on the buckled wooden window frames, and the grouting between the granite blocks had loosened and fallen out.

Inside, a greasy-haired guy had his face hidden behind a dog-eared copy of *Fiesta*, open at Readers' Wives. His black biker boots were on the reception desk, the soles cracked, heels worn beyond repair. When he saw Vicky, he closed the magazine and sat up straight. His name was Noah – unusual in Glasgow – the only notable thing about him. He wore a leather jacket, de rigueur in his universe, the collar up over a black T-shirt with I'M WITH STUPID on the front. His teeth were crooked, the backs of his hands and most of his fingers covered in faded tattoos. Noah's job was to strong-arm anybody who started bother or knocked the pros around, and to make sure the punters paid for what they wanted.

Drunks always got a slap because they didn't fight back.

Noah considered it a perk of the job.

Vicky hated coming here and rarely did. It depressed her. If things had gone a different road, this could've been her fate. Even the prettiest girls ignored the lines on their face, the coarsening skin, and overstayed their usefulness. After a while, it was about survival rather than money. The very freedom they craved becoming something to fear, something to dread. Until Rafferty, or whoever owned them by then, replaced them with a younger version of themselves and sent them to this.

She shuddered, thanked the Higher Power that had plucked her off that path and stepped into the rain to meet the car.

22

Patrick's assessment of Boyd: a hard man but not a thug – certainly not a gangster – failed to reassure me when faced with a guy who had less and less to lose the longer he stayed on the run. I faked a casualness I didn't feel and pretended I wasn't surprised to see him. 'You're wet, Dennis. Sit down.'

He straddled the chair like they did in cop movies. On another day, it might've been cool. Not today. With rain running off the end of his chin, it didn't get there.

'I called Diane. She told me.'

'Did she tell you why?'

'I can guess. McDermid's dead. Or Davidson. Whoever did it, I'd like to shake his hand.'

'Don't be so fast to congratulate them. They haven't done you any favours. The opposite: every policeman in Glasgow has your description, and they're all convinced you're a double-murderer.'

He peeled off his herringbone coat and hung it over the chair. Underneath his jacket the front of his shirt was sodden. Boyd had come to make a point and wasn't leaving until he had. 'I thought I'd convinced you Wilson wasn't me?'

'Convinced is too strong. Planted a seed of doubt would be nearer the mark.'

'But not now? Now you think I squared things with McDermid.'

'Somebody did. To be fair you're just about everybody's favourite suspect.'

He snorted at the gullibility of people and took me to task. 'Let me ask you a question, Charlie. Do you believe in fate?'

'Never given it much thought. Should I?'

Boyd brought a crumpled packet of cigarettes from his pocket, a casualty of the weather. 'I'll level with you. Coming across your ad in the phone booth at Central Station was good news for me. I was desperate. It was as if God had changed his mind and decided to pitch in on my side, know what I mean?'

I had no idea.

'After Strathclyde Park I felt better than I'd done in a long time. I had hope. That's what you gave me. All I had to do was stay ahead of the police and let you get on with it.'

'Naïve. It wasn't ever going to be that simple.'

'Naïve.' He rolled the word round his mouth, savouring its meaning. 'A pretty fair description of me my whole life.'

'But you survived. No easy trick to pull off.'

'Don't confuse surviving with living. It's not the same. Not even close.'

'Where've you been?'

He blew smoke at the wall and returned to the taciturn character I'd met in the car.

'Here and there, you know.'

'What do you want?'

'Good question. Been asking it myself. The answer is you're still the best chance I've got of proving I didn't kill Joe Franks.'

'Then you're in big trouble, Dennis. Bigger than you realise.

The only way to clear your name is for a witness to confess to perjury, and we're running out of witnesses.'

'No thanks to me. I still didn't do it.'

'I believe you.'

His expression froze. 'You do?'

'Absolutely. A guilty man wouldn't have come here. Pity my opinion doesn't help you. You or me. If we find Willie Davidson and get him to talk there might be a chance. But I'm staying clear of what's going on right now. And my advice to you hasn't changed. Turn yourself in.'

'Not happening, Charlie.'

'They'll get you in the end. And suppose Davidson goes the same way as the other two. It'll be three charges of murder you'll be facing.'

'Not if you stay on board. You say you believe I'm innocent. All right. Prove it.'

'Dennis, you're a wanted man. Just being here puts me over the line. Here's the deal, and it's the same deal. I'll do my best to get to Davidson before whoever killed Wilson and McDermid does. But you were never here. We've never met. And the case I'm on is ancient history.'

Boyd stuck the cigarette in the corner of his mouth, and – the only word for it – chuckled. He lifted his coat and struggled into its soggy folds. 'So, you'll help but only on Joe Franks. The rest's getting a wide berth?'

'Right. Anything else is too dangerous.'

The skin under his eyes crinkled. It was the first time I'd seen him smile. And I got what a younger Diane had seen in him. Maybe still did. At the door, he stopped and grinned again. Not bad for a man hunted by every policeman in Central Scotland.

Dennis Boyd said, 'Who's being naïve now, Charlie?'

* * *

The storm raged into the night before blowing itself out, lowering the temperature and clearing the mugginess from the air so we could breathe, replacing it with the familiar West of Scotland summer weather of weak sunshine and a breeze stiff enough to make you believe it was autumn. I slept badly and woke early with the image of Dennis Boyd standing in the doorway.

A break in the downpour gave me the chance to walk to NYB without getting soaked. The unexpected visit was on my mind. My original instinct to turn Diane Kennedy away had been on the money. Meeting Boyd – not once but twice – put me in the position I'd tried to avoid. On a stack of bibles, I could swear no knowledge of exactly where he was hiding, but I knew he was in Glasgow. Keeping that kind of information from the police made me, if not quite an accessory to double murder, at least guilty of obstruction. Claiming to be working on the Joe Franks case already seemed laughable. Whether Boyd was guilty or innocent – then or now, to use his expression – didn't come into it.

DS Andrew Geddes was the last man I wanted to see, but in NYB there he was, still scribbling away.

As a police officer, he'd experienced the worst of human behaviour. He didn't let it poison his opinion of his fellow man; it was poisoned to begin with.

To the world, Geddes presented a brusque, sometimes rude, persona. Knowing him better did little to alter the perception. In reality, he was both brusque and rude – though he saw it as plain speaking – and easy to dislike. We disagreed on many things. Occasionally, just occasionally, he lowered his guard and let me in and I saw that behind the grumpy façade was a decent guy, admittedly a grumpy decent guy. He should've gone further in the police force and would have if a determination to go his own way hadn't held him back. In terms of promotion, he'd dragged his heels. Younger guns were leaving him behind, mainly because climbing the greasy pole wasn't one of his talents.

He was busy and didn't notice me. I left it like that. Given who'd been in my office, the less contact I had with the law, the better.

Michelle smiled from behind the bar. I said, 'On your own? How's it going?'

'Better. But Jackie still doesn't speak to me unless she has to.'

'She'll get over it.'

'I'm not so sure. If it wasn't for the customers I would've already quit.'

'Nice, are they?'

'Very. Pat's invited me to have a drink with him on my day off.'

'And will you take him up on his offer?'

'I think so.'

If Gail found out she'd kill him.

The door to Jackie's cubbyhole was shut. I opened it and wished I hadn't. Her head rested on the desk; she was crying. Jackie Mallon was a tough lady; seeing her like this caught me unprepared. I blurted out, 'You all right, Jackie?'

She looked up at me, her eyes filled with tears, and nodded. 'I'm okay, Charlie. Got the blues, that's all.'

I knew the feeling.

23

To someone who didn't know better, the woman might be asleep. She seemed at peace, her breathing quiet and steady, her blonde head turned to one side. Vicky Farrell knew better. The flush on the skin wasn't natural. The drug had done that.

When they'd carried her sobbing to the room at the end of the corridor on the third floor and tied her with rope to the metal frame of the bed, Vicky had let them. They'd stripped the duct tape from their victim's mouth, her pleading the saddest thing Vicky had ever heard. Sean would make a terrifying enemy – Vicky had always known that – but this, this was worse than she'd expected, even from him.

She felt ashamed. If there had been a way to avoid being involved, she'd gladly have taken it. But there wasn't. Not unless she wanted to take Kim's place.

In a few hours, the men who'd brought her would come back and the process of sending this woman to hell would continue. The young guy with them had understood what he was doing: while the others held her, he'd lifted the woman's arm, wiping a spot on the inside near the elbow with a pad dipped in alcohol so as not to infect the area, then set about locating a vein. He'd ignored her muffled cries, inserting the needle at a shallow angle, pointing towards her heart. Vicky guessed he was a user. Then, he'd pulled the plunger back, checking the blood that rushed into the syringe was black and slow. It was and he applied pressure to the injection site. His work was done.

* * *

Dennis Boyd counted the crisp twenty-pound notes onto the dresser. Diane had been generous; there was plenty left from the first envelope, and he still hadn't touched the second one. Since leaving the Holiday Inn Express at Strathclyde Park, he'd stayed in a bed and breakfast in Mount Florida, not far from Hampden, expecting to bump into other guests but he hadn't. Apart from the tired-looking man on reception when he'd arrived, he'd seen no one, which suited him.

Time to move on. Again. But where to? Every newspaper headline screamed about the horror in Bellshill. For sure, the police wouldn't be considering other lines of enquiry. He was *It*. Whoever the real killer was knew exactly what he was doing.

Paying the bill was the tricky part. Trying to seem relaxed when relaxed was the last thing he felt. The man at reception made small talk about the weather and took his money. 'Was everything okay for you?'

Boyd faked it. 'Yes. I'll recommend you.'

'Did you fill in our Customer Service Questionnaire?'

He admitted he hadn't.

'Then could I ask you to put a review on Trip Advisor?'

Boyd had never used Trip Advisor. His accommodation needs

had been unaltered for a decade and a half. He paid his bill and left, glancing back to see if the receptionist was following him with his eyes. He wasn't; he was safe.

In town, Boyd bought a *Daily Record* and walked to a haunt from his previous life, a stone's throw from where Hughie Wilson had been beaten to death. It hadn't changed. Downstairs, he had the place to himself and ordered sausage, fried egg, beans, toast and coffee from a cheery waitress. While he waited, he read the latest news: the police had confirmed the identity of the man discovered in the garage as Liam Peter McDermid. The link between the victim and Wilson – not difficult to piece together – dominated the story. An old picture of Boyd took up half the front page above a recap of the Joe Franks trial. He stared at it, wondering if he'd ever really been so young, fingering the spectacles in his jacket pocket.

In the toilet, Boyd put them on. From the mirror the truth of his situation stared back at him: the disguise was laughable. Charlie Cameron was right. It was only a matter of time before he was caught.

Back in his seat, he laid the envelopes on the table – one thin, one thick – and studied them. Diane's cash – generous though it was – wouldn't last forever. Eventually, it would run out and he'd need work to survive. When that day came, he had to be far away. The killer could've finished what he'd started: the third witness might already be dead. If so, he could forget it – there would be nowhere to hide; the cliché about throwing away the key would become reality.

Reluctantly, he realised Diane's suggestion about the night train to London might have been the best option. When she'd made it, only Wilson had been murdered. Now McDermid had joined him and it was too late. Police would be watching every major transport link and Dennis Boyd knew he should have listened when he had the chance.

The waitress came back with his breakfast. His or Desperate Dan's, Boyd couldn't make up his mind. He spent the next thirty minutes ploughing his way through it; miraculously, he had an appetite. The mountain of food made a vivid picture on the plate and Boyd had an idea.

He bought jeans, three T-shirts, a brown corduroy jacket and a pair of casual shoes, paid cash, and stuffed the clothes Diane had given him in a rubbish bin. In an art shop in Queen Street, remembered from the old days, Boyd bought a bundle of sketch pads and a set of charcoal pencils.

In Barlinnie, where every day was like a week and every year a lifetime, a man with a gift got respect. Inmates hadn't left their vanity on the outside. Boyd had sketched some of the most dangerous men in Scotland. His talent had given him a daily purpose that saved his life. It could do it again.

* * *

Exhaustion from the fight she'd put up at the house and the effects of the drug meant Kim had slept the night away – a troubled sleep, filled with demons only she could see, moaning, calling out a name – Rosie – thrashing so violently the ties at her wrists were all that stopped her rolling off the bed onto the floor.

The room was shabby and smelled of sweat. In the weak light cast from a dusty bulb dripping cobwebs, Vicky Farrell had watched from a chair in the corner. After the soulless sex with Sean, she'd listened to him coldly describe the sickening destruction he planned for the mother of his child. Vicky wanted no part of it. She'd learned long ago that refusing Sean Rafferty wasn't an option.

She remembered the newspaper images of the couple on the register office steps, the new bride lifting the white satin hem of her dress off the ground, waving at the crowd. At her side, her smiling husband, proud of his new wife.

What had she done to deserve this?

Kim opened her eyes, unsure where she was, until the hellish nightmare rushed in and she screamed, 'Where am I? What've you done to me? Please, my baby. Let me go to my baby.'

Vicky reluctantly opened her mobile, hearing the words, hating herself for uttering them. 'She's awake.'

* * *

Kim strained against the ties fastening her to the bed, sobbed Rosie's name into the pillow and gave up. It was hopeless. She'd been a fool. Imagining Rocha would choose her over Sean had been inexcusably stupid. The terrible cost of believing the Spaniard's honeyed words was losing the only thing that mattered to her.

From the moment she'd allowed him to caress the nape of her neck with his finger he'd sensed a conquest to add to his collection. From then, it had all been a game. Confessing he'd bedded Sean Rafferty's wife, even if it meant signing her death warrant, wouldn't cause Emil Rocha a second's concern. On the contrary, whispering her betrayal in her husband's ear would've been sweet. Playfully asking how Sean would react if he discovered what she'd done, knowing he was going to tell him, was shocking and cruel.

Apart from the brief phone call, the woman in the chair hadn't spoken. Kim desperately tried to reach her. 'He's going to kill me; you understand that, don't you? My blood will be on your hands. Your hands! You'll be a murderer.'

Her voice was on the edge of hysteria; Vicky pretended to ignore it. Kim wouldn't let her.

'How can you stand by and let him do this? How can you?'

Silence.

Then the pleading, disturbing and sad and awful to listen to. 'Let me go, please. I'll disappear. All I want is my little girl. You're a woman, maybe a mother, this—'

As soon as Vicky spoke, she regretted it. 'He isn't going to kill you.'

Not getting drawn in was the only way to survive – refusing to see the prisoner chained to the bed as a human being. In her life, Vicky Farrell had done things she wasn't proud of but nothing like this.

Kim kept on. 'You don't know him.'

Vicky wished that were true. She said, 'I've known Sean Rafferty longer than you.'

'Then, you realise he's capable of anything. Rosie's just a child. A child! I'm her mother. She needs me. Please, I'm begging you.'

'You're wasting your time. I can't help you. Nobody can.'

It was the truth; crossing Sean would mean it was her shackled to the bed, her arm they injected, her on the painful road to addiction and prostitution on the streets. Vicky had to block out the pathetic cries and stay strong no matter how difficult it was. Anything else was suicide.

Kim said, 'I need to go to the bathroom.'

'Not yet.'

'I need to.'

'I said, not yet.'

'When?'

Before she could answer, the door opened and the guy from earlier came in, smiling as if he were meeting an old friend.

Kim saw the syringe in his hand and screamed.

* * *

Buchanan Bus Station was in Killermont Street; the irony didn't escape him. Behind the ticket counter a man who looked to be in his mid-forties managed to answer his question about the next bus to Oban without making eye contact: a skill first-timers in prison quickly learned.

According to the station clock he had two hours to spare; he deserved a drink. Standing at the bar in The Counting House at George Square seemed long ago; so much had happened it was difficult to take it all in. He strolled down Renfield and turned left into Drury Street. The Horseshoe Bar was a Glasgow institution, the kind of pub he'd missed. At lunchtime it was busier than most watering holes in the city. Boyd asked for the whisky Diane had ordered on Paisley Road West – Johnnie Walker Black Label – and a half-pint of lager, and pushed one of her twenty-pound notes across the dark-wood bar. The whisky was smooth. He let the atmosphere wash over him and felt himself relax. Maybe Cameron would do the impossible: find the third witness and get him to confess. Boyd signalled the barman for a refill, surprised to realise he was actually enjoying himself. By the time he'd downed his third, he'd started to believe.

New clothes and the alcohol made a difference. Boyd felt good. On his way to the bus station he thought about buying a couple of cans of beer, changed his mind and settled for a sandwich and a bottle of water instead. The Horseshoe Bar had been fun. But nothing had changed; he was still on the run. Better not to kick the arse out of it.

The Citylink bus reversed away from the stand and into the

early afternoon traffic as the sun broke through the clouds. Boyd watched Glasgow disappear. Soon they were on Great Western Road, then at Anniesland Cross where Diane had taken him on his first day of freedom.

Her again.

She'd been in court every day, sitting at the back, pale and drawn, staring straight ahead. Not once had she looked at him. Boyd had understood what was going through her mind and had worried about her almost as much as himself. They had no future together. He didn't kid himself about that. Nevertheless, Boyd cared about her. He had few friends; she was one of them. Eventually, he'd stopped thinking about Diane Franks and when the car pulled up outside Barlinnie, Boyd hadn't recognised the woman behind the sunshades.

Time was a bastard.

He closed his eyes and fell asleep remembering the curve of her neck and the softness of her skin in Newton Mearns, and woke to the majesty of Loch Lomond. Boyd swore under his breath. Drinking at lunchtime was a bad idea; he needed to be alert, on the ball. So far, he'd been lucky – if he didn't count being the prime suspect in two murders.

At Inverbeg, some passengers got off and others got on. Boyd checked his fellow travellers out: tourists mostly, photographing everything without appreciating any of it. He didn't blame them; he'd done his share of taking life for granted and been given a hard lesson in return.

Tarbert came and went. The driver changed down gears as the road began to rise. Across the calm dark water of Loch Long, the village of Arrochar seemed to shelter in the brooding beauty of Ben Lomond in the distance behind it. They passed a man painting the hull of an upturned boat on the rocky shore; he stood back to admire his work and smiled, satisfied with what he'd done. Boyd envied him.

Making love to a woman, savouring a fine whisky – even painting a boat on a sunny afternoon – were the simple pleasures of a free man. More important than revenge for lost years. Dennis Boyd would gladly settle for them.

24

I hadn't seen Pat Logue since the day we'd found McDermid's body in the garage in Bellshill. Patrick was a rolling stone. Now and then, as he put it in his football patois, he 'took a dive'. I'd learned it was better not to ask. When he had something, he'd be back.

Weak sunshine broke through gaps in the clouds and the air was warm. I hoped it was shining wherever Dennis Boyd was. He'd done well to stay on the run this long, though he couldn't keep out of sight forever. Every day put him closer to capture. I needed Pat to find Willie Davidson before the killer did, but Patrick was distracted. I hoped whatever he was doing included finding the missing witness.

On many occasions in the past, Andrew Geddes would've been the first person I asked for help. Almost always he'd come through. With this, we were on different sides. If he even suspected I'd met Dennis Boyd, our friendship wouldn't save me.

Jackie was behind the bar in NYB. She wasn't crying now, but she looked different; I didn't know why. There was no sign of Michelle.

The man I was looking for was reading *The Herald* at a table by himself. I took my coffee over and said hello, trying to sound laid-back. 'Good morning, Andrew.'

Geddes glanced up at me without moving his head. 'Is it? Seen this?' He tapped the headline on the front page. 'Guy in Bellshill got murdered about half a dozen times.'

'Nasty?'

'Very.'

'You involved?'

'Unfortunately, no. Could've done with a high-profile prosecution right now. Big Sandy landed it.'

'Sandy?'

'DI Sandy Campbell.'

'Don't know him.'

'He knows you. Every copper in Glasgow knows you, Charlie. Not meant as a compliment, by the way.'

I faked innocence. 'What do you reckon?'

'The press has it about right. Makes a change. Dead guy was a barman called McDermid, a witness in an old murder trial. Testified against a guy called Dennis Boyd. Got him fifteen years.'

Pretending wasn't easy. I did my best. 'Old news, isn't it?'

'Would've thought so, except the night Boyd got out of Barlinnie, another one of the witnesses was found in a car park at Charing Cross with his face caved in.'

'And you think this Boyd did it?'

'Looks helluva like it. One might've been a coincidence, but two?'

'Surely Boyd would figure he'd be the obvious suspect. Nobody would be that stupid.'

Geddes folded the paper and sighed. There was pity in his eyes. 'You're naïve, Charlie. Anybody ever tell you that?'

'It's been said, Andrew.'

'Not the best quality in a man in your profession. Listen, and get this into your head. People are thick, criminals especially. They get caught because they fuck up, otherwise we wouldn't have a snowball's. Brilliant masterminds only exist in books and James Bond movies. Your average criminal is just that: average. Don't credit them with brains. They haven't got any. It's clear as the nose on your face what's happened. Boyd couldn't wait to get even. For years, it's all he's thought about. First thing he does is find Wilson – a scumbag in his own right, by the way – and end him. What it would look like didn't come into it. After that, he gives us the mummy in a Bellshill garage.'

Andrew shrugged. 'Wilson and McDermid sent him down. In Dennis Boyd's twisted thinking, they deserved it. So now they're dead. Got a better theory?'

I did, though not one I could share.

'Where is Boyd?'

'That's the question. Nobody's seen him apart from his sister. He left her house, supposed to be going for a couple of beers. As you do when you haven't had a civilised drink in a while.' He paused. 'Notice I didn't say when you haven't had a drink. Can get anything you want inside these days. Fucking all-inclusive holiday. The governor could be Thomas Cook.'

Conditions in Her Majesty's prisons was one of Andrew's pet poodles. I let him rave. 'So, Boyd's on the run?'

'For the moment. Seen it before and it always ends the same way. They run out of money, out of options or just lose the will to keep going. We'll get him. Bet that nice West End flat of yours on it.'

'What if Boyd doesn't care about getting caught? What if he's done what he set out to do? Evened the score. Nothing else counts, including going back inside for the rest of his life.'

Andrew sat back in his chair. 'But he hasn't, Charlie.'

'I don't follow you.'

'He hasn't "evened the score". There were three witnesses.'

'I assume the other one's in protective custody.'

'He would be if we could find him.'

'You mean you don't know where he is?'

'I mean we don't know.'

'Is that a no-idea-don't-know or a last-seen-don't-know?'

'Willie Davidson's last known address was in Largs.'

'Largs?'

'With his married daughter. He lives with her. At least, he did. Not there now. And if he's got half the savvy you credit these types with, he won't return until Dennis Boyd's out of circulation.'

'She must be worried sick.'

'I'm told she is. We've got people watching the house.'

If Andrew had been paying attention, he would've noticed my expression change. He wasn't. He opened his newspaper and added a gruesome image to take with me. 'Then again, the guy might be in a lock-up somewhere, Tutankhamuned-up.'

I turned to go.

'And by the by. I've got a date for the promotion interview.'

On another day I would've been happy to chat about his prospects. Not today. I had to contact Patrick. 'You ready for it?'

He kept his eyes on the page. 'As I'll ever be, Charlie. Ready as I'll ever be.'

* * *

Outside NYB I punched Pat Logue's number into my mobile. He answered on the first ring. 'Charlie. Well timed.'

'Patrick, be careful. The police are watching Davidson's house.'

'I know.' He sounded relaxed. 'Got a couple of men in a car

across the street. Clocked them right away. They searched the place yesterday.'

'But didn't find Davidson.'

'Because he isn't there.' Patrick was enjoying himself. 'The game's moved on. An hour ago, the daughter went to the supermarket. Bumped into the back of another car in the Tesco car park. No real damage. Her fault, no contest. Her nerves are shredded. The driver started givin' her a hard time. Lucky I was there to smooth things over. I got her calmed down enough to give her insurance details and told him in future to watch how he spoke to a lady. She was shaken up about it so I took her inside and bought her a cup of tea. Nice woman. Must take after her mother.'

I held my breath. 'You're telling me you've talked to Davidson's daughter?'

'Yep. Turns out she went to school with my cousin. Small world or what?'

'Did she say where her father is?'

'He left as soon as he heard about Wilson. Olive reckons he knew he was in danger.'

'Olive?'

'Yeah. Her name's Olive. Olive Devlin. She was a teenager when her father testified against Boyd. Doesn't remember much about it. This last year Davidson's been on a short fuse, flyin' off the handle for no reason. In the beginning, she thought it was dementia. Now she knows he was scared.'

A man's freedom hung on my next question. 'Did she tell you where he is?'

'I've been down here for two days. Best customer Nardini's ever had. The bump in the car park was jammy but it was the cousin that swung it. Gave her one of your cards.'

He was winding me up. 'Stop fucking about, Patrick. Did she tell you where he is?'

'Her dad's treatin' himself to a wee holiday. She's pretty sure he's at a bed and breakfast on Arran. Davidson and his wife – she's dead by the way – spent their honeymoon in Whiting Bay. Been going there two or three times a year.'

'Did you get the address?'

'Now you stop fuckin' about, Charlie. 'Course I did. Want me to hop over?'

It was an easy question to answer. The pace was picking up, and with Dennis Boyd somewhere out there on the run I had to act fast. Face to face with a terrified Willie Davidson might be the only way to know the truth about the testimony that had already resulted in the brutal murder of two men.

I looked at my watch. 'No. Meet me at the ferry in an hour.'

My hand was on the doorknob when the phone on the desk rang. Time wasn't on my side. I picked up the receiver. The voice on the other end was well spoken and polite.

'Mr Cameron?'

'Yes.'

'This is Barry McCabe from Turner, O'Neil and McCabe. You were anxious to speak to my father.'

'I still am. Is he back from his cruise?'

Barry hesitated. 'Not yet. He took a bad turn. They're flying him and my mother home today. The Spanish doctors think it's best.'

'I'm sorry to hear that. Is he all right?'

'He says he's fine. Then he always says he's fine. I'm calling to tell you I've no idea when he'll be able to see you. My mother just wouldn't allow it.'

'Of course. I understand.'

'My father retiring was her idea. She pushed for it otherwise he'd still be in harness. Growing up all I remember is my dad working. Even on Christmas Day.'

'I'm sorry he isn't well. I was looking forward to talking to him.'

'Perhaps you'll be able to when he's stronger.'

'I hope so. Tell him to look after himself.'

'Too late for that, I'm afraid. My dad's a man who goes his own way. If you knew him, you'd understand. Goodbye.'

25

Vicky was expecting Sean's call. When it came, she almost didn't answer and let her mobile ring out a dozen times. Hearing his voice, knowing he was responsible for the horror in the room, was more than she could stomach. Through the night, sitting in the chair with the noises of the brothel seeping through the paper-thin walls – giggling girls and loud men; drunken laughter and angry growls; faked orgasms that went on for minutes, and, from somewhere nearby, the crack of leather against flesh – she'd realised Sean was an animal with no bottom to his depravity. That didn't excuse her from going along with it. But she had, because, like most of Glasgow, she was afraid of him.

His voice was casual, relaxed, almost as if he'd phoned to catch up with a pal he hadn't seen in a while. 'How's it all going?'

Vicky wanted to shout, 'How do you think it's going, you fucking monster?' Instead, she said, 'She's asleep.'

The news displeased him. 'Asleep! Wake her up. The faster the craving starts, the sooner we can move to the next phase. My darling wife is at the beginning of a new career, one she's admirably suited for. And I don't mean a West End girl.'

'It's hard to watch.'

Sean laughed. 'You're a great fuck, Victoria, excellent value for money, and you do a good job running the girls, but it's fair to say you never were the brightest button in the box, isn't it?'

The insult was old; he'd used it before to remind her of her place.

'I do my best, Sean. I do what you tell me.'

'Yeah, well, I'm telling you to wake the bitch up. While you're at it, make her eat. Don't want her dying on us and getting off easy.'

She took a deep breath and appealed to a sense of decency she knew didn't exist.

'Sean... you and I go back a long way... are you certain you really want to go through with this? I mean, whatever she's done, however bad it was, surely this—'

'You volunteering to take her place? 'Cause that can be arranged. As for strolling down memory lane – you're a hooker, a pro, Victoria. Bought and paid for. "Had more pricks than a second-hand dartboard."' He sniggered at his joke, then cut it short. 'Don't go all sentimental on me, for Christ's sake, eh? That isn't our arrangement. Give me a bell when the withdrawals start like we agreed. Details. I want details, the juicier the better. And you're right, we do go back a long way – first tart I ever had. They say you never forget the first one, don't they? Maybe that's why I've always liked you. Be a good girl and don't force me to change my mind.'

* * *

Vicky stared at the mobile in her hand; trying to reason with Sean had been a waste of time. Whatever line his wife had crossed she was paying for it now. More than retribution. This was revenge Vicky Farrell didn't have the stomach for.

Down the hall, a couple were arguing, the man's voice deep and low, the female yelling, accusing him. Every profession had rules. In hooking the most important one was: get the money first. It sounded as if somebody had forgotten it.

Vicky realised she was still holding the phone. Instinctively, she called Tony. He answered, his usual cheerful self. 'To what do I owe this honour?'

Vicky lied. 'Nothing. I was thinking about you.'

'Good to know. You all right?'

'Fine. I'm fine. Just a bit flat. I'm only on for a minute. When will I see you?'

'South coast tomorrow. Up north after that. You sure you're okay?'

The temptation to tell him the truth, that she was forcing another woman into addiction so a gangster could put her on the streets, was overwhelming. Vicky felt her resolve cracking. 'I... I have to go.'

'That's a short minute.'

'I'm sorry.'

He sensed her mood. 'Look, there are services in a few miles. I could pull in. We can talk.'

She faked it with another lie. 'No, no. Time of the month. Got the blues. It'll pass.'

Tony didn't believe her. He said, 'I love you, baby.'

'You can't know how much I needed to hear that today.'

* * *

Sean Rafferty watched a kestrel glide effortlessly over the river and land in the trees on the other side. It wasn't a visitor; he'd seen it more than once. Kestrels were birds of prey. Killers who survived by adapting to changing conditions. Sometimes they were even found in the heart of a city. Sean could identify.

He stepped away from the window. The conversation with Vicky Farrell told him something he hadn't known: Vicky was losing it. Getting sensitive in her old age. He had a lot on his plate. When things were back on track, he'd deal with her. A shame because, at the height of her powers, she'd been prime, no denying it. But that was then.

Her biggest mistake hadn't been questioning what he was doing, unwise though that was. It was the appeal to some imaginary bond between them, the 'you and I go back a long way' bullshit, that made him want to fucking throttle her for presuming they were, in some bizarre way, equals.

A younger Vicky would've known better. This Vicky didn't.

From the room next door, he heard his daughter's high-pitched giggle and smiled. The nanny seemed to be working out; Rosie had taken to her. He'd told the agency in Bath Street he'd need help for at least a year – probably longer – and asked them to send somebody experienced, somebody mature. Somebody he wouldn't spend valuable time thinking about jumping – life was complicated enough.

Spain was an hour ahead of Scotland; Rocha would be waiting for his call. His threat about the next shipment being the last wasn't serious – they both had too much to lose. It was a show of strength, a reminder he held the big cards. True. For the moment, at least. But in playing his unnecessary game to prove his superiority, he'd made an error.

Fucking Kim was one thing. Gloating about it was something else.

Elephants – and Sean Rafferty – never forgot.

The day would come. When it did it would be sweet.

Two thousand miles away, Rocha went into his prodigal-son act, unaware his insinuation at Glasgow Airport had reminded Rafferty he was in bed with a snake. And like all snakes, sooner or later, he would bite.

'I take it you're calling with good news, am I right?'

'Absolutely.'

'The problem has gone away?'

'It's sorted.'

The Spaniard said, 'Then, our plans can go on uninterrupted.' He lowered his voice, suddenly sincere. 'I never lost faith in you, Sean, I want you to know that. Business is business but your friendship is precious to me. As for the woman...' he sighed, 'you're better off without her. I'm assuming she's—'

'It's sorted, Emil.'

'Good, good. And how is your daughter? How is Rosie?'

'She's fine. We're both fine.'

'Perhaps you can bring her here someday. Children have an energy a tired old man can only envy. Give her a kiss from me. We'll speak soon.'

The line died. Rafferty slowly shook his head. Once upon a time, not so long ago, Emil Rocha was the most impressive man Sean had ever met. He'd wanted to be him. Not any more. The Spaniard had underestimated Jimmy Rafferty's son. A mistake. Their agreement would be reinstated, they'd continue to profit together, but the spell was broken.

Elephants and Sean Rafferty...

26

The Caledonian MacBrayne ferry from Ardrossan dipped and rose, throwing small lines of spray into the air and onto the bow. The morning's early promise had delivered a beautiful day and I was standing as far forward on the top deck as they allowed, shading my eyes against the sun. Ahead, spread across the horizon under a blue sky, the island of Arran might have been Tahiti.

Over to my left, a shout went up. People pointed at the grey-brown dorsal fin of a basking shark gliding through the water. When the creature rolled, giving us a sight of its white belly and huge open jaws, the watchers broke into applause. One of the crew, wearing green oilskins and a woolly hat, smiled; he'd seen it all before and hadn't forgotten the thrill of that first time.

Pat Logue had done an amazing job. Because of him we had a chance to discover the truth behind the testimony that had doomed Dennis Boyd. He was waiting for me when I returned to the car deck, leaning against the door with his eyes closed and his face turned towards the warm light.

With Patrick, the philosopher was never far away. Whatever

he'd had to drink brought it to the surface. 'Crossin' water always puts your troubles behind you. Ever noticed that?'

'Can't say I have, Patrick.'

'"The sea, once it casts its spell, holds you in its net of wonder forever."'

He was at it again. I didn't remind him the spell hadn't been strong enough to drag him away from the bar. He sighed and stretched. 'Guess who said it.'

'Haven't a clue.'

He was immune to my apathy. 'It's an obvious one.'

'Wouldn't know where to begin.'

'All right, I'll tell you. Jacques Yves Cousteau.'

'Very good. Now let's get our heads in the game. Where're we going?'

'Lamlash.' He checked his watch. 'Davidson's probably in the pub.'

A man after his own heart.

'Which one?'

'Not too many to choose from, Charlie. Olive says her father goes to The Pierhead Tavern or the Bay Hotel. Spends most of his time gettin' bluttered.'

* * *

From the ferry we drove the three miles from Brodick to Lamlash, where two dozen small boats lay at anchor in the bay. Scotland the wow! Today, my mind was on other things.

I parked in the car park opposite the pub. Outside, a group of blonde-haired female backpackers were drinking lager and enjoying the weather. Inside, the bar was busy. I scanned the faces, not sure who I was looking for, illogically certain I'd recognise him. Davidson was in his seventies. Nobody came close.

Behind me Patrick said, 'Maybe we've missed him.'

A sign directed customers to the terrace bar. We followed it upstairs. The terrace was full; all the seats were taken. Nobody there was Davidson's age.

Patrick said, 'He isn't here.'

In the distance, a lone figure at the end of the pier, gazing towards the Holy Isle, caught my attention. 'Yes, he is.'

I ran towards the flotilla of small boats at anchor with Patrick at my heels, our footsteps heavy on the stone jetty. Davidson was in a world of his own and didn't know we were there until I called his name. He turned slowly, with an effort drawing himself to his full height, one hand gripping an almost empty half-bottle of Famous Grouse. The whisky hadn't brought him peace: dark stubble covered his jaw and his eyes were red from crying. He wiped them on his sleeve like a child and stared through us.

Thanks to Pat Logue, Dennis Boyd might still have a chance to prove his innocence: we'd found the third witness.

Before I could introduce myself, Davidson spoke, his voice thick with booze. 'Leave my daughter be, you hear? She isn't part of this.'

He was expecting somebody else. I didn't enlighten him. Not yet. He growled an impotent demand and took an unsteady step forward. 'Leave her out of it.'

Olive's father was older than his years, his thin grey hair a match for his face. The one concession he'd made to the sunny day was a white shirt, open at the neck, under a wine cardigan worn with charcoal trousers. I tried to picture how he must have looked on the witness stand fifteen years earlier: tidy and clean-shaven, clear-eyed and plausible, describing a man running from Joe Franks' house who looked like Dennis Boyd.

All lies.

Time had paid him out for whatever he'd done; the fingers of his left hand trembled uncontrollably and not through fear: Willie Davidson had Parkinson's.

His voice cracked, he pushed his chest out, dredging courage from somewhere deep inside, and in a strange way, though I knew what he'd done, I admired him. 'Go on. Get on with it. Get it over with!'

Letting him give himself away would've been easy – he was drunk and it would've been cheap. I didn't have the stomach for it.

'You've got it wrong, Willie. We haven't come to harm you.'

His expression crumbled. His arms dropped to his sides like someone who'd reached the end of the line. 'Then what the hell do you want?'

'To talk about Dennis Boyd.'

As the realisation he wasn't about to die sank in, he set aside what was probably the one noble moment in his entire life and reverted to who he was, who he'd always been. 'Nothing to say about him. To you or anybody else.'

'You sure, Willie? You sure about that? I'm not. Your testimony convicted an innocent man. Yours and McDermid's and Wilson's. The only one above ground is you, though not for much longer. Thought we were them, didn't you? They'll be here soon enough. Whoever did McDermid and Wilson is coming for you. They can't let you live.'

Patrick said, 'If I can track you down so can they.'

'Willie, you're in danger. Let me take you to the police. They can protect you.'

He didn't seem to understand the words. I tried a different approach and pointed at his quivering hand. 'What've you got to lose? Make it right before it's too late.'

Davidson wasn't in the mood to make anything right. His crisis had passed; he was regaining control. 'Boyd beat Joe Franks to death. Bastard got what he deserved. I saw him there. It's what I said then and it's what I'm saying now.' He forced out an unconvincing laugh. 'So, you and the police can fuck right off!'

He pushed between us and lurched down the pier to the shore, still clutching the half-bottle. I called after him. 'Willie! Don't be a fool! Go to the police!'

Davidson turned, gave me the finger and, with the afternoon light dappling the bay, slurred a mouthful of untruths. 'He did it! Boyd did it! He's fucking guilty!'

* * *

Vicky heard the floorboards creak under his boots as he crept along the corridor. He was predictable, she'd say that for him. This time, he'd made a mistake – he hadn't reckoned Vicky would still be there. Most of the girls could tell stories about Noah, a disgusting user, probably the sleaziest individual to cross the threshold in Renfrew Street. Every night he paid at least one of them a visit. Having him to protect them was another sad irony in a life full of them.

She lifted a piece of metal pipe from the corner, feeling the cold solidness of it in her palm, and crouched. On the bed, Kim Rafferty snored in an exhausted sleep not destined to last – when she wakened, the craving would be waiting for her and the nightmare would continue. Vicky was determined this guy wouldn't be part of it.

The door opened; Noah stood in the shadows like Frankenstein's monster, letting his eyes adjust before coming into the room. He probably weighed as much as Vicky and Kim Rafferty together, a scuzz ball trying to take advantage. If he'd known the woman he was after was Sean Rafferty's wife, he'd have acted very differently. Men like this weren't brave; taking advantage of vulnerable females was his stretch. Tony was worth a hundred of him.

She allowed the would-be rapist two more steps, then swung the pipe through the air. It thudded against his shin, he screamed, fell to the floor and she was on him, crashing the metal against his arms and legs, beating him as he whimpered and crawled back the way he'd come.

When he'd gone, she closed the door, put the pipe down and dropped into the chair.

Kim would never know. Nobody would.

Vicky had won a small victory. Better than none.

27

The ferry trip back to Ardrossan was very different from the outward journey. My appreciation of the beauty around me had diminished; the combination of Davidson's drunken wretchedness and too much sun bleached whatever fragment of hope I'd had. My thoughts wandered to Dennis Boyd. The odds of proving his innocence in a fifteen-year-old case had never been great. Now, because of my misplaced sense of fair play, there were no odds. It was over. Davidson's claim remained unchanged: he'd seen him running from Joe Franks' house.

Joining Patrick in the bar instead of going on deck had seemed a good idea. It wasn't. He was in no better shape. We drank muddy coffee and didn't speak until the announcement for drivers to return to their cars blared over the Tannoy.

In Glasgow, I dropped him at NYB. Before he got out, he said, 'So that's it, Charlie. Can't win them all.'

'That's it for you. I'm not done. Boyd didn't murder Joe Franks. I intend to prove it.'

He shook his head and scratched his goatee. I heard a lecture – or maybe another quote – coming. It was neither; it was a rebuke. 'What is it with you? Used to think it was determination. Now I'm not so sure. Could be ego. This was a turkey from the start. Should never have got involved. For your own good, it's time to get uninvolved and you can't see it.'

'Not as simple as that.'

'Yeah, it is. The third witness was our last chance. We found him and he's sticking to his story. Give it up, man, before somebody decides you're too bloody nosy.'

* * *

I stayed in the office until the shadows on the wall faded to black, mulling over the confrontation. The last forty-eight hours had been manic, and my mistake on Lamlash pier weighed heavily on me. A skewed sense of honour had consigned an innocent man to a second term in prison and left another at the mercy of a killer. Davidson didn't want to go to the police. But he was drunk, not thinking straight. I should have taken the decision out of his hands.

The list I'd made – was it really only two days ago? – lay on the desk. I picked it up, tore it into pieces, dropped them in the waste-paper bin, and headed for the door. Pat Logue was right: the case was a bust.

My mobile rang just as I was pulling into the car park. 'This is Yannis Kontogiannakis. You called.'

The English was good, spoken in an accent as thick as olive oil.

'Yes, I did. Thanks for coming back to me. My name's Charlie Cameron. I'm a private investigator. I wanted to speak to you about a man you used to do business with: Joe Franks.'

'Joe. I don't understand. Joe died a long time ago.' Suspicion edged into his voice. 'Who did you say you were again?'

I told him, leaving out Dennis Boyd and double murder. 'His family has asked me to look into what happened to him. My problem is it's impossible to find anybody who knew him.'

'I see.' I could hear him turning over his reply. 'Well, we worked together for many years. I liked Joe. He was a fine man. We were a good team. I'm not sure what I can tell you.'

'Look, do you mind if I call you back? I'm in the car.'

'Are you phoning from Scotland?'

'Yes.'

He laughed. 'The way you speak takes me back. And you're in luck. I am in the UK for a few days. First London, then Edinburgh.'

'Great. Can we meet? I'm in Glasgow. I'll come to you. Anywhere you say.'

'No need. I love Glasgow. It'll be a good excuse to see it again, though, like I said, I don't know what I can tell you.'

'I just need to understand how the last deal went down, and anything you can think of that might throw some light on who killed him.'

'But I was told they caught the man.'

'That's the problem, Mr Kontogiannakis, I'm not sure they did.'

* * *

Dennis Boyd sat on the old shooting stick he'd found late on the first day in a musty shop that looked as if it hadn't had a customer in decades. He had paid for it – as he did with everything – in cash.

On the concrete viewing platform, next to McCaig's Tower, casting a critical eye over his efforts, it was almost possible to forget he was Scotland's most wanted man. Boyd had bought a set of light pencils he'd forgotten to get in Glasgow, and a cap. When added to the glasses Diane had given him, the transformation was complete.

People stared; Boyd was fine with that. He saw them out of the corner of his eye putting him down as eccentric without connecting him with the face on the front page of every newspaper in the country. Hiding in plain sight.

Below, Oban harbour curved in a horseshoe, Mull shimmered in the distance and a CalMac ferry returning from the islands broke a path through the water, leaving a white line in its wake. In prison, Boyd's artistic talents had been an escape. Revisiting them now heightened his appreciation of things he'd missed. Like Diane's soft body spread like a banquet. He smiled at the memory and added a few deft strokes to the picture, knowing this was how he should have spent his time instead of squandering it. No use regretting it. Painting took discipline. His younger self was headstrong and impatient, lacking the ability to stay with it. He'd been given a gift – no doubt about that. It wasn't enough. This was where he'd ended up. Being wise after the event did nobody any good.

The call to Diane the previous night had left him depressed. The news wasn't good. For hours, he'd walked the town's unfamiliar streets searching for a way to prove his innocence. He'd been a fool; he realised that now. Better to have taken her money and got on the London train. Instead, he'd rejected the idea, pinning everything on an ad in a telephone booth. How crazy was that? Cameron had actually found Willie Davidson, but the lying bastard was sticking to his story. The last hope, the only hope, was gone. There was nothing more the PI could do. His advice hadn't altered: Boyd should surrender himself to the police. A non-starter. Going back to prison wasn't an option even if he had to live in a cave for the rest of his life.

A middle-aged woman stopped to admire his work. Under her arm was a rolled-up copy of *The Scotsman*. Boyd wondered if she'd read the article about him and carried on as if she wasn't there, playing the part of an artist lost in his art.

She said, 'You really are very good.'

He mouthed a modest 'thanks' and adjusted the glasses, hoping she'd go away.

'Do you sell your work? You should.'

Boyd shook his head. 'It's just a hobby.'

'Well, I'd buy it. I'd love to have something like that on my wall.'

His one thought was to get her to go. On an impulse he handed the sheet to her and took her by surprise. 'Then have it.'

'Are you sure? I mean... it's very kind of you.'

'Not at all.'

'It might be worth a lot of money someday.'

'Then we'll both be in luck.'

The woman turned to go and changed her mind. 'Would you sign it for me?'

'Of course.'

Boyd wrote on the bottom and gave it back. The woman read the name, savouring the moment. 'I'll cherish it. Thank you again, Mr Franks.'

28

The voice on the other end of the line was defiant. Willie Davidson's opinion of me hadn't improved, though at least this time he was sober.

Our meeting on Lamlash pier had convinced me that if he was Boyd's last hope, then Dennis Boyd had no hope. How much of our conversation Davidson remembered was anybody's guess. Enough to make the call, apparently. I hadn't expected it, and what he had to say was a game changer.

He didn't introduce himself and came straight to the point. 'I'll tell you what you want to know. There are conditions.' He paused and I imagined him checking over his shoulder to make sure he was alone or, more likely, topping up his whisky.

'Where did you get this number?'

'From my daughter.'

Pat Logue had told me he'd given her my card.

'I'm listening.'

'Take Olive somewhere safe. They've already threatened her. It won't end there. They'll do anything to stop me from talking.'

Davidson sounded spooked. As well he might be. 'Who will?'

His nervous snigger travelled down the line. 'You must think I'm a clown.'

'All I'm asking is who we're up against.'

'That's all you're asking? When Olive's beyond their reach, you'll know what you want to know.'

'Which is what, exactly?'

'Who murdered Joe Franks and why. I told her to expect you. Do it now. And one more thing. I don't want Boyd near me.'

'I'm not his keeper. You'd better hope he doesn't find you.'

The defiance roared back. 'I can take care of myself.'

The last time I'd seen him that hadn't been true; he'd been crying. Agreeing wasn't difficult. And what choice did I have? Davidson was ready to cooperate, which meant Dennis Boyd would have the proof he needed to clear his name.

'Where are you?'

The snigger made a comeback. 'Go fuck yourself. Do as I say or Boyd goes back inside for killing Wilson and McDermid.'

'He didn't kill them.'

'He didn't kill Joe Franks, either. Look where that got him. Get my daughter out of harm's way. Once I've spoken to her, I'll talk.'

'Consider it done. Now cut the crap and be in my office at two o'clock, or she's on her own.'

It was a bluff, an attempt to even the score for Lamlash. Davidson cut the connection. I checked my watch and called Patrick. He sounded his usual upbeat self.

'Morning, Charlie. What can I do you for?'

'Need you to go to Largs. Olive Davidson's been threatened. Her father's just off the phone. He won't talk until he's certain his daughter's safe.'

Patrick was a good man; he didn't ask questions. 'I'm on my way. Let you know as soon as I've got her.'

I needed Diane to persuade her old boyfriend to trust me and do what I'd wanted him to do from the very beginning: give himself up.

Ritchie Kennedy answered the phone. When I told him who I was he shouted to his wife and left me to wait. It seemed the atmosphere in the Kennedy household hadn't improved. A minute later Diane said, 'Mr Cameron? Didn't expect to hear from you again after last night. Has something happened?'

Explaining would take time so I didn't. 'Boyd has to turn himself in. Today.' Before she could speak, I raced on. 'I can prove he didn't murder anybody.'

Her reply was breathless. 'Really? That's wonderful news. Wonderful. But how is it possible? Last night you said—'

'Davidson's changed his mind.'

'Why? I don't understand. Where is he?'

'This is the best chance Boyd's ever going to have. Tell him I want him in my office at three o'clock. He has to be there.'

'He will be. I promise you he'll be there. And thank you.'

I hesitated before making the final call, conscious it might mean the end of a friendship. Andrew was a copper twenty-four hours a day. His reaction to what I had to tell him was easy to predict: he'd go mental.

In my head I ran over what I was going to say, searching for the right words and coming up dry. Because there were no right words. I glanced at my watch: ten thirty-five. For the moment, at least, I didn't need them. Davidson would be here at two. If Diane did as I'd asked, Boyd would follow an hour later. To make it work, Andrew had to have heard Davidson confess before Dennis Boyd showed. What went down after that wouldn't be up to me.

His brusque voice sounded in my ear. 'Charlie.'

'Good morning, Andrew.'

'Good, is it? You must know something I don't. What can I do for you?'

The cynic was in residence.

'Can you be in my office at one-thirty?'

'Of course. I'll just drop everything.' He gave a jaded laugh. 'Am I allowed to ask why? Any chance of giving me a clue how you want me to spend the tax-payer's hard-earned money? They pay my salary, in case you've forgotten.'

'It's important. Really important. That's as much as I can say.'

'So, it's a mystery.'

'Andrew, trust me, it's important.'

When it suited him, Andrew was a paid-up member of the Awkward Squad.

'You'll have to do better than that, Charlie.'

I had to persuade him without giving away too much.

'An innocent man's freedom is at stake.'

Andrew was a hard guy to reach; he sucked air through his teeth. I could almost see his mock-serious expression. 'Dramatic. I'll give you that.'

'You've known me long enough. If I tell you it's important it's because it fucking is. I'll answer every question you have at one-thirty and then you can decide if I'm being dramatic or not.'

The silence from his end seemed to go on forever. Eventually, he sighed. 'This better be good. This better be very good or you and I are going to fall out.'

He'd got that right.

I breathed a sigh of my own. 'It is, Andrew. Really good.'

An hour later, Pat Logue called. 'Got her, Charlie. Olive's safe. She's talking to her father right now.'

All the players were on the board. There was nothing more for me to do but wait.

* * *

At exactly one-thirty, the door opened. Geddes hesitated for a second in the frame before stepping inside. We didn't shake hands or say hello and I realised my friend Andrew wouldn't be coming.

DS Geddes placed the chair against the wall, sat down and folded his arms across his chest. His expression told me everything I needed to know. I made a stab at breaking the ice. 'Thanks for coming.'

He brushed the pleasantry aside and made a show of checking his watch.

'Let's hear it, Charlie.'

A couple of hours considering what to say and how to say it hadn't helped. Reluctantly, I'd decided, for better or worse, to tell the tale without justification or excuse – lay it out as it had happened and hope Andrew could see it from my side of the fence.

I began with Diane Kennedy's trashy performance and her failed attempt at coy manipulation; her teary sob story about the murder of a husband she hadn't loved – probably never loved – her robust defence of the man found guilty of killing him, and her loyalty, which stretched to giving him money to get away from Scotland to start a new life somewhere else.

Geddes listened stone-faced. Merry widows didn't move him.

The meetings with Dennis Boyd – in Strathclyde Park and in my office – I left out. This conversation was going to be difficult enough without admitting I'd been in contact with a wanted man. One look at Andrew's tightly drawn features told me I'd made the right decision.

His breathing was as even and controlled as a Zen master. He must've been dying to interrupt, even if it was only to tell me what a prick I was.

There was sweat on my brow and my hands felt clammy. I

soldiered on, wisely omitting discovering the body in the garage in Bellshill and the anonymous telephone call to the police. Who was I kidding? By the time I got to Lamlash and Davidson, the detective in Andrew Geddes would have put the pieces together and know I was up to my neck in it.

My voice echoed in the room. 'This morning, they tried to intimidate Davidson's daughter. It backfired. He's agreed to share the secret he's lived with for fifteen years: who killed Joe Franks. He's coming here at two. We'll have the truth about three murders – Franks, Wilson and McDermid. But it isn't Boyd – he's been set up for a crime he didn't do. Twice.'

Geddes pushed himself out of his seat and left. Five minutes later, he came back and sat down without a word. And that was how it stayed. Over the years I'd seen the best and the worst of Andrew – this was new.

Two o'clock came and went. Davidson didn't arrive. At twenty past, when there wasn't any sign of him, I started to worry and decided to make a call. On my way to the door, Geddes caught hold of my arm. 'Don't try to warn him off, Charlie. It's gone too far for that.'

Outside, I phoned Davidson; the number was unobtainable. My fingers were trembling when I called Patrick Logue. 'Has Olive heard from her father?'

'No, she hasn't. Something wrong, Charlie?'

'I hope not.'

Traffic slowed at the lights on Cochrane Street, the drivers unaware of the drama unfolding on an afternoon in Glasgow. I looked up and down to see if Davidson was lurking in a doorway, too afraid to go through with what we had agreed. I didn't find him because he wasn't there. Panic washed through me. Without his testimony, Boyd was walking into a trap.

Back in the office, I tried to change the rules. 'Listen,

Davidson swore he'd tell the truth about Joe Franks as soon as his daughter was safe. Boyd is giving himself up on my say-so and he expects to be treated fairly.'

'He will be.'

'Even if this guy goes back on his word, promise me you'll hear Dennis Boyd out. Promise me, Andrew.'

'I will.'

I needed to believe him.

The minutes ticked by with my heart pounding in my chest. On the half-hour, Geddes' mobile rang. He opened it and listened, his eyes never leaving mine. When he spoke, his voice was cold and flat. 'I understand.'

He closed the phone and went back to his Easter Island impersonation, and for thirty minutes nothing happened. Nobody moved. Nobody spoke. At three o'clock, with the tension at breaking point, footsteps sounded on the stairs, the door opened and Dennis Boyd walked in. He looked at me, then Geddes, and back at me.

'What the fuck's going on?'

'It's all right, Dennis. This is a friend of mine.'

Boyd sneered and hooked a thumb in Andrew's direction. 'A friend? He's got cop written all over him.'

Geddes leaned against the wall as if what was going on had nothing to do with him. Boyd lurched towards me, his hands gripping the edge of the desk so tight the bones of his knuckles threatened to break through.

'I trusted you, Cameron. Diane trusted you. You set me up.'

'No, Dennis. They threatened Davidson's daughter. We've got her safe. He's supposed to come here to tell the truth.'

'Where is he?'

'Look. Sit down and calm down. Davidson might still come.

Andrew's here to listen to what you have to say. He's a good guy. This is your chance to tell your side. Take it.'

Suddenly, the door burst open and four uniformed policemen rushed in followed by a tall man with a pencil moustache, a self-satisfied smile playing at the corners of his mouth. The uniforms grabbed Boyd and forced his hands behind him; he didn't resist.

'Told you before, Charlie, you're naïve. Can't be "friends" with a copper. They don't do friends.'

The detective in charge ignored me, gave a curt nod to Andrew Geddes and went into his spiel. 'Dennis Boyd, I'm detaining you under Section 14 of the Criminal Procedure (Scotland) Act, as I have reason to suspect you may be guilty of a crime punishable by imprisonment, namely the murder of Hugh Wilson.'

The rest didn't register. I couldn't breathe; I was numb. It was as if the oxygen had been sucked from the room. Boyd didn't look at me when they took him away. Geddes had only spoken once since the start of my futile explanation, to warn me against tipping Boyd off. He pushed himself off the wall; for him it was over. But I had to know.

'Why? Why, Andrew?'

The question seemed to confuse him. 'Why? You can't be serious.'

'You made a promise to hear him out.'

'And I will. In an interview room in Govan, not here.'

'Boyd's innocent. When Davidson shows up, he'll swear to it.'

The detective's skin was the colour of bread dough, his lips a bloodless line, the anger in his eyes a match for Dennis Boyd's. Yet his voice was steady because, in the end, he was a copper doing his duty.

'No, he won't, Charlie. He won't be swearing to anything. His body was fished out of Lamlash Bay. That's what the call was about.'

'You knew he wasn't coming?'

He didn't answer and walked to the door. 'You've got some explaining to do. I'll tell DI Campbell to expect you.'

PART III

29

After Andrew Geddes left, I couldn't move; the sky had fallen on me. What had happened was like being in a car crash, too fast, too much to take in. The truth about so many things had been within touching distance.

Or, so it had seemed.

I'd let Boyd down. Again. I'd known it was the policeman in the room with me, and I should've guessed how he'd react. But fuck! He was supposed to be my friend. All I was asking him to do was listen, then, if he wasn't convinced, do what he had to do. But give the guy a chance. For fuck's sake, give him a chance.

Suddenly, the anger that had been building since Geddes had exploded and I raced down the stairs and into the street. Andrew was outside NYB and glanced round just as I grabbed his shoulder and threw him against the window. I expected him, pinned to the plate glass, to defend himself. He didn't; his arms hung by his sides. Our faces were inches apart; there was no fear in his eyes. He goaded me in the dull monotone I'd heard in the office.

'Fancy adding assaulting a police officer to the list, do you?'

'As a matter of fact, yes.'

I swung my fist and connected with his jaw. He staggered and fell to one knee. Before I could hit him a second time, strong arms circled my chest and dragged me away. Alex Gilby's voice was in my ear. 'Easy, Charlie. Whatever it is, don't make it worse.'

Geddes touched the trickle of blood at the corner of his mouth and came towards me.

'Not clever, Charlie. Not very clever at all. And here we are again. How often do you need to be told? If you'd wanted to be a copper you should've joined the force. I've warned you to stay on your own side of the street 'til I'm sick saying it. You don't listen, do you? The great Charlie Cameron always knows better.'

A crowd of people had come out from NYB, no doubt enjoying the excitement of seeing two grown men squaring up. Jackie Mallon was one of them. I shrugged free of Gilby. The urge to beat Andrew's righteous head to a pulp was fading.

He said, 'Told you every policeman in Glasgow knows who you are. Didn't tell you why. You're famous for sticking your oar in where it doesn't belong. A well-intentioned amateur. But an amateur just the same.'

'You've got a short memory. You wouldn't have a hope at promotion if it wasn't for me serving results up to you on a plate. The number of times I've solved a case for you seems to have slipped your mind. The amateur doing your work for you because you and your pals in blue are so fucking incompetent.'

The veins in Andrew Geddes' neck thickened; his hands became fists. He was on the edge but he was going to hear what I had to say. 'Fifteen years ago, an innocent man went down for a crime he didn't commit.'

'Not according to the jury.'

'Stop hiding behind the verdict. Your lot got it wrong. Whoever did it is leading you by the nose just like they did the last time. Davidson admitted it wasn't Boyd. He was going to confess to perjury and tell me the real killer's name.'

'Except, he didn't. Which knocks the backside out of your story and puts Dennis Boyd in the frame.'

Frustration boiled up in me. 'Talk sense. Pretend you're a real detective and try thinking for a change. Boyd came to give himself up. Why would he do that if he was guilty?'

Andrew poured contempt on my explanation. 'And that's where we part company, Charlie. You deal in theories and notions about justice. Professionals don't have that luxury. They're only interested in facts. In this case, the facts say that for a decade and a half, Dennis Boyd planned his revenge on the witnesses who spoke against him, and took it in a car park at Charing Cross, in a garage in Bellshill, and this morning in the Firth of Clyde.'

'You're choosing the easy road and you know it. You fucking know it!'

Andrew glanced at the onlookers and back. I was past caring who heard; it was the truth. 'You completely blanked the fact Davidson confessed to me. Didn't want to know because it made your old mates look bad. That's what I really can't take. You never gave Boyd a chance.'

'Not here to dole out chances. My job is to catch suspects. Guilty or innocent doesn't come into it. That's somebody else's call. You'll be lucky not to find yourself up on a charge after this.'

'So, as long as you can tick a box, everything's all right?'

Geddes brushed dust off his trousers and didn't answer. 'You've crossed the line for the last time. From now on keep out of my way. I'm not telling you again.'

'Don't worry. Your side isn't for me. Never could be.'

He shook his head and grinned his trademark grin, unamused. 'You're memory's selective, Charlie. As I recall you've got it wrong plenty of times.'

'But it didn't cost some poor bastard fifteen years of his life, Andrew. That's the difference.'

* * *

Geddes walked away without a backward glance. Alex Gilby laid a hand on my shoulder and guided me into NYB; the crowd went back to minding their own affairs. The exception was Jackie, who stood at the door, watching me.

Alex led us to a table and signalled to the bar. A large whisky appeared in front of me. 'Drink this, it'll do you good.'

'It'll take a lot more than that.'

His eyes wandered over my face. 'Want to talk about it?'

'Too late for talk.'

'Okay, but, whatever happened, you and Andrew will get through it. Even the best friends fall out sometimes.'

Alex imagined I was worried about the fight; he was wrong. At that moment, I couldn't have cared less about Andrew Geddes. My concern was for Dennis Boyd.

I trusted you... you set me up

'I'm okay, Alex. Really.'

He left and I changed my mind about the whisky. Jackie was at my elbow. I expected a lecture; it didn't happen. 'What was that about?'

When I didn't reply, she answered her own question. 'Andrew can be a hard guy to get along with. You do better than the rest of us. For it to go that far, he must've crossed the line.'

'We both did, Jackie.'

'It happens.' She patted my hand. 'Don't let it get to you.'

Maybe I imagined it – for a second, I was sure her eyes filled up. Like Alex, she meant well, though I doubted she was right. Geddes had a long memory and, as his ex-wife, Elspeth, had discovered, putting the past behind him wasn't one of his gifts. Right now, I was with him on that. Dennis Boyd had trusted me. I'd trusted Andrew. We'd both come out on the losing side.

Jackie laughed softly and got up. 'Have to admit you lead an interesting life, Charlie.'

'Is that what it is? I was wondering.'

'Have another whisky. On the house.'

'No. I'm fine.'

'Sure?'

'Absolutely. I'll have to make a statement. Better get it over with.'

She took the hint and left. I opened my mobile and punched in Pat Logue's number.

'Charlie. What's happenin'?'

'Long story, Patrick. Get Olive to Helen Street. Ask for DI Campbell.'

'Did it go okay?'

I sighed, wishing I hadn't turned down Jackie's offer. 'It went the way it went.'

'As bad as that?'

'Yeah. As bad as that.'

* * *

At Govan police office, DI Campbell was in fine spirits; not surprising, in his position. Thanks to me, a wanted man had fallen into his lap, and the detective inspector was disinclined to hold his good fortune against me. I told him how it had been, minus the parts he didn't need to know. The policeman sat back in his chair, relaxed, not bothering to fake interest, as though he'd already decided whatever I had to say wasn't important.

He let me finish and took over. 'Amazing how your name

keeps cropping up, Charlie. You're a friend of Andrew Geddes, is that right?' He moved a pen around his desk. 'Bit of a dour bastard, between you and me. Would've got on well with John Knox, if you know what I mean.'

I knew.

'He'd throw the book at you and not think twice. Can't say I blame him. You've a reputation for sailing close to the wind. Not everybody appreciates that.'

I let him do the talking; he preferred it that way.

Campbell turned his attention to a ragged fingernail. 'Me, I'm inclined to take a different view. Truth is I'm grateful to you. There's a man downstairs in the cells who wouldn't be there without Charlie Cameron. Besides, you represent a tonne of paperwork I can do without. So why don't I do us both a favour? If anybody asks, you've had your knuckles rapped. We'll need a statement. Then you can go. But remember, you've been long enough in the game to know the rules. Police business isn't your business. In future, stay clear.'

'There's nothing to stop me investigating anything I like so long as I don't break the law.'

He frowned. 'Not a good idea, Charlie. You tend to get lost and go for a wander.'

'When can I speak to Boyd?'

'System's against you. Have to wait your turn.'

'So when?'

'He'll be charged later this afternoon with his lawyer present and appear at Glasgow Sheriff Court tomorrow. The next time you meet him he'll be on remand in Barlinnie.' He sniggered. 'After what happened today, you'll be top of his visitors list. I'm sure he'll be delighted to see you.'

DI Campbell was enjoying himself. I hated to spoil his fun but it had to be done.

'Dennis Boyd didn't do it. The real killer is still out there. Ask Boyd where he was this morning. I bet he was nowhere near Arran.'

'Already did. Claims he was in Oban. But he's lying.'

'You can place him at the scene of the crime, can you?'

Doubt flickered in Campbell's eyes. He reached for an answer and found it. 'We'll get what we need. Don't worry on that score. He's going back inside.'

'Unless he's a magician he can't be two places at the same time. Putting him on the island shouldn't be difficult. Somebody must've seen him: at Ardrossan or on the ferry. But you can't and you won't because he's telling the truth. And, if he wasn't in Lamlash, he couldn't have killed Davidson. So, who did?'

The certainty faded from Campbell's face. I stood up; the interview was over.

'Got your work cut out, unless, of course, you settle for the easy target like last time.'

* * *

Getting drunk was an attractive proposition, and the bottle of Famous Grouse in the bottom drawer of my desk was calling. I could've resisted, put up a fight, but sometimes giving in just felt like the right thing.

The first couple of shots came straight from the neck and when the fire hit the back of my throat, I knew I didn't want to stop; willpower was having a holiday. The awful sequence of events – from Davidson's mid-morning telephone call to brawling in the street with Andrew Geddes – rolled over me. I'd been lucky it was DI Campbell's case. He was telling the truth when he said Andrew would have nailed me to the wall.

Pointing out the weakness in Campbell's case had been satisfying but it didn't change anything. Coupled with the history between them, Boyd's admission he'd been in the car park where Hughie Wilson died would be enough to bring a murder charge.

According to Pat Logue, two police officers had taken Olive Davidson away. I didn't envy any of them. Patrick had done everything asked of him. None of it was down to him. The same couldn't be said for me. By the time I thought about getting myself a glass, the bottle was edging towards half empty and it didn't seem worth the inconvenience. I put my feet on the desk and closed my eyes.

Diane Kennedy didn't bother to knock; she threw the door open and came in. Without make-up she seemed old and I could see she'd been crying. I braced for an angry tirade. It didn't come. She ran to me and fell into my arms, sobbing uncontrollably. 'Charlie, Charlie. It's so unfair.'

Just what I needed: a hysterical woman.

The perfect end to a perfect day.

* * *

Since Noah's midnight visit, Vicky hadn't gone back to her flat, sleeping fitfully in the chair rather than her own bed. Tony sensed she was struggling and called every day to speak to her from wherever he was. She made an effort to sound upbeat and cut the exchanges short before he could probe too deeply.

He was a good man. But even good men had their limit. This life wasn't his; how much longer would he put up with her rejections before he'd had enough and offered his love to somebody worthy of it? For all his worldliness, he was in some ways an innocent. The night they'd met she'd been in a bar in Miller Street, off George Square; he'd asked if he could buy her a drink and sat down. It had taken an hour to suss he didn't know what she was.

When she'd told him, he'd carried on as if she hadn't spoken. Eleven months later the relationship was strong, except Tony wanted more. So did she. Fear made her settle for what they had and she prayed he would, too.

Time had no meaning for Kim. She was still being sick, had no interest in food and ate little. Mars bars were the mainstay of a diet that, along with the 'H', brought a dramatic weight loss, most noticeable on her face, arms and legs. At the beginning she'd cried. Now, she waited for the next fix, eyes open, staring at the wall, deep in depression.

The knock on the door startled Vicky. She opened it, stepped into the hall and found Noah waiting. 'Mr Rafferty called. Says he wants her earning. Got a john at the desk looking for a woman.'

'She's too ill.'

'Mr Rafferty says—'

'I couldn't care less who says, she can hardly stand. She isn't in a fit state to work.'

'You tell him.'

'No problem, I will. If he wants to make money off her, he'll have to wait or he'll have a dead junkie on his hands.'

Noah had delivered his message and came closer, cigarette smoke and the sickly smell of cheap wine floating like a cloud around him. He bared his bad teeth. 'You nearly broke my fucking leg, bitch.'

Vicky wasn't fazed. 'You're lucky it wasn't your skull. I'll speak to Sean—'

Noah sneered. 'Sean, is it? Big mates, are you?'

Vicky was going to let it go, then changed her mind. Putting the wind up this animal would be fun. 'Now you mention it, yeah, we are.' Vicky faced him down. 'I covered for you. Otherwise, you would've been out on your fat arse ages ago. Not any more. It's personal. Any idea what would happen if he hears about your nightly habit of sampling the merchandise without paying? He'll cut your bastard heart out and throw what's left in the Clyde. Ask yourself why Sean Rafferty is interested in what goes on here.'

The threat found its target – Vicky saw it in Noah's eyes.

'As for your customer, send him to somebody else. This one isn't for sale.'

30

Opening my eyes was painful. I closed them again and tried to figure out why I felt so bad. The answer arrived like jagged fragments from a bad dream: the look on Dennis Boyd's face when he realised he'd walked into a trap; Alex Gilby pulling me away from Andrew Geddes outside NYB; and Diane Kennedy's tears on my neck. I drew the duvet over my head and lay until the nightmare moved on. Eventually, I stumbled blindly to the shower and began a reluctant recovery that wouldn't include eating.

The hot water helped. After a while I felt good enough to make a will, but decided to face whatever had to be faced. Getting myself together was a slow process. When I was ready, I called a cab to take me into town – it wasn't a difficult decision considering my car was where I'd parked it the previous afternoon. While I waited, I forced down a cup of coffee and struggled to make sense of the previous day. Unfortunately, I succeeded.

Excuses weren't hard to find; I had no use for them. Blaming Willie Davidson's no-show for what had happened was too easy. If I could find the third witness, so could the killer. Shortly after his telephone call to me, Davidson was dead and with him Boyd's last slender hope of clearing his name. Dennis Boyd had been set up; I was sure of it. The witnesses had committed perjury for money. Their paymaster – whoever he'd been – had murdered Joe Franks.

I'd been accused of being naïve. On recent evidence, the verdict was guilty as charged. Discovering the killer's identity had always been a long shot. Now it was impossible.

Over his shoulder the taxi driver made a stab at cheery conversation but gave up when it was clear I wasn't interested in talking. At George Square, I got out and walked the rest of the way. Usually, my first stop would be NYB. Not today. I'd no wish to run into Andrew or Jackie Mallon, or anybody else. I had to think. To do that I needed to be alone.

A wall of whisky fumes hit me as soon as I opened the office door. The bottle on the floor against the wall caught my eye. Of course, it was empty. I lifted it and dropped it into the wastepaper basket; it fell with a dull thud on top of Diane Kennedy's cigarette butts. Apparently, the No Smoking policy had been suspended.

So how long had she been here? What hopeless promises had been made? I shuddered at the thought. Unless something unexpected came along, Boyd was headed back to Barlinnie. As Andrew Geddes never tired of reminding me, his guilt or otherwise was a decision other people would make. The ability to prove it, one way or the other, was the only thing that mattered. And on that, I'd failed.

Around eleven-thirty, my mobile rang. I thought of not answering it and changed my mind. 'Charlie Cameron.'

A voice with a heavy accent said, 'Mr Cameron. It is Yannis. How are you?'

I lied. 'I'm fine.'

'My business in Edinburgh will be finished this morning.

Then I will come to Glasgow on the three o'clock train. Where will I meet you?'

My heart wasn't in it but the Greek was going out of his way to help. 'I'll be at Queen Street station when you arrive.'

'Great. See you then. Goodbye.'

I'd forgotten about the Greek. It probably wasn't important now. Pat Logue stuck his face round the door. 'Two words, Charlie. Su perb. But you couldn't hold on, could you?'

'Come again.'

'To stick one on that pompous arsehole. All this time I've waited, and when it finally happens, I'm somewhere else.'

'You didn't miss much. It was not my finest hour, Patrick.'

He came in, closed the door behind him and sat down. 'With respect, I'll be the judge of that. Jackie says you laid him out. Were the scales suddenly lifted from your eyes and you saw him as he really is? Did you remind him how many of his cases you've solved?'

Patrick's enjoyment was undisguised. Punching a policeman – especially this particular policeman – appealed to him.

'Sorry to disappoint you. It wasn't like that.'

He picked the whisky bottle from the waste basket and held it in the air. 'How do you come to be assaulting an officer of the law? Nothing to do with alcohol, I hope.'

'We had a disagreement. It got out of hand.'

He let it go and became serious. 'I called you last night. Mobile was switched off. Guessed you wanted space.'

Good guess.

I brought him up to date on how it had been: from Davidson's non-appearance and Andrew's betrayal, to Boyd's reaction and the conversation in Helen Street with DI Campbell. He listened without interrupting. When I stopped speaking, he summed up where I was. 'And you're blaming yourself?'

'Yes, I am.'

He waved an admonishing finger and hit me over the head with one of his quotes. '"Better to be punished for making the right decision than live with the guilt of making the wrong one." Write it down. Seriously, anybody would've done what you did.'

'No, they wouldn't. I should've held back until Davidson told his side of it. Instead, I was in too much of a hurry.'

Patrick didn't agree. 'Yeah. Bring him in before he got caught. Hindsight's a wonderful thing, Charlie. The one mistake you made was to trust a copper.'

I held up a hand; he wouldn't be stopped.

'No. It's the truth. You acted in good faith. The same couldn't be said for your pal. Not blaming him, mind. Just doing what he knows. Guys like him never have a day off. Can't help themselves.'

'Nice of you to give me a pass, Patrick. Coming to me for help is the worst move Dennis Boyd's made.'

Patrick wasn't having any. 'Talk sense, Charlie. Nobody else would've given him the time of day. You did. And got a witness to admit he'd perjured himself at his trial.'

He used his thumb and forefinger to make his point. 'You were this close to proving the jury got it wrong fifteen years ago. Who else could've done that?' He answered his own question. 'I'll tell you. Nobody.'

I thanked him for his faith in me. 'Except where does it leave us? Which reminds me, the Greek Joe Franks bought stones from is coming through from Edinburgh on the three o'clock train from Waverley.'

'Want me to meet him? What's his name?'

'Yannis.'

'Does he know anything?'

'Doubt it. According to Boyd he's a good guy.'

Patrick got up to go. 'I'll be there. And by the by, I spoke to

Olive this morning. She's gutted, as you would expect. Willie Davidson might've been a rat, but he was still her father.' He changed the subject. 'Anything coming up? Could use the cash.'

* * *

I didn't catch up with Patrick again until close to five in the afternoon. Too late. He introduced his companion like a long-lost brother. It had taken less than an hour for these kindred spirits to recognise each other and begin the celebration.

Pat raised a glass and said, '*Yamas*! Means cheers in Greek, Charlie.'

'Thanks for explaining that.'

Patrick was enjoying himself too much to notice the sarcasm. He nudged my elbow and pointed. 'This is a great guy. Liked him as soon as I saw him.'

Yannis let his new best friend do the talking. Diane had met him just once, fifteen years and twenty kilos ago – her description was out of date; the black hair had thinned and was streaked with grey, sunglasses he wouldn't have much use for pushed up off his grinning moon face.

I wanted to speak to him; this wasn't the moment. These guys were serious drinkers and they were headed for a session. I made my apologies, ducked out and left them to it.

* * *

There was a smile in his voice. There always would be even when he was ordering somebody's death.

Sean Rafferty imagined Rocha dressed in a white lightweight suit and sandals, casually inspecting his nails, relaxing in the shade of his fucking orange tree, while other people made his money for him. Not far away, a naked woman would be in the swimming pool – probably young, definitely beautiful. Rocha wouldn't hurry; no matter how long he took, she'd wait. Emil Rocha was who Sean Rafferty aspired to be – the man who had it all. Except, his perfect life, like everything about him, wasn't so perfect, as the presence of the armed guards at the gate and on the walls testified. Rocha had many enemies. Someday, one of them would get him; his time on earth would prematurely end with his suntanned face in the dirt and Rafferty would be looking for a new partner. Until then...

The Glasgow gangster faked it. 'Emil, this is a surprise.'

'A pleasant surprise, I hope.'

Unease rippled Rafferty's skin: a call from the Spaniard was rarely good. Usually, it meant he was unhappy. And Emil Rocha didn't keep his unhappiness to himself.

'Always.'

'I was thinking about you and decided to give my friend in Scotland a call. How are things?'

'Fine, Emil, everything's fine.'

'You deserve credit for how quickly you handled our problem. I appreciated it.'

'It was necessary. Thank you for bringing it to my attention.'

'As you say, Sean, it was necessary. Though, I took no pleasure in it, I assure you.'

Liar, he'd relished every second – before, during, and after. Especially after, brazenly revealing he'd had sex with Kim, rubbing Rafferty's nose in it, daring him to react.

'I'd like another look at the land you showed me. Send me a report. Perhaps, I was too hasty.'

'Did the Menorca project fall through?'

Rocha paused, the phony bonhomie faltering, and Sean realised there had never been a Menorca project; the drug lord had invented it. He'd been on his way to spend the afternoon with Kim, correctly assessed the implications of her unfaithfulness for himself and decided not to get more deeply involved with a man who wasn't in control of his wife.

if she's willing to betray you to me, she'll betray both of us to the police

it's merely a question of when

'Oh, that. The individuals who approached me had interesting proposals. I turned them down.'

A conversation with Rocha was a masterclass in duplicity. Sean imagined him sipping an espresso, waving to the girl in the pool. 'Opportunities are like autumn leaves, my young friend. Thick on the ground. The skill lies in choosing which ones to pick up. We can continue with our plans.'

'I look forward to it, Emil.'

'As do I. And, Sean, one last word. A serious man wouldn't have to learn the same lesson twice.'

The line died. In Glasgow, Rafferty trembled with rage. Rocha's tone had been friendly. Underneath the façade, the bastard was warning him.

Again.

* * *

Rafferty hadn't seen his wife since they'd taken her screaming from the house in Bothwell. The Spaniard's phone call had stirred his hatred for the bitch. Coming here hadn't been in his plans, yet he couldn't stay away – his thirst for revenge was too great; he had to witnesses it for himself. He stood by the filthy bed, looking down at the sleeping Kim, his features lit with an intensity Vicky had only seen at the height of sex. Sean swept Kim's hair away with his finger so he could see her face. His lips parted in a grin. At the final of Miss Scotland, surrounded by lovely women, she'd shone.

She wasn't shining now.

He stepped back and spoke to Vicky out of the side of his mouth without taking his eyes off Kim. 'Wake this bitch up. I want to speak to her.'

Vicky swallowed her disgust. 'Sean... she—'

He turned, his voice dripping menace. 'Don't fucking argue with me.'

Vicky gently shook Kim's shoulder. Her eyes opened – she saw her husband and cowered from him.

Rafferty said, 'Sorry to break into your beauty sleep. Got a message I thought you'd want to hear.'

He held the mobile out and pressed play: Rosie was in her walker. In the background, Sean encouraging her. 'Wave to Mummy. That's a good girl. Wave to your mummy. Ask her when she's coming back.'

On the bed, Kim whimpered like a wounded animal, unable to take her eyes from the screen, tears falling silently. Vicky had known Sean Rafferty was a heartless bastard, but this... The absolute cruelty of it stunned her.

He closed the mobile and nodded. 'She's ready to start earning. Make it happen.'

'Who'd want her in that state?'

He smiled. 'You'd be surprised. She can have twenty-four hours. That's it – I've waited long enough.'

He caught the look in her eyes. 'Get it done, Victoria. No more excuses. And somebody fix that fucking light outside.'

31

Patrick Logue's dubious claim to fame was that he'd never had a hangover. Today that boast was under pressure. He was subdued; his face was pale, his eyes bloodshot, his usual bonhomie absent. Underneath the table his hands would be shaking. It didn't take second sight to know how the night before had ended; Patrick had met his match and was suffering. I ignored his pain and asked a question, although the answer was in front of me. 'So how did it finish with Yannis?'

His reply was short on detail. 'Fine.'

'Where did you end up?'

'Got round a few places.'

Patspeak: he couldn't remember.

'You were getting on like a house on fire when I saw you.'

He faked a smile that died on his lips. 'He's an interestin' guy.'

'What did you find out yesterday, anything?'

He took a breath deep into his lungs and let it out slowly. This was a trial for him and he was clearly struggling.

Patrick changed the subject to something more important. To him. 'Don't happen to have a beer, do you, Charlie?'

I reached into the bottom drawer of the desk and brought a bottle of Chivas Regal out. 'No beer. Give you a shot of this if it'll help.'

The secret of serious drinking was flexibility. He eyed the bottle. 'I'll take it.'

The whisky disappeared in a couple of gulps. I gave him another and watched the colour return to his cheeks.

'So, back to Yannis. Did he have anything we can use?'

Patrick shook his head.

'Nothing we don't know already, Charlie. But I'll tell you one thing, the Greeks can't half drink. My finances are beleaguered.'

'Meaning what?'

'I'm buggered. Don't suppose you could sub us a—'

I beat him to it. 'Don't you ever give up?'

He accepted the rebuke and rubbed his hands together, the Patrick of old reborn.

'Worth a try, Charlie, always worth a try. What's the next move?'

'We've run out of witnesses. That just leaves what connects them. Get me the link, Patrick, just get me that link.'

* * *

Yannis arrived at five minutes to ten and, in contrast to Pat Logue, was relaxed and fresh: a different man from the glassy-eyed whisky drinker. I remembered the grin – it was still there. From behind it, he studied me. In his business, over the years, the Greek was bound to have come up against heavy characters. He'd survived and I understood why: there was a strength and an easy charm I hadn't noticed yesterday. The ponytail dropping to his black T-shirt must go down well with female tourists: very Shirley Valentine.

I filled him in on my interest in Joe Franks; he didn't comment.

'When we spoke on the phone you told me Joe was a fine man.'

His features cracked in a smile revealing white teeth and he replied without answering my question. 'The Scottish are like the Greeks. Unfortunately, the weather is not so good.'

I tried again. 'How well did you know Joe?'

'For more than twenty years he was my friend. We drank together many times. Always it was Joe who took me home. Always. In the morning I didn't have to look in my pockets to see if my money was still there. Do you understand? I trusted Joe Franks and he trusted me.'

'Did he have enemies?'

He slapped his thigh as if I'd made a joke. 'A successful man can't go through life without making enemies.'

'I mean serious enemies.'

'I understand what you're saying. I've dodged more than one bullet in my time. Ours can be a dangerous game to be in. But Joe was a good man; a man you could rely on. He never took chances.'

'Would it surprise you to hear he was broke?'

Yannis shook his head. 'I wouldn't believe it.'

'Why not?'

'Because. It's impossible.' He drew his fingers through the once-black beard, glanced round the room and slowly came back to me. 'You never met Joe Franks. He knew his business. Diamonds, rubies, emeralds: he could assess their quality in his sleep. Joe didn't make a bad deal in his life.'

'Did he tell you about the last deal he was involved in?'

'Sure, we respected each other's opinion and spoke all the time. He used to joke that my country invented diamonds because the word diamond comes from the Greek word *adamas*, meaning invincible.'

'Did you tell him to be careful?'

The question puzzled him. 'Joe was a professional. There was no need.'

'Then why did he keep the last parcel – the one that got him killed – in his home instead of in the office safe?'

I was suggesting his friend had been reckless or, worse, a fool. The Greek's dark eyes mirrored his displeasure; he defended the dead jeweller. 'If Joe kept them at home you can be certain he had a good reason.'

His loyalty was admirable. I moved past it. 'Except somebody murdered him, Yannis. Somebody stole those stones.'

We stared at each other across the desk until he said, 'Do you think it was me?'

My reply was blunt. 'I don't know. Was it? According to Dennis Boyd, you argued. Three hundred thousand pounds was mentioned. What was the row about? Were you involved in the deal?'

He nodded, appreciating the candour, and I knew this man had nothing to hide.

'No. Joe wanted me to come in on it but I was stretched in other directions and couldn't. He got frustrated and we argued. An hour later, he called me and we laughed about it.'

'Did the stones ever surface?'

'No. After Joe died, I waited for them to come on the market. They never did.'

'Would you have recognised them?'

'As a package yes, the individual stones, no. There are other signs.'

'Like what?'

'Provenance.' Yannis saw the blank look on my face. 'The

seller and the documentation he provides. If he has none...' He let me finish the thought.

A light went on in my head. I'd been coming at it from the wrong angle. In a case with so many unanswerable questions it might still be possible to discover who had fenced the diamonds. 'If they didn't pass through the usual routes, what would happen to them?'

He smiled at my lack of knowledge. 'A parcel like this would be blood in the water, attracting sharks from many places.'

'Who else did Joe work with besides you?'

'Over the years, many people, too many to remember. Always ones he'd done business with before. No, to find the truth you will have to go in another direction.'

Yannis looked me in the eye and I knew what Joe Franks had known: the Greek was a straight-shooter. I said, 'Did Joe seem different to you?'

'Yes. Towards the end he became quiet. His marriage was in trouble so I assumed that was the reason.'

'Did you ever meet his wife?'

'Once. In Chania. She came with him on a trip.'

'What did you think of her?'

He scratched the beard. 'A fine-looking woman. Apart from that I don't remember much about her.'

There was no more to say. At the door, the Greek shook my hand in an iron grip. 'Let me know what you find.'

'I will. I promise, I will.'

He seemed satisfied. 'Your friend Patrick is another good man. Very smart. I envy him. Where does he find the time to read so many books?'

I could've told him. It was better he didn't know.

* * *

Apart from losing a good friend, the rift with Andrew was a blow. Often in the past he'd used his connections to help me with a case. The deal was straightforward: I pretended to listen to him grumble about misuse of police resources and said nothing when he barked his usual question, "Do you imagine I'm working for you, Charlie?" and he'd be back a couple of days later with the information. Understanding the official thinking on where Joe Franks' diamonds had gone would've been useful. Too bad that option didn't exist any more.

Diane Kennedy was the next best thing. The last time I'd seen her she'd been distraught, breaking her heart, sobbing on my shoulder over Dennis Boyd. I'd expected her to blame me; she hadn't. Her conviction that her old lover was being set up again to take the fall for something he didn't do was so strong my involvement was overlooked and earned me a pass – a more generous assessment of my efforts than my own.

When I called, she sounded relaxed. 'We're at home all day.'

Domestic harmony? Or maybe she was warning me Ritchie was there and to be careful about what I said.

Diane opened the door, radiant in beige trousers and a scarlet blouse tied at the front, though the lines on her face told the real story of what she was going through. I followed her into the lounge. Over her shoulder she said, 'Can I get you anything? Tea? Coffee? Something stronger?'

'I'm fine, thanks.'

Kennedy glanced up, expressionless. She sat beside him on the couch. 'I'm surprised to hear from you again so soon. With Dennis in prison I thought that would be the end of it for you.'

'That's not my case. You hired me to look into Joe's death, remember? That's what I'm doing. What happened to his diamonds?'

Kennedy answered for her. 'They were never found.'

I ignored him and put my next question to his wife. 'Apart from losing your husband, no insurance meant you lost out on a small fortune. Did the police speculate on where the stones may have gone? There must have been follow-up?'

The surprise she'd admitted a moment earlier played on her face. 'None that I know of. They thought Dennis had stashed them before they arrested him. I assumed the killer laid them off to a fence.'

'You mean the real killer?'

'Yes.'

'But they spoke to you about them.'

'They did, of course they did. More than once. And what a waste of time that was. They interviewed me at the station the day after the murder. Later, they came here asking questions about the diamonds. I was still in shock. My husband was dead. I didn't twig at first until I suddenly realised where it was going. They thought I might have been in on it.' Kennedy patted his wife's hand. 'Treated me like a bloody criminal, if you want the truth.'

I threw sympathy her way. 'Family members are always prime suspects.'

She hugged herself like a child. 'I couldn't get through to them that I didn't even know Joe had stones in the house. He was so secretive towards the end. Hardly said a word. They changed their tune when they found a second diamond and Joe's blood in Dennis's car.'

'Did you get them back?'

'We did. Eventually. Got a decent amount for them, too. God knows what the whole lot was worth.'

'Who did you sell to?'

Diane said, 'Joe kept me away from the business so I hadn't a clue. I used a guy in the Arcade who probably ripped us off. I just wanted the nightmare to end. Except, thanks to my late husband, I needed the money.'

Her present husband gently massaged her shoulders. Relations between them, so obviously strained because of her connection to her former flame, must have improved. I guessed Boyd being in custody might have something to do with it.

'Then, you can't tell me anything?'

She shook her blonde head. I turned my attention to Ritchie and caught him off guard. 'Weren't you in business with Joe Franks at one time?'

The implication didn't escape him; he reacted. 'No. I approached Joe – must be eighteen years ago – about maybe getting together.'

'What did he say?'

'Wouldn't consider it. Turned me down flat. Told me to stick to what I knew. Good advice. Though something good came out of it. I met Diane.'

A look passed between them; time for me to go. At the door I said, 'Did you speak to Boyd about the visitor list?'

'Yes,' she said. 'You're on it. He's expecting you at eleven o'clock tomorrow.'

Kennedy put his arm round his wife and grinned fiercely at me. His rival was in prison and likely to stay there. He allowed the satisfaction to show. I guess he couldn't help himself. From where he stood it had worked out all right.

He said, 'Apart from his sister you're the only one who wants to see him.'

32

I didn't go back to the office; I went home and called Barlinnie. Boyd had no visitors scheduled for the next day. Now, he had me.

From what I'd seen, Ritchie and Diane Kennedy were trying to put their marriage back on track. Good for them. Kennedy struck me as a difficult guy to like and Alex Gilby reckoned he was a hard taskmaster to work for. On our briefer than brief acquaintance, he'd managed to be boorish without saying very much, a singular talent. Living in Dennis Boyd's shadow couldn't have been easy; the battle for his wife might have been going on since the beginning.

But he'd won. At least, he thought he'd won. The memory of Diane sobbing on my shoulder suggested that whatever had existed between her and Boyd was far from finished.

At ten minutes to nine at night there was a knock on my door. I opened it to find Andrew holding the bottle in his hand up to let me see the label: Johnnie Walker Blue Label.

'Any idea how much this stuff costs? They say only one in ten thousand casks makes the grade. All bollocks, probably. But it's bloody good stuff. And it should be at the price.'

I stood aside to let him in. I'd known Andrew a long time; this was him apologising – or as close to it as he was liable to get. My anger hadn't disappeared but turning him away would be churlish and, besides, he was right: Blue Label was bloody good stuff.

'We'll need four glasses.'

'Why four?'

'Two for the whisky, two for chilled water. It's how you drink it, apparently.'

I did as he asked and watched him pour. He handed mine to me and lifted his own.

'May you be half an hour in heaven...'

I completed the toast for him '...before the devil knows you're dead.'

He nodded. 'Cheers, Charlie.'

We sat for a while, alternately sipping the mix of old malt and grain and the water. On some levels Geddes was a complicated man, on others there was a disarming simplicity to him. Problem was, you could never be sure which Andrew was going to show up. If it had been me bringing a peace offering, it would've been rejected. Some people were like that.

I gave him time to come to the point of his visit, glad he'd made the move. When he didn't, I said, 'What's the latest with the promotion interview? Got a date yet?'

He took a drink from his glass and gave a grimace that had nothing to do with the neat whisky. 'To tell the truth, been thinking about pulling out.'

'Why?'

'You know why.'

'No. I don't.'

'What if they turn me down? Am I supposed to keep taking orders from jumped-up uni students with five minutes' experience of real police work for the rest of my life? Because I'll tell you, Charlie, whatever else, that isn't happening. I just can't do it.'

'Agreed. Except they won't turn you down.'

Andrew wasn't convinced. 'Thanks for the vote of confidence. Appreciated. You don't get how tough it'll be talking to superior officers about how great you are. Not advisable to bullshit men who've seen it and been it.'

'Don't. Just tell them what they want to know.'

'Which is?'

'Your record. The fact you've got the highest solve rate in the city. Andrew, you're a great detective.'

He stared at his shoes and shook his head slowly. 'No, Charlie, *you're* a great detective. They trained me and gave me resources. That's the difference. You're a natural.'

A compliment from Andrew Geddes was a rare thing. He said, 'I was wrong. I should've stuck to the deal with Dennis Boyd. I've lost it since this whole promotion thing started.'

'He didn't do it.'

The old Andrew surfaced – by-the-book, black-and-white Andrew. 'That's for the court to decide. I'm talking about trusting you, trusting your judgement.'

It had taken a lot more than the price of a bottle of expensive whisky to bring him here. I didn't push it. He leaned across and topped our glasses up.

I said, 'Need some more water?'

Geddes drew me a look. 'What do you think? Marketing crap. Like telling a room full of detective chief inspectors how good you are.'

'In your case, it's the truth.'

He savoured his drink and remembered something. 'By the by, I went to see Boyd today. Owed him an apology, too.'

'So you agree he isn't guilty?'

He tilted his head and his expression changed. 'Not at all. That's for—'

I interrupted. '—the jury to decide. You said.'

He smiled into his glass. 'Scoff away, Charlie. Have to tell you it doesn't look good. DI Campbell can't tie him to Bellshill or Lamlash. Yet. But that won't matter. One murder will do. And the car park in Elmbank Gardens fits the bill. Boyd admits he planned to track down the witnesses who'd spoken out against him. He doesn't deny finding Wilson's body. Just as well. Left his fingerprints at the scene. My guess is he's headed back inside. Shotts probably. For a revenge killing they'll throw away the proverbial key. "Prosecuted to the full extent of the law" as they say.' He finished his drink and stood. 'Sorry to be the bringer of bad news.'

For a moment I thought he'd forgotten the bottle of Blue Label. Wishful thinking.

'Want me to call you a taxi?'

'No, got the car.'

'You're driving?'

He stepped away and peered at me. 'Might be a great detective, Charlie, but sometimes I wonder about you.'

'How so?'

'Told you before, you're naïve. I mean, what're the chances of me getting stopped?'

He took my silence as an answer. 'Exactly. See what I mean?'

At the door we shook hands. 'I'm visiting Boyd tomorrow.'

Andrew didn't try to hide his surprise. 'Why, for Christ's sake? It's all over bar the shouting. Let justice take its course.'

'Justice has nothing to do with it. Got that from you. And I want to ask a favour.'

Geddes sighed whisky fumes over me. 'Oh, yeah? Not the only one around here who's naïve, are you? Spit it out.'

'Can you find out what happened to the diamonds stolen when Joe Franks was murdered?'

'You can't be serious.'

'I am. At the time, what was the thinking?'

He considered the question. 'Should be something in the original file. Assuming it still exists. Chances are, it doesn't. Too long ago. I'd get myself another client if I were you.'

I didn't answer him. Andrew had already lost interest. An encouraging sign: it meant normal service between us had been resumed.

33

The room at the end of the corridor was as it had been the night Kim Rafferty arrived bound and gagged: the threadbare carpet, the shabby second-hand furniture and the cobwebs hanging from the dusty bulb were unchanged. But the figure on the bed was a different Kim, her eyes dull, set back in dark sockets, the once glorious hair lank and lustreless. Except for when the pains in her body got too bad, she didn't struggle to free herself or cry, and when the guy with the syringe came through the door, her arm went out to receive what he'd brought.

On the days he didn't come, Vicky Farrell's shame was more than she could bear.

Drugs had never been a part of her story; she'd seen what they could do and was afraid of them. Witnessing Kim Rafferty's craving up close was a reminder it could so easily have been her climbing the walls, moaning, willing to do anything to make it end.

After his last visit, Sean had stopped calling, as though the terrible vengeance he'd authored no longer interested him. That wasn't it. His will was being done – all he needed to know.

Kim whimpered, 'Where is he?'

Vicky gave the answer she'd given a minute earlier. 'He'll be here.'

'When? Tell me when. I need it.'

'Soon.'

Kim buried her head in the filthy pillow. 'I'm bad. You don't know how bad.' She retched. 'I'm going to be sick. Give me something. Please. Please!'

'No, you're not. There's nothing in your stomach.'

A wave of abdominal cramps gripped her insides and sweat broke over Kim's body; she cried out and drew herself into a foetal position. 'You're killing me. I'm going to die. Where is he?'

Vicky heard herself and wanted the ground to open up under her. 'He'll be here soon.'

'I need it NOW! NOW!'

'Soon.'

* * *

Contacting Sean again would be a dangerous mistake – he'd made very clear what he wanted her to do and wouldn't appreciate it. Vicky had no choice. People mistakenly thought becoming hooked took time. It didn't. For some, just once would do it. Giving Kim a fix every other day meant the drug never cleared her system. Instead of diminishing, her dependence grew until she was a full-blown junkie. She was probably close to that now. And bad as that was, it wasn't the main problem – something in the woman had died. Kim Rafferty was fading fast.

Sean sounded irritated, even before she spoke. 'I'm busy, Vicky. What do you want? And before you start, choose your words carefully or me and you will be falling out.'

'She can't handle much more. Her body won't take it.'

'Since when did you become a doctor? Must've missed that bit.'

'I'm with her all the time. I see what's happening.'

'You're getting soft, Victoria. She deserves everything she's getting and more.'

Vicky bit back what she wanted to say. Rafferty lowered his voice. 'Don't question me. It'll be over when I say it's over and not before. Get her through it. If it's too much for your delicate disposition, I'll get somebody else, and you and I can have a chat about your future, how about that?'

'I'm trying to help. She's sinking.'

'Good. Tell me when she's sunk. Meantime, like I already said, put some customers her way.' He laughed. 'If nobody will take her, give her to Noah. See how she gets on with him. Can't imagine it'll be a problem for her.' He paused. 'Thing is, Vicky, you know fuck all about her, or what she's done. Don't call me again unless you fancy going down the same road. That can be arranged.'

* * *

Vicky had been one of the most dependable people in his organisation.

Had been.

Threatening her cost him nothing and Sean had meant every word. In his universe, unconditional loyalty was a given. They'd had good times – he hadn't forgotten them – but if she was going soft, she was no use to him. He tapped his mobile and spoke to the man at the other end of the line.

'Vicky Farrell's wandered off the reservation. I want eyes on her, day and night.'

* * *

Seeing Dennis Boyd wasn't something I was looking forward to; he'd trusted me and I'd let him down. Finding himself back behind bars on a murder charge was his reward.

In the waiting room, tired acceptance on the faces of dull-eyed women told the real cost of breaking the law. To many of the kids with them, their father would be a barely remembered stranger, who smiled and said their name a lot. The smaller ones – not yet old enough to understand – clung to their mothers and cried for attention they couldn't give. What must it be like to go through this twice a month?

I didn't know and didn't want to know.

Everybody was given a seat allocation and, after a short wait, we were led upstairs to the visiting room. Vending machines along one wall and a play area softened the experience. But not by much. Then, the prisoners were brought in.

Boyd came towards me and sat down across the table. I hadn't expected him to shake my hand and he didn't. With the way things had gone, I had to be top of Dennis Boyd's shit-list. But when he spoke any resentment was under control. 'Had an unexpected visitor yesterday.'

I feigned surprise. 'Yeah? Who?'

'Your not-so-friendly policeman pal. DS Geddes.'

'It isn't his case. What did he want?'

Boyd bared his teeth in a failed smile. 'Fucked if I know. Maybe thinks he should have heard me out before calling his mates.'

'Did he say that?'

Boyd glanced at the other visitors. When he brought his attention back to me, he was grinning. ''Course not, but you were mentioned. Got the impression he rates you.'

Just not when it counted.

'What did he say?'

Boyd shrugged. 'Some guff. I switched off and let him talk. So, where are we with this?'

His question took me by surprise. 'What do you mean?'

'I mean, where are we?'

Our eyes met, his were hard and clear; he was serious. He said, 'What's done is done, Charlie. We both acted in good faith and we both got screwed. Get over it. But this thing isn't finished. I didn't kill those lying bastards. Only wish I had.'

He leaned towards me to make his point and I smelled cigarette smoke on his breath. 'Although unless you start doing your job I might as well have.'

That statement revealed the truth about how he really felt. Boyd wasn't as fatalistic as he was making out. Throwing accusations of blame around, even with some justification, wouldn't get him anywhere and he was sharp enough to appreciate it. Dennis Boyd needed me and he knew it. I was all he had, all there was.

'Okay. After Joe Franks was murdered what happened to the diamonds, any ideas?'

He drew away. What I was asking amused him. 'I had a long time to think about that. Some nights it was the only thought in my head.'

'So?'

'Two options: pass them on to a single buyer or shift them a bit at a time.'

'What would you do?'

'Wouldn't steal them in the first place.'

'Suppose you had.'

Boyd looked around the room. When he returned, he gave me an answer. 'A bit at a time is easier. Handing them off as a parcel is quicker. Arguably safer with only one person involved. More control of where and when the stones surface. If they do surface. Could still be in somebody's safe.'

'Fifteen years on? Not likely.'

'Everything that's happened to me isn't likely.'

He was on the edge of feeling sorry for himself; nobody would grudge him that, only it wouldn't get us anywhere. I steered the conversation back to the robbery.

'Were there dealers Joe didn't trust, maybe someone he'd had problems with in the past?'

Boyd shook his head. 'No. Joe Franks was in business a helluva long time. He only worked with people he trusted.'

'Give it some thought. Up 'til now, the focus has been on the murder. I want to concentrate on the diamonds. Find who bought them and we're a giant step closer to finding who sold them.'

I stood. Boyd stayed where he was. Again, neither of us offered to shake hands. He grinned up at me.

'Something funny?'

'Not a fucking thing. Just glad to see you're still on it, Charlie. Knew I'd picked the right man.'

* * *

Driving into the city, Dennis Boyd stayed with me. His strength was admirable. For a guy who'd spent a decade and a half behind bars for a crime he didn't commit he was doing all right. Better than all right. Freedom had been short-lived. He'd been on the run from the first day. On my say-so, he'd turned himself in, expecting his side of the story would be heard; a promise – mine – that proved to be false. Yet, he'd still been able to smile. If the circumstances were reversed, I doubted I could stand being in the same room as me.

By the time I got to Glasgow I wasn't in the mood for work.

Reluctantly I climbed the stairs to the space Alex Gilby had given me to compensate for losing the office above NYB, which had been finished in a got-a-great-deal-on-this-paint colour. Nothing else explained the dodgy shade; the smell hung in the air. When he'd told me the decorator he intended to use was an old friend called Matt Black, I only just managed to keep my face straight.

'Matt Black? Good, is he?'

'The best. Been in the game all his life.'

'Matt Black.'

'Yeah. Why, do you know him?'

Alex didn't get it. Sometimes things were so obvious we were blind to them – like why three seemingly unconnected witnesses would perjure themselves in the common cause of convicting Dennis Boyd. Because, if Boyd was innocent of killing Joe Franks, that was exactly what had happened.

I sat down, tilting the chair so my head could rest against the wall, closed my eyes and searched for the link between Hughie Wilson, Liam McDermid and Willie Davidson: 'nonentities to a man', to use Pat Logue's phrase. Taken together, the power of their testimony sealed Dennis Boyd's fate.

An hour later, no nearer an explanation, I walked round to NYB. Patrick was at the bar with the dregs of a pint in front of him. Usually, he'd have the next one lined up ready to go. Today, he was pacing himself, spinning out his money. The reason was behind the bar: Michelle. I tapped him on the shoulder and drew him to a seat away from the distraction of the new barmaid's cleavage.

He faked interest. 'What gives, Charlie?'

'Nothing, and that's the problem. Been out to Barlinnie visiting a guy who'd love to be doing what you're doing right now.'

'Dennis Boyd.'

'The very same.'

Pat Logue still wasn't paying attention; he shot a glance over my shoulder to Michelle chatting to a guy in his late twenties. Patrick said, 'How's Boyd holdin' up?'

'Better than I would be. Bloody case has hit a brick wall. Be a good moment to change that, otherwise Boyd's going away for a very long time.'

I had his attention at last.

'Can I take it you haven't found anything?'

'Sorry, Charlie. Nada.'

'Meet me in my office in ten minutes.' I pointed towards Michelle. 'And bring your brain with you.'

He accepted the criticism and nodded. 'Wee head's been doin' the thinkin'.'

'Unless we find something, Boyd has no chance.'

'I'll finish my pint and be right with you.'

I was cramping Patrick's style; it couldn't be helped. I needed his mind on the job. If it wasn't, he was no use to me. He was headed for trouble – if Gail caught him, likely as not, she'd throw him out – but it was his own business. Mine was proving Dennis Boyd was innocent.

Ten minutes after I arrived in Cochrane Street the door opened and Patrick came in, pulled a chair up to the desk and sat down. 'Okay, I'm here.'

'The original case against Boyd was based on circumstantial evidence.'

'A bloodstain and the diamond in the back seat of his car.'

'Convincing so far as it went, though probably not enough to get a conviction. The testimony of three witnesses – strangers to each other – put the verdict beyond doubt.'

Pat said, 'There has to be a connection, doesn't there?'

'Right. What did a bouncer, a joiner and a barman have in

common fifteen years ago? Start with the bouncer and the barman.'

'Already did, Charlie.'

'I realise that, Patrick. This time dig deeper. Go all the way back. Did they ever work the same gig? After that we'll see where the joiner fits.'

'I'll do my best.'

'No word on who bought Joe Franks' diamonds?'

'Not a whisper. Problem is, it wasn't yesterday.'

'Then make a list of dealers. Maybe one of them will talk. Come back to me as soon as you get anything. Anything at all.'

'Understood.'

His fingers drummed the table. I recognised the sign; he was about to ask for a sub. In the end he thought better of it and got up to go. 'What would men be without women, Charlie?'

'You're going to tell me.'

'Scarce.'

'Who said it?'

'Mark Twain.'

On his way out the door I tossed one of his own lines at him. '"Keep it in your trousers." Who said that, remind me?'

34

The guy with the syringe had come later than usual. When he'd finally shown up, Kim was in agony, eyes rolling crazily in her head, clawing at herself, tearing the ropes tying her to the bed. Crying. Pleading. Begging. As the high had faded, she'd fallen into a dwam and gone to sleep, weaker than ever. Nothing mattered any more. Not even her daughter. What she'd done wrong – whatever it was – had cost her everything. And still Sean wasn't satisfied. For him, revenge was like sex; he always needed more. With Vicky's help, he'd reduced the mother of his child to a junkie. What remained of the beauty queen was a shell, sad and sickening to watch, and Vicky had to get out of the room.

Downstairs, Noah's piggy eyes studied the titty magazine in his hand. He knew his boss was there but didn't look up. Savages like him never learned: he had no better angels to appeal to. In the long run it wouldn't go well for him. Somebody would fight back – a short, violent, unexpected struggle, leaving blood on his leather jacket and a pair of scissors sticking out of his neck. That day couldn't come soon enough for Vicky.

She stood on the front steps worn down by countless male

feet, the blue neon sign above her still blinking in and out. She breathed the cool night air, forcing herself to be calm. The conversation with Sean had finished her; she'd come to the end of the line. Tony had asked her to leave Glasgow and go away with him more times than she could recall. She'd seen disappointment cloud a little deeper in his eyes with each refusal and despised herself for hurting an uncomplicated guy who couldn't begin to understand how she felt about Vicky Farrell.

Except, the excuses didn't make sense any more, even to her. Noah wasn't the only one it would end badly for: she remembered Rafferty's threat and shivered with fear.

get it done, Victoria

Vicky fingered the mobile in her hand, reluctant to make the call that would draw Tony into her world, knowing if she did there was no going back. When he knew the truth – the awful sordid truth, worse than anything he could imagine – the decision would be his.

Hearing his voice soothed her. She said, 'Where are you?'

'Just dropped off a load in Carlisle. Why?'

'When can you get here?

* * *

At half past two in the morning, under a starless sky, Glasgow was a drab collection of empty roads, stationary cars, and darkened shop windows. Noah hadn't been on the desk in Renfrew Street – probably off forcing his attention on another poor unfortunate – and Vicky had been able to slip out unnoticed. She wasn't happy leaving Kim alone in case the animal decided to try his luck a second time. But there was no other way. They were in the end game. Twenty-four hours from now, Rafferty's broken wife would be desperately selling herself on a corner of

Blythswood Square to anybody who'd have her, her addiction snapping at her heels like a rabid dog. Sean would remember Vicky questioning him and turn his malign focus on her; she'd be the one whimpering for the guy to stick the syringe in her arm. And it would begin; everything she'd witnessed – the pain, the humiliation, the unspeakable degradation – all of it, would be hers.

Kim would survive without her for a little while – she'd have to.

Vicky found a parking space and walked to the all-night café near Woodlands Road she'd been in with Tony seven or eight months earlier, when he'd asked her to marry him and received the first of many rejections. He'd gone quiet when she'd answered and for a week, Vicky hadn't heard from him. Maybe it was his silence or perhaps she'd got used to having him around, but she'd called and suggested they have dinner. Since then, turning him down had become a running joke between them, though Vicky suspected that, inside, Tony wasn't as amused as he pretended.

At twenty past two in the morning the place was busier than she expected. Tony was already there, the cup of muddy coffee on the table almost finished. He kissed her and anxiously searched her face. 'What's going on, baby?'

Vicky burst into tears and hid her face behind her hands. 'I'm so ashamed.'

Tony let her cry it out. When she was done, she wiped her eyes and looked across at him, self-loathing staring out of her. 'How can you possibly want to marry somebody like me?'

He didn't hesitate. 'Because you're a good person and I love you.'

'I'm not good. Nothing like good.'

'Yeah, you are. You don't see it. I do.' He sighed. 'Vicky, grow up. Do you seriously imagine I haven't checked it out? Of course I have. Eight months ago. I figured you'd walk away when the time was right. For you. For us. And now, we're here.'

She whispered, 'I'm scared, Tony. Really scared.'

'Scared? Of what? What's going on, Vic?'

Vicky couldn't bring herself to say it out loud and he reacted. 'That settles it, you're not going back. We'll leave now. This minute. In a few hours, we'll be hundreds of miles away. You'll be safe.'

She shook her head. 'No, no.'

'Then we're staying here until you explain why not. Putting your life in danger makes no sense. I won't let you do it.'

Vicky got herself under control. Tony loved her. He deserved the truth. She'd no wish to hurt him more than she already had but it couldn't be avoided. Describing the shabby room in Renfrew Street, the woman shackled to the bed and the guy with the syringe was hard for her to do, hard for him to listen to. Anger and revulsion in his eyes; Vicky wanted the ground to open up and swallow her.

Tony didn't interrupt or avoid her gaze. When she came to the end of her story, she lifted her chin defiantly. 'So, there it is. If you still want me, I'm ready to go, but I'm not leaving without her. I owe her that much. And you have to know what you'd be getting into. This is only the beginning.'

'Only the beginning of what?'

'Of Rafferty's revenge.'

'Revenge on who?'

'Me. I defended Kim, spoke up for her. That puts me on the other side. Anybody who isn't *for* Sean Rafferty is against him.'

do better or get another gig

She folded her arms. 'You don't understand – how could you?'

He sensed they were about to lose each other again. 'Yes, I do and I love you even more for it. Leaving Kim would haunt us for the rest of our lives. Sooner or later, it would tear us apart. We could go to the police.'

'With what I've done? No, impossible.'

This had been coming from the moment he'd asked if he could buy her a drink in the bar on Miller Street. And Vicky was right; he couldn't deny it. She waited for his answer. Tony toyed with his coffee and looked round the café. 'Then we get her out ourselves.'

'When?'

He pushed the cup away and put money on the table. 'How about right now?'

35

It made sense to take her car and leave the lorry. On the open road it was a beast, in the city, a cumbersome liability. Vicky studied Tony out of the corner of her eye, only too aware what he was risking. He stared ahead, his expressionless face pale and shadowed in the street light, maybe having second thoughts. Who would blame him? How many guys would do this for a prostitute? If they got caught, retribution would be swift and final – they'd both die horribly. Silently, she made a promise to herself: when this was behind them, she'd marry Tony, live wherever he wanted them to live, and be the wife he deserved.

He said, 'Don't try to bring anything. In and out, like we agreed.'

'She's weak, hardly able to stand. She may not be able to walk.'

'I'll carry her. If we get separated, meet me back at the café.'

Vicky reached across and found his hand. 'Don't worry about me. Whatever happens, get Kim away. It's her Sean really wants.'

'I will, but if we get—'

'The café, yeah, I've got it.'

She parked in the aptly named Hill Street, pulled Tony to her and kissed him. 'I love you, you know that, don't you?'

He smiled. 'Finally.'

'I didn't say yes the first time you asked me, because—'

He put his finger to her lips. 'I understood then and I understand now. Let's do this thing so we can get on with the rest of our lives, eh?'

'If Noah's on the door, let me handle him.'

Tony smiled. 'No,' he said, 'that bastard is mine.'

* * *

There was no sign of the doorman; his titty magazines were there but he wasn't. They climbed the stairs, bare boards groaning beneath their feet, echoing against the peeling walls. Vicky shivered, more afraid than she'd ever been. Behind her, Tony tested every step, not trusting his weight to it until he was certain it wouldn't betray them, listening for the shouts that would mean they'd been discovered.

Without him, without his courage and strength, Vicky would've run, even though she'd never forgive herself for deserting Kim Rafferty.

After what seemed like an age, they reached the third landing and tiptoed to the room. The house was still, devoid of the usual mating noises, and they began to believe they were going to get away with it. Vicky turned the handle, gently pushing the door open, half expecting the loathsome Noah to be waiting on the other side, smiling his broken-toothed smile. He wasn't. In the weak light, Kim lay semi-conscious on the bed, more dead than alive. The high had lasted a mere ten minutes before her eyelids fluttered and closed and she passed to the land of the lost.

She hadn't returned. Maybe would never return. Vicky couldn't allow herself to believe that.

Kim's once flawless skin had the pallor of old cheese; livid cold sores marked her cracked lips, each shallow breath like a death rattle.

Vicky cradled her thin frame in her arms, whispering reassuring untruths. Tony untied the ropes fastening her to the bed. Her eyes opened, no recognition in them, and Vicky redoubled her lies, frantically trying to reach her.

'Kim, Kim, it's okay, it's okay, you're safe. We're getting you out of here.' She took off her coat. 'Help me get this on her.'

Somewhere outside, a car door slammed, then another. Vicky went to the grimy window; three men were heading for the house. Further down, a Mercedes turned the corner into Renfrew Street: Sean. How could he have known?

She yelled to Tony. 'Go! Go! There's a back door, use it! The keys are in the ignition.'

He lifted Kim up. 'No chance, Vic. Not without you.'

'I'll be okay. Do it!'

'I can't leave witho—'

'We haven't time for this.'

'Rafferty isn't a fool. He won't believe you. And if he doesn't, he'll—'

'He will. Yes, he will. I'll make it look like somebody took her. For Christ's sake, before we all die in this shithole. Please, Tony!'

'I love you, Vicky.'

'And I love you, too.'

The instinct to survive kicked in. Tony was right – convincing Rafferty his wife had been abducted was her only hope. Vicky knocked the table over, grabbed the grubby bedclothes and dragged them onto the carpet, as if there had been a struggle. It wasn't enough. Not nearly enough.

She wasn't brave, far from it – she had no choice. Vicky steadied herself, heart thumping, not sure she could go through with it, images of Kim's ravaged body, physically and mentally broken, flashing through her mind. They'd do the same to her and worse. The hurt in Tony's eyes when she'd forced him to leave her behind haunted Vicky. This was her fault. Her doing. He was a good guy – too good for a scrubber like her – who should never have been part of this filth.

If she ever wanted to see him again, just one dreadful option remained. Vicky stepped back, took a deep breath and smashed her face as hard as she could off the edge of the open door: the blow bit into her forehead like an axe, cutting through the flesh on the brow to the bone, instantly mutilating her. A bomb exploded in her head, blood and unimaginable pain blurred her vision and she dropped to the floor. Somewhere in her brain, angry voices drowned in a storm breaking against an ancient shore; Vicky recognised the metallic taste in her mouth.

Then, nothing.

36

She came to on the floor surrounded by strange faces. Across the room, Sean Rafferty sat in the chair where she'd watched his wife's descent into a dark place, his fingers steepled in front of him. He tilted his head and spoke to one of his men. 'Get her a glass of water.'

Vicky's clothes were covered in blood, her head felt like it was coming off her body and one side of her face was numb. She mumbled, 'I couldn't stop them, Sean. I tried. There were too many.'

Rafferty played with his ring. 'Can you describe them?'

'Not really, it all happened so fast.'

He put his hands together, applauding slowly, and came towards her. The punch rocked her head back on her shoulders; fresh pain lanced her brain and Rafferty hunkered down next to her. 'I'm disappointed in you, Victoria. I mean, really disappointed. Let me ask, because I'm curious. What is it about me makes you believe I'm a fucking idiot, eh?'

'Sean—'

'Shut it, bitch! Don't lie to me. There's been somebody on

your tail since you started having second thoughts about the job. Knew you were building up to something. You and your boyfriend. I hoped you wouldn't be so stupid.' He sighed and held out his arms. 'But there you go.'

Rafferty paced the spartan room, shaking his head. 'Don't insult my intelligence with your fairy stories. We go back a long way, said it yourself. Knowing what you know about me, I'm surprised you'd try that crap on.'

He took hold of her chin and forced her destroyed face up to the light. Vicky trembled and pulled away. 'Oh, Victoria, that's nasty. You're no fucking good to me now. Your price just went through the floor. Lucky for you not everybody has my standards.'

Rafferty tired of the game and walked to the door. He spoke over his shoulder to Vicky huddled on the floor. 'You and Noah are pals, right? He'd love to have some fun with you.' He laughed. 'Doesn't mind if they're ugly, do you, Noah?'

Noah's tongue ran over his lips; he nodded and grinned.

'And in case you're expecting your boyfriend to come riding in on his white horse and save you – forget it. He'll never find you where you're going. When you're good and ready, you can take my whore of a wife's place on the street.'

* * *

The next morning the air was heavy, the sky grey. The forecast was rain and lots of it. I gave NYB a miss and went to the office, feeling flat. A phone call and a voice I hadn't heard before straightened my mood. 'Can I speak to Mr Cameron?'

'Speaking.'

A sigh came down the line, as if the person on the other end had come to a decision and was relieved. 'This is Anthony

McCabe. I handled Joe Franks' accounts back in the Battlefield Road days. You talked to my son, Barry, about Joe.'

'Yes. He was helpful but couldn't tell me anything.'

'Those files were long gone, I'm afraid.'

A shaft of sun pierced the cloud cover, found the window and splashed golden light across my desk. I took it as a sign.

'Barry told me you hadn't been well.'

'That's true. Fact is, I'm still not great, one of the reasons I'm keen to meet up with you.'

'You live in Arran, don't you? I can come to you. Tell me when.'

'Actually, that won't be necessary. I'm in Glasgow today seeing a consultant. I'll come to you.'

'Excellent. What time?'

'Just got off the train at Central Station. How about now?'

'Great. My office is in Cochrane Street.'

'I know. See you soon.'

At last. Who better than his accountant to tell me the truth about what kind of businessman Franks had been? I waited ten minutes, then went downstairs to find the promised rain beginning to look less likely; the clouds were breaking up. Behind them the sun was flipping a coin, trying to decide what kind of weather the city was going to have.

A taxi with two passengers in the back pulled into the kerb and a woman, petite and well dressed with steel-grey hair, got out and glared at me, before turning to attend to the man with her: the accountant had brought his wife.

With the driver's help they got him into a wheelchair. Even that small effort visibly drained him; his face was the colour of putty, he struggled for breath, and I understood why Mrs McCabe wasn't pleased. When he saw me standing by the door, he raised a hand and tried to smile. The woman paid the driver, fussed with her husband's coat the way a mother might do with a child, and pushed the chair towards me, her first words revealing exactly how she felt.

'Are there stairs? Because if there are, forget it.'

McCabe started to protest and was immediately overruled. 'No, Tony. It's crazy you're even here. I shouldn't have allowed it.'

I stepped forward and shook hands with both of them. His fingers were cold, the skin stretched so tight I could feel every bone, and his eyes were watery. Losing weight had left deep hollows in his cheeks. He looked what he was: a man not long for this world. I wouldn't have bet on him lasting to the end of the week, yet, against his best interests – and no doubt fierce and justified opposition from his wife – he'd made the journey to meet me. There had to be a very good reason.

Mrs McCabe's handshake gave perfunctory a bad name; it was over in a second, our fingers barely touching. The message was clear: we'd just met and already she didn't like me.

McCabe stared up from the chair. 'Hate to admit it but she's right. Then, she usually is.' He gestured to his wife. 'This is Julia. Never go anywhere without her and not just because of this.' McCabe tapped the wheelchair's metal frame.

At his side, Julia's lips tightened in a half-hearted attempt at a smile that died still-born on her lips, and in her face I saw the pain of knowing her husband – the man she'd probably loved for most of her life – wasn't going to recover.

The physical differences between them were stark: where he was friendly, she was terse and tightly wound; his pallor was bloodless, her face was flushed, as if resentment was choking her. McCabe's eyes, glassy and weak, seemed fixed on the edge of weeping; his wife had long passed that point. Julia McCabe looked like someone who hadn't had a night's sleep worth a damn since long before their holiday had been cut short.

I put a hand on the accountant's shoulder. 'No problem. We'll do the simple thing.'

He sounded relieved. 'Is there somewhere nearby we can go?'

'Absolutely. Place called NYB. It isn't far and the coffee's good.'

Julia McCabe pounced. 'Tony isn't allowed coffee.'

Her husband offered a veiled apology for her abruptness. 'Afraid she's right again, Mr Cameron. Doctor's orders.'

'Then it'll have to be something else.'

The little talking he'd done had exhausted him and we made our way in silence to the Italian Centre. Beside me hostility rolled off his wife. Who could blame her? Her husband should be at home in bed, not being bumped around Glasgow.

In NYB I cleared a path to a table over against the wall. Mrs McCabe ordered a latte from a waitress I didn't recognise. I asked for an espresso. The accountant surprised us. 'Brandy,' he said.

His wife started to argue; he dug in his heels and defied her. 'Damn it, woman, I want a brandy and I'm going to have a brandy, because whether I do or don't, it won't change a thing. Drop the pretence; nobody's buying it.'

It was harsh. Julia's lips trembled and her head went down. She might have cried if she hadn't been all cried out. McCabe ignored her and spoke to the waitress. 'Something decent. And a little water, if you don't mind.'

The atmosphere had suddenly become charged. I changed the subject. 'What time is your appointment with the consultant?'

The question was asked in innocence, but my timing was off. Mrs McCabe exploded. 'Oh, for God's sake! You're supposed to be an investigator. Are you blind? There isn't an appointment. There won't be any more appointments. Tony only said that so you'd think he had a reason for being in Glasgow in case you were too busy to see him. Silly old fool. Told him he was off his head. He wouldn't listen.'

McCabe snapped back. 'I do listen.'

'No, you don't. You haven't listened to me more than twice in fifty years. If you had we wouldn't be where we are, and you know it.'

She sounded angry with him, and she was, but really what I was hearing was sadness from a woman who was out-of-her-mind scared. Ill health had driven a caring relationship to the brink.

McCabe's eyes met mine: look what I have to put up with, they said.

The waitress came back with our drinks. He lifted his with a trembling hand and sipped it. I asked how it was. He set it down on the table before he answered. 'Not bad. Not great.'

Forcing the conversation would get me nothing. I waited until he was ready to continue. It was McCabe's story; he could tell it how he liked, when he liked.

Finally, he cleared his throat and began. 'The Joe Franks I knew was a good guy – at least, according to his own lights. Like so many of us, he was honest up to a point. In business, he was straight as a die, known for it. To my knowledge that didn't change.'

McCabe let the implication sink in. Julia's eyes didn't leave him.

'That said, the personal side of his life was something else again. Hooking up with Diane was a mistake made in the heat of the moment. The attraction was mutual: he had money and she was a great-looking woman any man would be happy to be seen with. Of course, it didn't last. Diane started running around behind his back. So far as I could see, Joe lost interest before she did. All he really cared about were stones.'

None of this was news. Dennis Boyd had told me the same. McCabe took another sip of the brandy. 'Most of it is common knowledge. What isn't well known is that it wasn't Joe's first marriage. Or the first mistake he'd made with women. When our paths crossed, he was a man with a secret. As his relationship with Diane soured, he realised just how much damage he'd done.'

'To his first wife?'

'And to the girl.'

McCabe saw the look on my face; his cracked lips parted in a smile. 'That's right. Joe Franks had a daughter. His wife was pregnant when Joe left her and set up home with Diane. Never saw her again, far as I know.'

Skeletal fingers caressed the glass but left it on the table – maybe his protest had run its course. The accountant needed a breather. I obliged by recapping what he'd said.

'Okay, so Franks had been married before. When he met Diane, he left his wife.'

McCabe shook his head. I wasn't getting it. 'No. Leaving her for another woman would've been bad enough. Leaving her pregnant was what he couldn't live with. I told you, Joe had his own values. In his book, that was about the worst thing he could've done.'

'If he was as good a guy as you say he was, why do it?'

The accountant shrugged. Under his coat I guessed he was a bag of bones. 'He didn't know. For more than a decade he didn't know he had a daughter until one day a fourteen-year-old girl turned up at his office in the Argyll Arcade and introduced herself.'

37

We sat while McCabe thought about whether there was any more to add. His wife hadn't touched the latte she'd ordered; by now it would be lukewarm.

'He asked me to send them money; it wasn't enough for him. His marriage to Diane was already in trouble. From then on, there was no saving it. The past ate away at him.'

'What did he do?'

'He accepted nothing that had already happened could be altered. But the future...'

He let the potentials hang in the air. 'Diane's carrying-on made it easy for him. He told me the story and asked me to help. Of course, I said yes. Then he instructed me to make new arrangements. So, I did. He was a man who wanted to right a wrong. As his accountant, there was a part for me to play.'

'These "new arrangements", what were they?'

He lifted what was left of the brandy and finished it in one swallow. His wife stared with empty eyes; she was losing him in more ways than one. Her influence, severe yet benign – at least for the moment – had reached its limits. I felt for her.

McCabe said, 'Like everybody, I'd heard the gossip. According to the rumours, Joe was going bankrupt. Supposed to owe money all over the place.'

'And didn't he?'

McCabe wiped his mouth on the sleeve of his coat and shot a glance at his empty glass. 'Julia, I'd like another brandy. What do you think?'

For the first time his wife softened. Her hand found his and something only they could know passed between them. 'Why not, Tony? If that's what you want, why not?'

'Will you join me?'

She blinked, a single tear ran down her cheek, and she smiled. 'That would be nice.'

'Brandy all right?'

'Brandy will be fine.'

He extended the invitation to include me. 'And yourself, Mr Cameron?'

'It's Charlie. Make it three.'

In an American diner in the centre of Glasgow, Tony and Julia McCabe had come to a decision to live whatever remained of life together and were happy about it.

I went to the bar. Jackie wasn't around. Neither was Pat Logue. Maybe he was out chasing down information on the witnesses. I hoped so. When I came back with the drinks the McCabes were holding hands, whispering to each other. Anthony McCabe seemed suddenly stronger: a man reborn. He added water to his glass. 'Where was I?'

I reminded him. 'The arrangements Franks asked you to make.'

'Yes, yes, I remember. Joe had reached a crossroads. His daughter showing up pushed him closer to doing what he'd already been thinking about doing.'

'Leaving Diane.'

'Not just leaving her. His money was the only reason she'd married him. I suppose he could tolerate that so long as there was something – anything – there. The daughter, her name's Karen by the way, gave him the chance to make things right.' McCabe paused. 'Right isn't the word.' He searched for the phrase and found it. 'To make amends.'

'And to get back at Diane.'

'That, too.'

'What was he planning?'

'Joe knew divorcing Diane was inevitable. She'd given up even trying to hide the affair. He needed to be sure there would be nothing – and I do mean nothing – for her. He got me to set up two new accounts: one for him, one for Karen.'

'And siphon money into them.'

'In the months before he was murdered, he was obsessed. It was all he thought about.'

'Who were the accounts with?'

'Bank of Scotland and the Clydesdale.'

The code: easy to crack it if you knew how.

'BS – Bank of Scotland, CL – the Clydesdale Bank, and TM for Tony McCabe.'

'Spot on, Charlie.'

'You were aware of it?'

'Yes. Joe told me he was keeping a record of how much he was taking from the business and everywhere else, though I would've worked it out in any case. After all, I was on the inside.

'To the world it looked like he was on the skids. Not the truth. Not even close. In his determination to leave her with nothing, he'd squeezed every last pound, and started missing bills. The mortgage hadn't been paid in months, the rent was behind in the

Arcade, and the business account and his old personal account had been cleaned out long since.'

His laugh sounded like an avalanche breaking on the side of a mountain – as if someone had told him a joke and he was only just getting it. It came at a price and Julia moved into the role of nurse, holding him until the coughing passed. 'I've often imagined Diane's face when she got the news.'

'It didn't take her long to land on her feet.'

McCabe glanced at his wife. 'I doubt it was her feet she landed on, Mr Cameron.'

'She married a guy called Kennedy. Ritchie Kennedy. Ring any bells?'

'Sorry, it doesn't. But God help him, he'll need it with that woman.'

'Did you know about the last deal Joe was involved in, the one that probably got him killed?'

'I had an idea something was going on, but not the details.'

'What happened to the accounts?'

Something clouded in his eyes; it might have been pride. 'I did what Joe would've wanted, contacted his daughter. She came to my office and signed for the account with her name on it. By then she was in her late teens and her mother had died. I said her father had been a good man, that even the best of us make mistakes.'

'Ever hear from her again?'

'No. Didn't expect to. What had to be done had been done.'

'What about the other account, the one Franks set up for himself?'

This was Anthony McCabe's moment, very probably his last moment in the sun, and he wasn't going to be hurried. His hand slipped inside his coat. When it came back it held a dark-blue book with a gold crest embossed on the cover. 'Sent it to them every six months to get it updated. Last time was six weeks ago.'

He handed me a white envelope. 'A letter of authority.' He tossed his prize on the table in front of me and watched it fall. 'See for yourself. If you're wise, you'll take some free advice from an old accountant: never underestimate compound interest. There's fifteen years of it in there.'

He finished his brandy and pushed the wheelchair away from the table; his work was done and he was pleased. His wife took her cue from him. She stood and again drew the coat around him, mothering him like before. He let her. The McCabes were back where they'd started: the two of them against the world.

When your time on earth was tight, decade-old questions about who had done what and why had little importance. It no longer mattered. In his shoes, detaching from the future was easy – he wouldn't be around to see how it played out. His wife wheeled him towards the door.

McCabe gave me a half-hearted smile. 'It's your problem now, Charlie.'

* * *

I waited on the pavement with them, though I needn't have bothered. Anthony McCabe had discharged his duty and passed it to me. Julia McCabe's lips were pressed together. In a strange way, she seemed satisfied, perhaps with good reason. There would be no more difficult trips to Glasgow and no more small rebellions from her husband. In that, at least, she'd won. Her eyes stayed on the traffic and didn't look at me. Nobody spoke. What was the point? It had all been said.

it's your problem now, Charlie

Finally, a taxi stopped and the struggle I'd witnessed before began again in reverse. When the ailing accountant was safely in the back seat, the driver stowed the chair and the passengers settled themselves for the journey to Central. The burst of energy McCabe had enjoyed in NYB was short-lived. His head lay back and he was breathing heavily. Whatever he was thinking he kept to himself – his wife would know but she wouldn't be sharing those thoughts – or anything else – with me.

When their car disappeared through the lights and into George Square, the first scattered drops of rain began to fall; the coin-toss in the sky had gone against the city. I headed to the office and climbed the stairs that had been too much for Tony McCabe. At the top, I closed the door behind me. Until this morning, the jeweller had been a man with a failing business and an unfaithful wife, a guy whose death at the hands of a robber was almost a welcome release from a life, professionally and personally, in freefall.

Except that wasn't how it had been. Mrs Franks wasn't the only one in the marriage who'd been unhappy.

I threw the bankbook on the desk, wondering what fifteen years of compound interest looked like, and sat down. The pages were dry, discoloured with age, with entries every six months as regular as clockwork. My finger followed them to the end and read the total.

Diane's husband hadn't been the fool she'd taken him for.

* * *

For a time, it had looked as though the forecast was going to be wrong. The steady drumming on the windowpane confirmed it wasn't. One of the things I'd never understood about Scotland was how, as soon as it started to rain, it suddenly, almost immediately, felt colder. Winter was still a long way off, at least in theory, but the temperature in the office seemed to have gone down.

The conversation with Anthony McCabe played in my head. In spite of his illness, he'd been determined to fulfil his responsibility. For a decade and a half, he hadn't known how until I'd given him the opportunity.

But what did it tell me, beyond the fact his old client, the jeweller, intended to get his retaliation in first? Diane had been in the dark about what was coming, blissfully unaware her husband was planning to leave her homeless and penniless. The accountant was clearly with Franks, his phraseology skewed in his favour, the disapproval of the woman he'd married undisguised. 'Diane's carrying-on made it easy for him,' he'd said, and followed it with an off-colour comment which I guessed was out of character – 'I doubt it was her feet she landed on, Mr Cameron.'

Then again, there was another way of looking at it: Diane hadn't known – still didn't know – Joe's wife had been pregnant when she hooked up with him. From everything I'd heard, being a husband wasn't his forte. Franks had proved it, not once but twice. Precious stones rather than people had done it for him. For a passionate woman a relationship with a man who sometimes didn't come home and slept in his office would be an unfulfilling experience. Seeking and finding attention outside their marriage was inevitable. And her husband wasn't blind; he had to have decided he could live with it. Until something changed his mind.

Maybe Diane had become too brazen, rubbed his nose in what she was doing. Maybe discovering he had a daughter was a painful reminder of his shortcomings as a spouse and he'd resolved to make things right, starting with the girl he'd fathered but never known. Or, unlikely as it seemed, perhaps it had been good old-fashioned jealousy. His wife taking Dennis Boyd as her lover had plunged her infidelity to a new low: betrayal. Affairs with strangers he could turn a blind eye to, an affair with the man he employed to protect him and his merchandise was something else.

* * *

The call from Pat Logue brought good news. 'Struck gold, Charlie. You were spot on. There is a connection, a very definite connection.'

Knowing who made it easy to guess why. As usual, the hard bit was the bit in the middle, the thing DS Geddes was obsessed with: proof.

Time to take it to the next level.

Andrew Geddes leaned his elbow on the table, a hand supporting his head. While he wrote, his lips moved as he muttered to himself. When he saw me, his expression didn't change; he nodded, crushed the sheet into a ball and dropped it on the floor beside the others. I'd no idea how long he'd been at it. I took a seat and waited. A stranger would've been hard-pressed to guess we were friends. Andrew said, 'Bloody paperwork. Never had any patience for it.'

'Still working on the promotion?'

He put the pen down, pinched the corners of his eyes and stared. 'Is that what I'm doing, Charlie? Been so long I'd forgotten.'

'Making progress?'

A noise at the back of his throat answered for him. 'Not so you'd notice.'

'What's the problem?'

The wrong question. Geddes couldn't hold his frustration in check. He kicked a paper ball and watched it roll across the floor.

If Jackie caught him making a mess of her bar, he'd be hearing about it. 'It's rubbish. A right load of old bollocks. Fuck all to do with anything. Yet, this is how they judge you. Who can tell the tallest tales, fib the biggest fibs.'

'Just play the game, Andrew. Whatever they want, give it to them.'

He pursed his lips and looked at me like a boy studying an insect he was about to squash: with a mix of fascination and pity. 'You really don't get it, do you, Charlie? I despise the whole fucking process from start to finish. They're asking me to make myself acceptable. They're asking me to lie.'

He was right, I didn't get it. 'Give them what they want. Lie if that's what it takes.'

'That what you'd do? Misrepresent yourself to get ahead?'

'What's to misrepresent? You're a first-rate detective, that's the truth. Sometimes we have to jump through hoops, so jump. In the end, all that matters is that Police Scotland has a new detective inspector 100 per cent committed to the job. And, with you, they will.'

Andrew held up a form and pointed to a question. 'This is the problem. Give an example of your leadership qualities.'

Off the top of my head I could think of a dozen.

'It's about selling yourself and I struggle with that. Anyway, enough about me. What do you want?'

I feigned offence. 'Well, that's nice.'

'Might not be nice. Bet it's accurate. What do you want, Charlie?'

'What would you say if I told you I'd found a link between the three witnesses?'

Andrew gave me another of his sad-case smiles. 'Since you ask, I'll tell you. I'd say that, as usual, you can't let it go.'

'Boyd needs somebody in his corner.'

'And that somebody happens to be you.'

'Proof isn't always easy to find. Wasn't that what you were just saying?'

'Not exactly. And it isn't the same thing.'

'No? Maybe I didn't hear you right. If you can't convince the people you want to convince, you'll be a DS for the rest of your career. If Boyd can't convince the people he needs to, he'll spend the rest of his life in a cell. So, yeah, it's not the same. Not the same at all.'

Andrew lifted the pen. 'Ever thought of going into the used car game, Charlie? Okay, I'm buying. What's the link?'

38

Andrew would've contacted DI Campbell and gone to the house in Newton Mearns. The policemen would be out of luck. I'd already tried; there was nobody home.

I'd left the city at the tail end of the rush hour, now dusk was falling, and in the gloom the approach to Daltallin House was impressive: a meandering single-track road overhung by trees. My tyres crunched over gravel, startling a pair of foraging rabbits. A crow swooped noisily from a branch and passed low in front, reminding me I was an unwelcome stranger in his territory.

Ritchie Kennedy was a workaholic who spent most of his time at his hotel. If he wasn't already here, sooner or later he'd show up. When he did, he'd find me waiting.

Suddenly, a black granite monstrosity rose against the darkening sky. Light blazing from leaded windows lent a charm the building would lack in the day. If gargoyles were your thing, you'd like it. I didn't.

All I saw was Joe Franks' money.

A line of expensive cars sat at the far side under a twenty-foot-high hedge. Kennedy's was one of them. He was a greedy man, greedier than most, and he'd drawn other greedy men to him: Wilson, McDermid and Davidson. Stealing the jeweller's wife hadn't been enough, he'd wanted it all.

I hoped it had been worth it, because it was over.

I pulled in beside a blue Lexus, got out and walked through the front door like I belonged. Inside, the staff on reception kept their heads down, too busy to notice me. When a fresh-faced waiter carrying an empty tray drifted past, I guessed he was on his way to the bar and followed. The décor was dark wood, polished brass and curtains it would take two strong men to carry: a male space. Not for me. To prove the point a group of business guys – ties loosened and jackets off – drank over-priced whisky their companies would be charged for from cut-glass tumblers, laughing like schoolboys at dirty jokes. One of them whispered the punchline, savouring the reaction. In an hour or two, whispering would be abandoned and the polite man behind the bar would cast anxious glances at the group, wishing they would call it a night before they offended somebody other than him.

At the door to the restaurant, a maître d' asked my name, ready to check it against a list of reservations. I stopped him before he could get started. 'I'm meeting Mr Kennedy.'

'Certainly, sir. Mr Kennedy's party is over by the window. Shall I tell him you're here?'

I smiled. 'That would spoil it.'

The Kennedys were at a table with four people I didn't recognise. Diane saw me first. 'Well, well,' she said, 'this is a surprise.'

Her husband swivelled in his chair, and when he realised who it was, his expression was hard to describe. He glanced at his dinner companions, regretting they were present, maybe sensing what was coming. His wife certainly didn't. She lifted her glass and said, 'So what's Charlie Cameron doing in darkest Ayrshire?'

There was humour in her voice. 'Has our culinary reputation reached you?'

She was wearing a cream blouse with a double-string of pearls at the throat and in the subdued light her eyes were wine-warm and provocative. I didn't answer. I was about to ruin her evening.

'The food isn't why I'm here, Diane.'

I ignored the other people at the table and spoke to Kennedy. 'Joe Franks was a simple man. Ever wondered what he would've made of how you spent his cash?'

Kennedy threw his napkin down in a show of frustration and disapproval. 'What do you want, Cameron? Just what the fuck do you want?'

Before I could answer, a collective gasp went up from the diners as police officers poured into the room. DI Campbell certainly liked to make an entrance, almost swaggering past the dumbstruck guests. He'd dreamed of moments like this and was enjoying himself. At the door, Andrew Geddes hung back, letting him make the collar that could so easily have been his. To climb the greasy pole, you had to be willing to play by different rules. Andrew wasn't. When would he learn?

Campbell drummed his fingers on the brilliant-white table-cloth, his eyes travelling over Kennedy and his friends. When he got to me, he paused; the DI was having a good day and didn't want it to be over too soon. He greeted me like an old pal. 'We must stop meeting like this, Charlie.'

The pleasure he'd taken arresting Dennis Boyd – a man who'd turned himself in – was fresh in my mind. I didn't like Campbell and wasn't amused.

'Suits me, Detective Inspector.'

'People could get the wrong idea.'

The joke fell flat and the smile disappeared – like everything about him, it had never been real – and he got on with what he'd come to do.

'Richard Kennedy, I'm detaining you...'

The familiar words drifted through the silent room. Two officers grabbed Kennedy's arms and handcuffed him. Diane seemed not to understand what was happening; she started to object. Her husband halted her in her tracks; his apology, an admission of guilt, silenced her. 'I'm sorry, Diane, it was an accident. I liked Joe. I never meant to hurt him.'

As they led him through the stunned restaurant his wife lost control, screaming, lashing out at the nearest policeman, tearing at her hair and, in the process, breaking the strand round her neck. Pearls bounced and rolled across the table and onto the floor. Her hands flailed wildly, knocking over her wine glass, her breasts heaving under her blouse.

'Bastard! Fifteen years, you lying bastard!'

She buried her head in her hands and cried, overwhelmed by the shock of discovering she'd married the person who'd murdered her husband and put an innocent man behind bars for a huge chunk of his life.

Her friends tried to comfort her; there were no words.

* * *

A sign hanging from the ceiling of the Bombay Cafe in St Vincent Street told anyone interested that ALL CHAI IS COMING STRICTLY WITHOUT OPIUM.

We were in a booth. Patrick was sipping a lager and studying the menu. I'd called to let him know what had happened at the Daltallin House hotel and he'd insisted on celebrating. This part of the city had upped its game in recent years and the Bombay Cafe stood out from the many burger joints surrounding it.

When I got there, he shook my hand. 'Two words, Charlie: result. Did the impossible, solved a fifteen-year-old case. You're some man. What do you fancy? Last time I was here I had the lamb Madras. Excellent. Could do worse.'

'Lamb Madras it is.'

He raised his glass in a toast. 'This is on me.'

There was something different about him; he seemed younger. Then I realised what it was: no goatee. He read my mind, stroked his smooth chin and answered the question I hadn't asked. 'Felt like a change. Must admit it takes a bit of gettin' used to.'

'Does Gail like it?'

He turned away. 'She hasn't said. Don't think she's noticed.'

I'd known Gail Logue almost as long as her husband. She was sharp – there was no chance she'd missed it. When it came to other women Patrick had form. Shaving the goatee was so obvious I wondered if he wanted to get found out.

'You're wrong. She'll have spotted it right away.'

He shrugged like he didn't care and returned to Ritchie and Diane Kennedy. 'How's she takin' it? Must be pretty shook up.'

'Devastated. How do you come back from something like that? DI Campbell's interviewing Kennedy as we speak. Some time tonight he'll be charged with murdering Joe Franks.'

'Because you kept pluggin' away Dennis Boyd's off the hook.'

'For the original crime, yes. Proving Kennedy killed the witnesses might not be so easy.'

He disagreed through a mouthful of pakora. 'The guy had motive and opportunity. He's goin' down. Will Boyd have been told?'

'Too soon. But I'm seeing him in a couple of days. He'll know by then.'

'The police were happy to let it all fall on him. Not you. Your pal must be pleased. Ungrateful bastard. Bet he takes the credit for Wilson, McDermid and Davidson as well. Does his promotion chances a helluva lot of good.'

Pat Logue wasn't there or he'd have seen Andrew let Campbell have the glory.

'He's a great detective, give him that at least.'

Further than Pat Logue was prepared to go; when it came to policemen, and Andrew Geddes in particular, his heart was hardened. The arrival of our main courses delayed his rejection of my assessment. 'If you say so, if you say so. Except nothin' would've been done if you hadn't kept with it. The people I know don't talk to coppers. Code of the West. His "great detective skills" would've got him exactly nowhere.'

'They wouldn't have spoken to me either, Patrick.'

'True enough, but I wouldn't have gone there if you hadn't pushed me to dig deeper.'

I let it go. Patrick's opinion wouldn't change. We gave our attention to the meal, which was, indeed, excellent. Any time the conversation got too close to Michelle he steered it back to the case. Patrick was incorrigible. He was going to do what he was going to do. It would take more than me to stop him.

* * *

At eleven-thirty, just as I was thinking about bed, Andrew showed up. It had been a long day and, in the doorway, he looked tired: there were lines on his face and at the corners of his eyes and mouth I hadn't noticed before. He handed me a bottle of Bell's. 'Thought we might need this.'

I weighed it in my palm. 'This celebration deserves better, don't you think?'

He smiled a knowing smile. 'What've you got?'

When I brought out the Johnnie Walker Gold Label Reserve, he nodded appreciatively. 'Won't argue with that.'

The whisky was clean and smooth; we enjoyed it in silence until Andrew said, 'Kennedy signed a confession an hour ago. Claims the jeweller was an accident.'

'A robbery that went wrong.'

'Yeah. And time's on his side. After fifteen years, premeditation won't be easy to prove.'

'What's he saying about Wilson and the other two?'

Geddes shook his head. 'So far, nothing. Campbell has another session scheduled for tomorrow. By then, hopefully, he'll have Kennedy's phone records. With any luck they'll show he talked to the victims shortly before they died.'

'Will that be enough?'

'Not nearly. Unless we can place Kennedy in the Elmbank car park, the garage at Bellshill, or on Arran, he might well get away with it.' He drew his fingers through his thinning hair. 'Good work on that, by the way. Bloody obvious now. What put you on to it?'

I told him. 'If Dennis Boyd was telling the truth, the witnesses had to be lying. Nothing else made sense. So why? What did a barman, a joiner and a nightclub bouncer have in common? Wilson didn't work where McDermid tended bar. And where did a joiner fit in? Only Davidson wasn't just a joiner, he specialised in shop-fitting.'

'Shops, clubs and pubs: Ritchie Kennedy.'

'Right. Kennedy used the money he'd got from Joe Franks' diamonds to buy a country house hotel with a Michelin-starred restaurant, but his roots had been humble: a couple of spit-and-sawdust pubs. Three of them and a club, to be exact. At some time, the witnesses – dodgy characters to begin with – were employed by him. When the robbery went wrong, he paid them to lie under oath.'

'And sent an innocent man to prison. Heartless bastards. Wonder if they ever gave a second thought to what they'd done.'

'Doubt it. For a decade and a half, they went on living their lives. Everybody would've been happy to hear that Boyd had died inside. Except it didn't happen. Dennis Boyd was a hard man – the reason the jeweller used him as a bodyguard – revenge kept him going. When he got out, he was coming after them and they knew it.'

'Kennedy most of all. Must've been terrified Boyd would beat the truth out of McDermid or Davidson.'

Andrew helped himself to another drink. 'The wife's in a helluva state. Just sinking in. She's a brassy piece, no better than she should be, but I can't help feeling sorry for her.'

The whisky talking.

'Campbell's invited me onto the case.'

'Payback for handing it to him on a plate?'

Geddes laughed. 'Doubt that. He's asked me to interview Mrs Kennedy. Doesn't fancy doing it himself so I am, first thing in the morning. Can't say I'm looking forward to it. Second husband murders the first husband? Christ.'

I didn't have advice for him. I said, 'The marriage to Franks was over. Her affair with Boyd was the last straw – he was divorcing her.'

'Even so.'

'What about Boyd?'

Geddes shook his head. 'Still the prime suspect in three murders.'

'Where's the motive? He needed them alive.'

Andrew toyed with his whisky. 'Try good old-fashioned revenge. Boyd knew he'd been set up and knew who was responsible. Unless we can put Kennedy at the crime scenes, what's changed?'

His assessment stopped the conversation in its tracks. Eventually, I said, 'I don't understand why you gave the arrest to Campbell. It would've made sense to push yourself forward, especially with your review coming up.'

He eyed me over the rim of his glass. 'Is that what I did?'

'That's what it looked like.'

'If I told you I'd spoken to the chief inspector before I called DI Campbell, would you believe me?'

'Did you?'

Geddes didn't reply; he hadn't spoken to anybody. It wasn't who he was. I said, 'Surely somebody will remember seeing Kennedy at one of the scenes?'

He stared wearily into his drink. 'We'll appeal for witnesses and hope somebody comes forward, otherwise the PF might be forced to go with manslaughter.'

'After what Boyd went through it doesn't seem right he isn't getting a better shake.'

Andrew finished his whisky and stood, his face flushed and more lined than when he'd arrived. He bit back his anger as best he could. 'Right? How many times do I have to say this? Right's got fuck all to do with it. The only thing that matters is proof.'

We stopped at the door. DS Geddes put a hand on my shoulder. 'You've got great instincts, Charlie. Better than anybody I've ever met. But the thing is, proof trumps instinct every time. You believed Boyd hadn't murdered Joe Franks and you were spot on. Wilson, McDermid and Davidson were scum, won't find many who'll disagree about that. But they're dead and somebody killed them. You can't see past Ritchie Kennedy. At the risk of repeating myself, where's the evidence?'

'It's obvious.'

'To you maybe. Not to a jury. Boyd's still the favourite.' Andrew counted on his fingers. 'One: it's common knowledge he intended to go after the witnesses because they lied on the stand. That's motive. Two: he admits he was at Elmbank Street car park on the night Wilson was beaten to death, as well as his fingerprints. That's opportunity.'

Geddes flashed his bad-news grin. 'Hate to be the one to break it to you. It isn't over. Not by a long way. Might be beyond even you, Charlie.'

It was the truth. After everything Boyd had been through it was hard to hear. I pretended I wasn't fazed and turned his well-worn argument against him.

'Motive and opportunity, I'll give you. But ask yourself, Andrew: is it proof?'

* * *

When I came through the main door of Helen Street police station, Patrick was waiting, clearly unhappy to be there. I understood. To the Pat Logues of the world, police stations were Kryptonite, avoided at all costs. I told the sergeant on reception who we were and why we were here. He wrote down our names and asked me to take a seat.

Pat whispered to me out of the side of his mouth. 'Everybody gives you the once-over in places like this. Guilty until proven innocent. Suspicious bunch of bastards. Good mind to tell them where to shove their statement.'

He seemed to have forgotten our presence wasn't exactly optional.

'Coppers have a look about them, ever noticed?'

'Can't say I have.'

He snorted his disbelief. 'Then you must be blind, Charlie.'

Hours ago, I'd been a hero. It hadn't lasted very long.

Two young constables on their way to their car happened to glance at us. It was enough. Patrick leapt on it as proof. 'See that? See what I mean.'

I didn't see.

He stared into my face, incredulous. 'Sometimes I wonder how you've managed to get through life, Charlie. Don't you realise these people would kick their granny if it got them an arrest?'

'Sorry, that hasn't been my experience.'

It was the wrong answer. He folded his arms and slumped in his chair. 'Then all I can say is you've been lucky. Bloody lucky. The rest of us aren't so fortunate.'

I tried the reasonable approach. 'Well, you do sail close to the wind.'

'Bit rich comin' from you, isn't it? How many times have you – what do you call it? – oh, yeah, "crossed the line"?'

'We're not talking about the same line, and it's always in a good cause.'

Patrick nodded, unconvinced. 'That how a judge would see it?'

'Depends on his definition of a good cause.'

'Does providin' for your wife and family qualify? "Men keep on the path of righteousness only because the road to the Devil is not yet paved."'

Like so many of his quotes, it killed the conversation and we waited until a uniform appeared and asked me to follow him. Patrick stared into space.

The interview room was the same as any interview room I'd ever been in: white walls, a table with a tape machine the size of a cigarette packet on top, and a couple of chairs on either side. A plainclothes detective I didn't recognise sat in one of them. As

I came through the door, he glanced up, then drew his eyes away.

A second officer, tall with a pencil moustache, leaned against the wall: DI Campbell. His smug smile when he arrested Dennis Boyd in my office hadn't impressed. He wasn't smiling now and, for a moment, I got what Pat Logue had been talking about; the feeling of being judged was hard to shake. There was no sign of Andrew.

Campbell spoke from behind me, playing to an invisible gallery, enjoying himself. Because of our efforts, a disturbing case had fallen into his lap signed, sealed and delivered. The credit – thanks to Andrew Geddes – would be his, even though the DI's contribution was zero. Gratitude would've been appropriate. Clearly it wasn't going to happen. Patrick was going to love this. Not!

'Fairly get around, Charlie. Don't tell me the arse has dropped out of the dirty-picture game? DS Wharton's going to conduct the interview. Pretend I'm not here.'

I'd do my best.

When it was over the DI opened the door to let me out in a show of mock civility. 'By the way, Charlie, he's still going down. You do know that, don't you?'

It took a second to realise he was talking about Dennis Boyd.

39

From the start my instinct had been to give Diane, Ritchie, Dennis Boyd and the whole ancient saga a miss and I hadn't been wrong. Ritchie Kennedy confessing to the fifteen-year-old killing of Joe Franks should've been enough, except it wasn't. Events had moved on. Pat Logue claimed God hated him; the Almighty really had it in for Dennis Boyd. Telling him he was the prime suspect in three murder investigations wouldn't be nice. I didn't get the chance. My mobile rang. Calling from prison meant time was tight; he launched right in as if our conversation in Barlinnie had never ended.

'You asked if there was somebody Joe didn't trust, Charlie. Somebody in the business. Well, I just remembered there was. Could well be nothing: a guy wanted to go into partnership with him. Had fuck all to do with me but, for what it's worth, I didn't take to him. Dapper. Dressed like a dodgy insurance salesman.'

'How long was this before Franks was murdered?'

'Six months, maybe less.'

'What makes you think he might've been involved?'

'He put a lot of effort into persuading Joe to cut him in.

Claimed he had connections. Took us to Casino on the Clyde one night to swing it. Spent a fortune.' He laughed. 'Should've saved his money. Joe wasn't impressed.'

'Cut him in on what?'

'Some deal Joe was trying to pull together. I could tell Joe wasn't pleased he'd found out about it.'

'The same deal that got him killed?'

Boyd stuck to what he knew. 'This was months before that, but, yeah, suppose it could've been.'

'You said us.'

'Joe, Diane and me.'

'Why were you included?'

'Joe wanted my opinion on him.'

'And what did you think?'

'Didn't matter in the end, they had a bust-up halfway through dinner. Joe told him to fuck off. Franks had spent most of his life in the stones market and here was this idiot telling him how he was going about it all wrong. Clown.'

'What was his name?'

'Graham Lennox.'

* * *

His last-known address, like Joe Franks', was an office above the shops in the Argyll Arcade. I put on a coat and headed out to find him.

In Queen Street, people sheltered in doorways waiting for the worst of the downpour to ease off. A woman with an umbrella almost took my eye out as she hurried past with her head down, her only concern getting where she was going before the rain got any heavier.

At the Arcade, a brass sign told me I'd come to the right place.

I knocked on the door and went in. Above my head a bell tinkled. The room was small, the air warm and musty. Apart from a desk, two chairs and a row of battered filing cabinets, there was nothing. I guessed the cabinets were for show and would echo the same emptiness as the rest of it. From somewhere a high-pitched male voice shouted, 'With you in a minute!'

The linoleum on the floor had been laid when the world was young, scuffed and torn, the nondescript design worn bare. Rain dripping from my coat formed a puddle like a miniature lake at my feet. When Lennox appeared, I was reminded again of just how long ago it had all been. Dennis Boyd described a pushy, dapper man; a crude wheeler-dealer determined to talk his way into whatever Franks had going on, who'd been rejected and maybe taken it personally. I'd expected my questions to be met with evasion and sleazy energy.

That man no longer existed.

Now he was granddad-who-does-hugs.

He was in his seventies, his hair – what was left of it – white and sparse, carefully combed over to cover the almost-bald head. The light-grey suit he was wearing was well matched with the maroon tie and grey shirt, the sleeves shot at the wrist revealing gold links with what I assumed, given the trade he was in, was a tiny diamond in each cuff. Lennox had the face of a man-child, smooth except for lines at his eyes. He wore a pair of horn-rimmed glasses, and his fingers were long and slim, the nails manicured. I guessed his hands would be soft – although he hadn't offered to shake mine – the hands of a man who hadn't done a day's work in his life. Graham Lennox was vain; appearance was what mattered. He wanted to look successful and might have pulled it off if it weren't for the down-at-heel surroundings giving the game away. I'd be willing to bet he was struggling to pay the rent.

No doubt some people would be fooled. I'd come across plenty of his type: he was a con man, pure and simple, older than when he'd tried it on with Joe Franks, but, under the skin, a con man just the same.

He peered at me over his bifocals while he dried his hands on a paper towel.

'Agnes, my secretary, is on holiday.'

In the over-heated room, the smell of Listerine drifted on his breath. Behind him, where the top of the wall met the ceiling, a spider hung suspended from a web, the gossamer trap already dotted with the remains of dead insects.

I almost laughed out loud. Lennox was at it: there was no secretary, no cleaner either. His fastidiousness didn't extend to his office. I played along with the fantasy meant to impress. 'No problem. I tried to make an appointment. The number just kept ringing out.'

He repeated the lie, adding to it for my benefit. 'As I say, my secretary's in Majorca, lucky woman. Anyway, you're here now. What can I do for you?'

His smile faded as soon as I told him. 'I'd like to ask a few questions about an old acquaintance of yours, Joe Franks. Remember him?'

Lennox's expression locked in place as his brain processed this blast from the past. I enjoyed putting a dent in his urbane act. To his credit, he recovered. 'No, can't say that I do.'

'Didn't you have dinner with Joe six months before he was murdered?'

He shook his head. 'Sorry, I couldn't have, don't know anybody called Franks.'

'Really? Weren't you keen to be part of a deal he was putting together? Maybe you've forgotten.'

His tie was straight; he straightened it anyway. 'When was this supposed to have happened?'

Lennox was an old dog, and, like every old dog, played to his strength: he already knew. When I answered, he dropped the act, leaned across the desk, and rubbed my nose in it. 'You're asking if I had dinner with somebody fifteen years ago.' He steepled his hands and slowly shook his head. 'I probably did. Didn't everybody? Didn't you?'

His buffed fingernails got his attention before he moved on to those showy cuffs. At first, my unscheduled appearance and questions about the past had fazed him. Not any more. Too much water had gone under the bridge; there was nothing to say.

Lennox was in control, detaching from a conversation that had no interest for him was easy, and he was probably already considering the fastest way to get me out of his office.

'I'd be more careful about where I got my information. I'm afraid you've been misled, Mr...?'

The old sorry-I-didn't-quite-catch-your-name gambit.

'Cameron. Charlie Cameron.'

'Whatever you've been told, Mr Cameron, isn't correct.'

I took a notebook from my inside jacket pocket and pretended to read from it. The page was blank. Graham Lennox wasn't the only old dog, or the only one with a talent for untruth. I hesitated, feigning confusion. 'The two other people who were there that night tell a different story.'

He sighed and cast around the room, hoping to find something to satisfy me. Over his shoulder, the spider dangled at the end of an invisible thread. Lennox said, 'What reason would I have to deny it?'

I had him.

'Let's suppose it's just slipped your mind and you did know Franks. None of us are getting any younger, right, Graham? Joe was putting a big deal together. You got wind of it and wanted in. I'm guessing you'd tried a few times to persuade him. Dinner was probably your last attempt.'

Lennox stared at me and didn't interrupt. How many nights' sleep had he lost worrying about what he'd done? When Dennis Boyd went down for a murder he didn't commit, this guy would've breathed a huge sigh of relief. And as months turned to years, maybe he really did forget – he would've tried, that much was sure. Time had covered the murder and the robbery the way autumn leaves gathered and banked against a headstone in a cemetery, until the grave beneath was obscured. But the body was still there. For Graham Lennox, spring had come to blow the leaves away and expose his guilt.

Me. I was spring.

A sheen of perspiration glossed his forehead. Sitting in his shabby office, I knew Boyd had remembered well. Lennox fingered his glasses. 'This is nonsense. All nonsense.'

Spoken without conviction. He didn't believe it and neither did I.

'Where's the proof?'

'Will two witnesses do?'

'Witnesses to what?'

'The dinner you can't recall. Fortunately, they don't have that problem.'

'Okay. All right. I wanted in on a diamond deal I'd heard he was planning. That isn't a crime.'

'No, you're right, Graham, it isn't. Though what happened after Joe turned you down most definitely is.'

'Don't be stupid. I didn't kill anybody.'

'You didn't. Ritchie Kennedy took care of that. I'm betting you were the guy who moved the gems.'

His jaw tightened, the well-cared-for fingers couldn't stay still.

But I had nothing beyond a dinner to use as leverage. Not enough. Not nearly.

Lennox pulled himself together. 'Time for you to leave, Cameron. Whatever you thought you were going to find here, I'm sorry to disappoint you.'

I shook my head. 'This is how it is: murdering Joe Franks was one thing, fencing the stones something else.'

Kennedy had confessed to killing Franks but wouldn't give whoever he'd passed the diamonds to. He might've made a deal with the prosecution; he didn't try. Lennox was a loser. Kennedy had nothing to fear from him. So why not cut the deal?

The clouds parted: he was protecting somebody. For certain, it wasn't Graham Lennox. Who did that leave?

I leaned against the back of the chair. Across the desk, Lennox's fancy clothes looked like they belonged to someone else. Blood drained from his face leaving it pale, childlike and vulnerable; his hands balled into trembling fists. Before my eyes he became what he'd always been: a wide boy whose reach had exceeded his grasp. His tongue ran over his lips again and left them still dry. Whatever else he was, he wasn't stupid; he was ahead of me. Remembering the past and seeing the future; knowing where this was going. And he was scared.

I said, 'You realise she'll crack, don't you? Give you up without a second thought. I'd get my version of the story in first if I were you. Make it easier on yourself. A man your age with your delicate habits – don't rate your chances. Dennis Boyd's done a lot of hard time because of you. He has friends inside. They'll remember. And they'll be waiting.'

Lennox opened his collar and dragged the tie away. Suddenly it was too hot for him.

'You're trying to fucking scare me.'

'In your shoes, anybody would be scared.'

I pushed him to the limit and moved towards the door. 'Suit yourself, except know this: my next stop is her.'

He cracked. 'Wait! For Christ's sake, wait!'

I stopped with my hand on the doorknob and turned to face him. He was shaking. Fear had worn the urbane polish away. What was left didn't impress. Graham Lennox was a sorry excuse for a human being.

But nobody's perfect.

40

Geddes cut me off before I could tell him why I was calling. He was wired about his promotion interview. 'This is not the best time, Charlie. Up to my eyes in it, mate. Need to finish my presentation for the shit show tomorrow. Bloody nonsense. Wasting time telling these wankers stuff that's in my file instead of doing the job.'

'When is it?'

'Nine o'clock at Helen Street.'

I tried to reassure him. 'Your record speaks for itself. Wouldn't worry about it if I were you.'

He laughed a bitter laugh. 'Nice of you to say so. I'm sure that'll carry a lot of weight with them. Except my record as a policeman isn't what concerns me.'

'What does?'

He sighed. 'Listen, the interview panel will be three people: two detective superintendents – probably from the east – who don't know me from a hole in the ground, and somebody from Personnel. Senior officers with a tonne of experience between them. They'll spot bullshit a mile away.'

'And?'

'They're bound to ask why I've waited so long to go for promotion. I would. Thing is, Charlie, I don't have a decent answer for them.'

He might not, but I did.

Geddes hurried on, keen to be rid of me. 'Okay, how can I help this time? And make it quick.'

'What if I was to tell you Dennis Boyd—?'

Andrew could be a cheeky bastard when he felt like it, and today he felt like it.

'D'you know your problem?'

I didn't, although he was about to tell me.

'Every case has to be tied in a great big fucking bow. Otherwise you're not happy.'

I let him dig the hole deep. When he finished his nippy assessment of me, I continued. 'What if I was to tell you Dennis Boyd was framed by Diane Kennedy? And what if I was to tell you I could prove it?'

* * *

I laid the story out, beginning with Diane discovering Joe was done with her and was planning to leave her with nothing. Andrew listened at the other end of the line as my tale gathered momentum, the pieces slipping into place: the robbery that had ended in the jeweller's murder, setting up Dennis Boyd to take the fall for it, and offering him money to go away when he came out of Barlinnie.

'Boyd refusing to go sealed Hughie Wilson's fate. The fifteen-year-old pigeons were coming home to roost unless they got him out of the way.'

Geddes wasn't a believer – not yet – but the impatience was gone. 'Which meant they needed to silence all three.'

'Right. And they did.'

He interrupted again. 'You know what I'm going to say, don't you?'

I knew. Of course I knew. 'Yes. Not hearing proof, Charlie.'

'Exactly right.'

'I tracked down the guy who fenced Joe Franks' stones.'

Whatever Andrew had been expecting me to say, it wasn't that. The sharp intake of breath gave him away. 'You're kidding. How the hell...?'

I told him Graham Lennox's back-to-the-wall confession about who he'd fenced Joe Franks' diamonds for: the missing link, blowing the lid off the whole mess.

Andrew was suddenly animated. 'Right, meet me at the house. I'll have Lennox picked up before he decides to go walkabout. Remember, from here on in this is police business. You're an observer, nothing more. Don't get involved or we'll be having words for real.'

'Understood, Andrew.'

He hesitated before he hung up and said, 'You're one of a kind, Charlie. Don't let me or anybody else tell you different.'

* * *

The red Audi was parked where it had been on my last visit. In a minute, faces would appear at windows and the neighbours would discover the kind of people they'd been living next to. As I walked up the path the curtains rustled, the door opened and Diane stood looking at me. 'Charlie? Didn't think I'd be seeing you again.'

She was wearing a white trouser suit over a sky-blue blouse, sunshades pushed back on her head: Diane Kennedy had got over the shock of her husband's arrest pretty damned quick.

'Going somewhere?'

We both heard the siren at the same time. Before she could reply, Geddes's car screamed round the corner. Diane raised a perfectly plucked eyebrow. 'Well, well. And to think it was me who persuaded you to take on the case. I underestimated you, Mr Cameron.'

She'd expected me to fail and Boyd to have had to leave Scotland.

Andrew got out and strode towards us, his face set hard. The words should've fazed her; they didn't. 'Diane Kennedy, I'm arresting you on suspicion—'

She held her hand up to stop him. 'I'm talking to Mr Cameron, do you mind?'

To me she said, 'You put it all together. How very clever of you.'

I didn't say it out loud, though I thought so, too.

Geddes broke in. 'It's over, Diane.'

'Is it?' She laughed. 'Had you all looking the wrong way for years, didn't I? Do you actually think a jury will be any different?'

The sun dipped behind a cloud and suddenly I felt cold. Or maybe it wasn't about the sun. There was no guilt, no remorse and, as they led her away, head held high, I wondered what it must be like to have such influence over people. There was more to the story than a handful of diamonds. Diane Kennedy was a singular woman, talented and flawed and, when it suited her, completely captivating. Seeing through her act had cost Joe Franks his life. But the awesome power remained; the spell she'd cast had only been broken when Lennox gave her up to save his own worthless skin. Diane had missed her vocation – as well as being selfish and ruthless, she was a consummate actress, her defence of her old lover Dennis Boyd a tour de force, so convincing it seemed impossible to believe anything other than that Ritchie had dragged her into the robbery and the cover-up against her will.

Wrong! It had been her from the start.

Far from being poor at picking men, she was brilliant – an unmatched manipulator: Kennedy, Boyd, Graham Lennox.

Yeah, even me.

* * *

Tony blinked and tried to stay awake. In the past week he could count on one hand how many hours' sleep he'd had. When his tired eyes gave in and closed, he saw Vicky pushing him to the door, pleading with him to go, and they snapped open, wild and afraid. He'd done what she'd wanted, listened to her, and would regret it for the rest of his life. But she'd been right: Rafferty would've killed the three of them without a moment's hesitation. He'd heard his men shouting to each other as he was going out of the back door. In another minute – less – Tony would've been trapped on the stairs with the unconscious Kim in his arms. They'd been lucky. Yet the truth brought no comfort. Vicky had sacrificed herself to save them. Part of him hoped she was dead. Thinking what Sean Rafferty would do to her if she wasn't was more than he could stand.

Kim had been burning with fever, seriously dehydrated from vomiting and diarrhoea, barely clinging to life. Without help she wouldn't have survived to walk the streets, the fate her husband intended for her. Getting her to hospital out of the gangster's reach had been the priority.

The following day he'd waited at the café until late, downing coffee after coffee until he couldn't taste them any more, desperately willing Vicky to come through the door and throw her arms round him. Gradually, hope died, replaced by paralysing fear. Returning to the vile decaying house in Renfrew Street was the one option left. Rafferty's men had been across the road, waiting for him to come back, but there was no sign of her. A beating would be worth it. Except they were obviously expecting him and would have taken a knife to Vicky's throat long before he'd got close enough to rescue her.

Since then, he'd been parked down the street from the brothel in her car, blinded by anger, tortured by guilt. Eventually, the thugs left. Believing he wasn't coming or because it was a trap? Every atom of his being was urging him to throw common sense to the wind. Finally, he couldn't stand it any longer and went to the door.

Noah was exactly as Vicky described him – a slovenly sleaze of a man. He instinctively knew who Tony was and started to get up from behind the desk. The punch broke his nose with a crack like a twig in the forest; blood sprayed over his magazine, he cried out and fell to the floor, howling. Tony followed him down and grabbed him by the throat. 'Where's Vicky? Where is she? Tell me, you bastard, or I'll beat you to a pulp.'

Noah didn't fight back – his kind never did. Terrorising helpless women was his stretch. His ugly teeth were stained red. He screamed, 'Sean took her!'

'Took her where?'

'Somewhere in the city.'

'Not good enough.'

'I can't tell you what I don't know.'

'Last chance.'

'I don't know.'

Tony drew his fist back, the agony of knowing he'd lost Vicky, maybe forever, powering the blow.

'Wrong answer.'

41

Geddes straightened his uniform and inspected himself in the mirror. Not bad, considering he'd had less than three hours' sleep. He didn't need his watch to tell him he was running late for the most important interview of his career. The DS couldn't have cared less: the job – the real job – had got in the way. Most of yesterday and well into the night, he'd interviewed Graham Lennox and Ritchie Kennedy, moving between the two, saving Diane till last. At half past five in the morning, he'd called time on the marathon sessions, satisfied he'd nailed it.

The contrast between the suspects was marked: Lennox was a lily-livered bastard who would've confessed to anything if it meant not going to prison. Geddes had taken that option off the table and watched the man crumble before his eyes. Two doors down, Kennedy had put on a very different show, sticking to his original story: Joe Franks had come home unexpectedly, they'd struggled, he'd fallen and hit his head.

'Whose idea was it to set up Dennis Boyd?'

Kennedy couldn't have been more definite or less convincing. 'Mine.'

'Where did Diane fit in?'

The deception started and his credibility faded. 'She didn't. Diane had nothing to do with it.'

The detective let him talk, recording every word. Along the hall, Lennox had told a different tale, putting Kennedy's wife squarely in the frame. It didn't matter; the mystery of Joe Franks' death had finally been solved.

One down.

Geddes had glanced at the clock on the wall – twenty-five to three – and moved on. 'Okay, Ritchie, for what it's worth, I believe you about Franks. So, who beat Hughie Wilson's brains out in the car park? Not going to tell me that was an accident, too, are you?'

'Dennis Boyd killed him.'

'Liam McDermid and Willie Davidson?'

'Boyd.'

'Not possible; he was miles away.'

Two hours later, Kennedy had realised the game was up. 'All right, it was me.'

'Then, I'll ask you the same question again. Where did your wife fit into it?'

'She didn't.'

Geddes had settled for what he had: it was a result.

But Diane had been the star turn. When they'd brought her to the room, she'd been confident there was nothing to fear because, just like Dennis Boyd, Ritchie would go down for her, except he'd do it knowingly. A couple of times, going over the details of how Joe Franks had died, she'd broken down, sobbing into her hands. Geddes had been chilled by her performance: the black widow, deadlier than the male, sacrificing one mate after another. It wasn't enough – Graham Lennox's testimony about who had brought the diamonds to him damned her and connected her directly to the crime.

* * *

Hearing the subject was going to be late raised a few critical eyebrows – the three-man panel wasn't used to being kept waiting. Assurances the officer was on his way did little for the mood. One voiced what the others were thinking. 'Bad start. Pity – the word is he's a good man.'

His colleague agreed. 'Not giving us much option, is he?'

At twenty past nine, the door opened and DS Andrew Geddes came in, saluted and apologised. It didn't go down well. 'Very glad you could join us, Detective Sergeant. Can we assume you've a solid reason for your tardiness?'

'I do, sir.'

'Care to share it?'

Geddes let them wait. Inside, he felt like cheering; it couldn't have played out any better. Thank you, Charlie. He cleared his throat. 'I've just charged Diane Kennedy as an accessory to the unlawful killing of her husband, Joe Franks, fifteen years ago.'

He paused to let it sink in.

'I've also charged Ritchie Kennedy with the murder of Hughie Wilson, Liam McDermid and Willie Davidson. When I leave here, I'll be charging Mrs Kennedy as an accomplice in those murders. She's in the cells downstairs.'

* * *

I saw Dennis Boyd just once more before he drifted out of my life.

I was reading *The Herald* and didn't notice him standing beside me until his shadow darkened the sheets in my hand and his ragged voice rasped a question.

'Mind if I join you?'

The eyes watching me were clear and, though the suntan had faded, the grey pallor of the prisoner was gone and wouldn't be coming back. His hair was longer and there was an ease about him that was new. Boyd's journey hadn't ended with the arrest of Ritchie and Diane Kennedy; in some ways that was only the beginning.

The publicity surrounding his case had made him a celebrity and a crowd of reporters had been waiting when he'd left the Big House for the second and last time. Since then, he'd become public property, an innocent man convicted of a crime he hadn't committed, who'd refused to stop fighting for the justice he'd been denied: the stuff of myth. A heavyweight Sunday supplement had already featured a black-and-white photograph of Boyd staring challengingly into the camera on its cover. Beginning on pages six and seven and continuing on twenty-eight, his remarkable story had caught the nation's imagination, opening doors beyond his wildest dreams.

Dennis Boyd was famous.

In every interview I'd read – and I'd read a few – he'd given me credit for his freedom. My phone was ringing off the hook. At this rate, I'd have to hire a secretary. I folded the paper and laid it aside. 'Sure. Sit down, Dennis.'

'Guessed you might be here.'

'Good guess. How are you?'

He dropped into a chair and considered his reply. 'I'm well, Charlie.'

'Where're you staying?'

'With my sister. Least, I was.' Boyd fingered the canvas bag at his feet. 'Left an hour ago. Need to find out who I am and all that.' He laughed. 'Sounds poncey when you say it out loud. I'm not comfortable being The Amazing Dancing Bear.'

'That how it feels?'

He nodded. 'Yeah, thought I'd get out of the city, disappear up north.'

'To Oban?'

'Worked before.'

'It did, didn't it? You're done with Glasgow?'

'Pretty much. Annie's been through a helluva lot, one way or another, she deserves a break. That's what she's getting. Besides, they say you should never outstay your welcome.'

I doubted he was in danger of doing that.

'I'm reading about a book deal – any truth in it?'

A smile spread slowly across his face. 'An Edinburgh literary agent has offered to represent me.' The idea amused him. 'Cart before the horse. I haven't written a word. Not sure I will, either. More interested in putting the whole thing behind me. Starting fresh.'

'Any idea what you want to do?'

'Buggered if I know. I've spent the last few days trying to answer that. Suddenly, I'm flavour of the month. Apart from the book thing, an art gallery in London has approached me about an exhibition of the work I did in prison.'

'Did you take them up on their offer?'

His laugh was like someone breaking rocks. 'Said I'd think about it.'

'What's to think about?'

He was pragmatic. 'No rush. It'll be there when I'm ready or it won't.'

if you can meet with triumph and disaster and treat those two imposters just the same

Pat Logue's obsession was rubbing off.

Boyd became serious. 'I owe you, Charlie. Won't forget it.' He took a sheet of paper from his pocket and put it on the table. 'Something to remember me by.'

Bold charcoal strokes formed a picture of a young man. The artist had been kind to his subject; the face was handsome, shining with optimism. Somewhere in there I recognised myself.

'Shaved a few years off. Thanks for that, Dennis.'

He grinned. 'Right back at you, Charlie. Take care of it, might be worth a couple of bob someday.'

We talked for a few minutes more, then I said, 'How do you feel about Diane now?'

Boyd's answer told me he'd learned the destructive power of resentment and wasn't willing to go there. 'We do what we do to survive, though, I have to admit, she had me fooled. Then again, maybe I fooled myself.'

'Don't we all?'

Dennis Boyd and his determination to go after the men who'd falsely testified against him had been the problem that refused to be resolved. Killing him was the obvious solution, yet she hadn't been able to bring herself to do it. Diane wasn't stone after all. Underneath the primal instincts of greed and self-preservation, a tiny ember of humanity still burned.

I didn't have the word for it.

Some might call it love.

Boyd slung the bag over his shoulder and got up to go. I went with him. At the door, we didn't say goodbye. We didn't say anything. Outside on the concourse, women in print dresses and sunshades toyed languidly with espressos under umbrellas advertising Absolut Vanilia; summer was coming and it felt good. The bank book the accountant had given me was in my pocket, along with the letter of authority he'd need to access the funds. What was in it was a long way short of fifteen years of a life. I'd already withdrawn my expenses. It seemed only fair Dennis Boyd should have the rest. I was sure his old boss would agree.

Boyd accepted it, an ironic smile playing on his lips, picked his way between the lounging bodies and walked into the sunshine; he didn't look back. Despite the lost time, it seemed a promising future lay ahead of him. With uncharacteristic brevity, Patrick Logue had summed it up in two words.

Re sult.

* * *

Later in the afternoon I took on a new case and turned down three more. Strange times, indeed. Where was everyone on those rainy Tuesdays when I twiddled my thumbs and wondered if I'd ever get another job? Just as I was shrugging on my jacket, getting ready to call it quits, a thought hit me: Dennis Boyd was going to 'disappear to Oban'. Why couldn't Kim Rafferty do something similar? Scotland wasn't safe for the ex-wife of the gangster and probably never would be, but I might just know the very guy who could help.

* * *

Yannis Kontogiannakis' Mediterranean voice rippled down the line. 'Charlie, this is a surprise. How are you? And how is my new friend?'

'We're both good, Yannis. You?'

He laughed. 'Yannis is always fine.'

Somehow, I believed him.

'How can I help you?'

'There's something I want to ask. If someone needed to drop out of sight...'

He jumped straight in. 'The south of the islands over the mountains to the coast is not only beautiful, Charlie, even

Interpol won't find you down there. We're not speaking about you, are we?'

'No, not me.'

'Tell me what you need me to do and it's done.'

His offer was generous. Too generous without understanding what he'd be getting into. 'This person has powerful enemies, Yannis. Dangerous enemies.'

He dismissed my warning. 'Life is dangerous. We Greeks have learned how to live and deal with such threats. And you, Charlie, who knows better than you?'

Pat Logue had been talking.

'And if this person had a child?'

'Even better. To save a young life is the best any man can do.'

I'd only met him briefly and I'd liked the Greek. Now, he had my admiration.

'Someone is going to be very happy to hear this. We'll speak soon.'

The conversation meant I had one more call to make. Turning Kim Rafferty away hadn't sat well with me and still didn't. Her husband was an angry man; the violence towards his wife would only get worse.

Living on a sunshine island was a lot of people's idea of heaven – Kim might see it as a prison sentence. I'd never know: her number was unobtainable and I guessed she'd figured out a way to escape without my help.

Pat Logue would be pleased.

42

The world kept turning. And in NYB, nothing had changed. Or so I thought. Jackie was on her own, busy with a drinks order; she seemed edgy. I picked up on her energy and wanted to ask again if she was okay. I remembered how my last attempt had gone and kept my distance. Jackie crying was a shock to the system – the Jackie Mallon I knew didn't do tears. Caused them? Absolutely.

I hadn't seen her man around lately – a good guy called Alan Sneddon – and wondered if they were having problems. It happened. She saw me checking her out, broke off from what she was doing and came over. 'I'm okay, Charlie, really. Thanks for the concern. It's hormones.'

'Hormones?'

'Yeah, I'm pregnant.'

I went round the bar and hugged her. 'That's wonderful.'

She made a face. 'I thought so. Now, I'm not so sure. I'm being sick fifteen times a day, my boobs are huge, and my feet are killing me. And this is only the beginning.'

'What's Alan saying to it?'

'Just what you'd expect. Delighted and scared.'

'Sounds about right. Shouldn't you be taking it a bit easier? Where's Michelle?'

'She left. Got a job with Santander.'

Patrick Logue arrived in time to catch the last part of the conversation. 'Who's got a job with Santander?'

'Michelle.'

He hadn't known. Michelle hadn't told him. Whatever had been going on was over. If he was hurt, he didn't show it. Pat was a survivor. With Michelle out of the picture, his marriage would probably survive, too.

Jackie said, 'She sent me a text, would you believe? Sorry, Pat, you'll have to make do with me.'

It was too good an opportunity for him to pass up. He said, 'Well, it's a bit unexpected, Jackie. You'll have to forgive my rough, manly ways, but don't worry, I won't tell Alan if you don't. Oh, and before it goes any further, you need to know, I'm a screamer.'

It got the reaction it deserved, though it made me laugh.

I lifted the early edition of the *Glasgow Times* from the bar, took it to my table and thumbed through it. On page nine, an item about the opening of a crèche in a factory in Stepps caught my attention. In the black-and-white picture a man held a child in his arms, smiling for the camera. Rosie Rafferty curled into her father.

Her mother wasn't in the shot.

Kim had been desperate to escape. When I hadn't been able to reach her, I'd assumed she had. That wasn't how it looked; the mother in her wouldn't have let her leave without her daughter. I didn't understand what it meant, but it didn't feel right.

I went back to the bar and showed it to Patrick. He blew the top off his pint. 'Not your problem, Charlie. Never was. As soon as she got herself involved with Sean Rafferty, Kim was in trouble.'

He was right. It didn't change the feeling in my gut.

'I could've done more. Should've done more.'

'And ended up in the river?'

'Not to help her was a mistake.'

A look I'd seen too often came into his eyes. '"We make mistakes. But we're human. And maybe that's the word that best explains us." Who said it?'

His timing was off. I'd heard enough of his bloody quotes and didn't appreciate hearing more. 'I don't give a damn. Do me a favour, put a match to that bloody book.'

'It's appropriate. Who said it?'

'Don't know, don't want to know.'

'Take a guess.'

'Nelson Mandela? Gandhi? Who?'

'Captain James T Kirk, Commander of the starship Enterprise.'

EPILOGUE

Rain fell relentlessly in thin sheets on the 'A' listed buildings on Blythswood Square, once the town houses of wealthy cotton merchants and shipping magnates. Sean Rafferty liked this part of the city. In another age, he'd have lived here; the history of the square appealed to him. Over his shoulder in No 7, Madeleine Smith had poisoned her lover with arsenic-laced cocoa and got away with it. Good for Madeleine. Rafferty was waiting for somebody who very definitely hadn't got away with it.

A taxi splashed to a halt outside the Kimpton Hotel, where a well-dressed couple sheltered in the doorway of the former home of the RAC Club under a black umbrella held aloft by the concierge. The man was bald, decades older than the woman. She was blonde and pretty, young enough to be his daughter, clinging to his arm as if they were on the edge of an abyss, instead of a wet pavement in the centre of Glasgow. Rafferty smiled – money got you just about anything. Which was why everybody wanted it. The concierge proved his point, slipped the tip into his waistcoat with the dexterity of a pickpocket and shepherded them through the puddles. An orange indicator flashed and the cab drew away, no doubt returning them to their comfortable lives in Whitecraigs, Dowanhill or Bearsden. Sean imagined them sharing a nice bottle of Chateaux What-The-Fuck with dinner, selected specially for them by the sommelier, the female fluttering her lashes, coyly pursing her lips, secretly hoping the wine, the two glasses of Courvoisier before the meal, and the Drambuie he'd drink after it would get her out of spreading her legs later.

Rafferty's driver pointed to a bedraggled figure coming up the hill from Waterloo Street, her cropped hair matted to her skull, the short skirt and high heels out of place in the filthy weather. She stopped at the corner, looking up and down, swaying slightly, obviously on something. Sean didn't blame her – if he spent every night doing what she was doing, he'd be on something, too.

The driver said, 'Is that her?'

'That's her.'

'Christ Almighty, she's pathetic.'

Rafferty smiled a second time. 'Isn't she just?'

A white Mondeo pulled into the kerb. The guy behind the wheel rolled the window down and leaned across to speak to her. The exchange was brief and the car pulled away. Rafferty understood why – one look at her face would be enough to put anybody off.

The driver said, 'He didn't fancy it. Know where he's coming from. You'd have to be desperate to take that on. Bloody desperate.'

'Fortunately, some people are.' Sean Rafferty tapped the dashboard. 'I've seen enough. Take me to Bothwell.'

* * *

Vicky was hurting. Every joint in her body ached; she needed a fix. Two hours, three at the most, to earn. After that, the city closed down and it would be too late. Thinking about not being able to score panicked her; an iron hand gripped her chest, her fingertips tingled with the anxiety attack already on its way. The guy appeared out of the rain and was beside her before she realised he was there. Something about him was familiar, though she couldn't place him. He squinted, amused, hard eyes assessing her. 'Well, well. Look what the cat dragged in.'

Vicky's brain wouldn't function.

He saw the confusion in her eyes. 'Don't remember me, do you? I remember you. How could I forget?' He laughed and stepped closer. 'No bells? That is disappointing. Made a lasting impression on your scrubber, though, didn't I?'

He grabbed Vicky's arm and slapped her against the railings. 'Kelvin. Got a right doing because of you. Spent five days in the Royal.' He slapped her; she stumbled and fell, tearing her tights, skinning her knee. Kelvin Hunter hauled her to her feet, caught a handful of her wet hair, and dragged her head up to the light. 'Jesus Christ! What the hell's happened to you? You weren't bad for a tart. Pick a fight with a bus, did you?'

Kelvin was enjoying himself too much to hear the car stop and the man get out. He threw Vicky to the ground, mocking her. 'Wear a mask. Who in their right mind would pay for that? Nobody—'

A hand gripped him and spun him round. The first blow broke his jaw, the second put Kelvin Hunter down – he wouldn't be getting up again any time soon.

Tony lifted Vicky Farrell to her feet and held her close as she sobbed into his shoulder. It had taken longer than he wanted, but he'd found her. He said, 'Come on, baby, we're done with this town. Let's get you home.'

ACKNOWLEDGMENTS

The fingerprints of many talented people are on this book. My thanks to the wonderful team at Boldwood books, especially, Sarah, and my editors Sue Smith and Candida Bradford, whose knowledge of the English language far outstrips my own. You make me better than I am. Beyond them and the fantastic energy they bring to everything they do are other people, too numerous to mention, who have made a telling contribution to the work. But, first, last, and always must be my wife, Christine. Writing is, by nature, an imperfect thing. Any errors that remain are my own.

MORE FROM OWEN MULLEN

We hope you enjoyed reading *The Accused*. If you did, please leave a review.

If you'd like to gift a copy, this book is also available as an ebook, digital audio download and audiobook CD.

Sign up to Owen Mullen's mailing list for news, competitions, updates and receive an exclusive free short story from Owen Mullen.

https://bit.ly/OwenMullenNewsletter

ALSO BY OWEN MULLEN

The Glass Family Series
Family
Insider
Hustle

PI Charlie Cameron
Games People Play
The Wronged
Whistleblower
The Accused

Mackenzie Darroch
Deadly Harm
In Harm's Way

Standalone
Out Of The Silence
So It Began

ABOUT THE AUTHOR

Owen Mullen is a highly regarded crime author who splits his time between Scotland and the island of Crete. In his earlier life he lived in London and worked as a musician and session singer.

Follow Owen on social media:

twitter.com/OwenMullen6
bookbub.com/authors/owen-mullen
facebook.com/OwenMullenAuthor

ABOUT BOLDWOOD BOOKS

Boldwood Books is a fiction publishing company seeking out the best stories from around the world.

Find out more at www.boldwoodbooks.com

Sign up to the Book and Tonic newsletter for news, offers and competitions from Boldwood Books!

http://www.bit.ly/bookandtonic

We'd love to hear from you, follow us on social media:

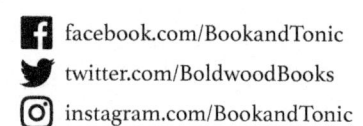

- facebook.com/BookandTonic
- twitter.com/BoldwoodBooks
- instagram.com/BookandTonic

Printed in Great Britain
by Amazon